# HARTE'S DESIRE

*Cynthia Harrod-Eagles titles available from
Severn House Large Print*

# HARTE'S DESIRE

Cynthia Harrod-Eagles

**Severn House Large Print**
London & New York

This first large print edition published 2008
in Great Britain and the USA by
SEVERN HOUSE PUBLISHERS of
9-15 High Street, Sutton, Surrey, SM1 1DF.
First world regular print edition published 2007 by
Severn House Publishers, London and New York.

British Library Cataloguing in Publication Data

Harrod-Eagles, Cynthia
  Harte's desire. - Large print ed.
  1. Female friendship - Fiction 2. Married women - Fiction
  3. Neighbors - Fiction 4. Chick lit 5. Large type books
  I. Title
  823.9'14[F]

  ISBN-13: 978-0-7278-7733-8

Printed and bound in Great Britain by
MPG Books Ltd, Bodmin, Cornwall.

# One

Polly woke luxuriously to the knowledge that it wasn't a work day so she didn't have to get up. Instantly, to her annoyance, she was wide awake, beyond all possibility of drifting off again. It was only a quarter to seven. On work days she could hardly drag herself out of bed, her eyes glued together, even if she'd had an early night. But on a day when she could have had a lie-in, sleep abandoned her in *chunks*. Why did that always happen?

Seth slumbered on blissfully. He never stirred until she woke him with a mug of coffee. Seeing that they got up at the right time was her job – had been ever since they first slept together (in *his* flat, because when she left home she'd shared with two other girls in furnished rented, and he was fastidious not only about bathrooms being spotless and not having hand-wash lying about, but about décor and furniture in general). As soon as she had started to share his bed, he had given up all responsibility relating to clocks and alarms, and would sleep until the Trump if she didn't wake him. Of course, geniuses *did* need a lot of sleep –

and to be fair to him, he did get up first on a Sunday after their lie-in and bring her tea, usually on a tray with a flower in a vase, which was sweet and romantic – though it did always make her wonder, with secret guilt for being so prosaic, what she was supposed to do with it.

His thing about alarm clocks had spread to the diary, too. She was the one who had to check it every day and tell him what he was supposed to be remembering. She suspected it had something to do with his mother, Sophie. Seth was an only child, and from what Polly gathered, Sophie had done everything for him until the (lamentably late) day he left home. Of course, he wasn't entirely helpless. He usually ironed his own shirts, saying she or Leela – whoever it happened to be – didn't do it properly. She admitted she wasn't too wonderful at ironing (too impatient, wanting to get it done so she could go on to something more interesting), but she always took extra care with anything of his; and Leela, their daily, was an artist. But if he could see a difference which she couldn't, so be it. His appearance was very important in his job, and he always looked – well, immaculate didn't cover it. A whole new word needed to be coined to cover his perfectionism.

She found she was too wide awake to lie still now. Once her brain started churning she had to move. She slid out of bed and went towards the bathroom, then paused a moment to look back at him. Their wonderful six-foot-wide bed had been made to Seth's design, hand-carved from Burmese pyinkado, and the pale sheets looked wonderful against the dark wood. Even more wonderful, of course, was Seth, looking simply sensational with his dark head cradled on the pale pillow.

The bedlinen was unbleached Ethiopian Awash cotton, with a seriously stratospheric thread-count (which Polly could never remember). Though she would never have dared admit it to Seth, thread-count was a teensy bit lower on her list of priorities than his. But when Seth had told neighbour Tom Butler, of the gay Butler-Benns, about it, he had opened his eyes wide and said, 'Oh. My. God.' And then he had turned to Polly and said gravely, 'You are *so* lucky to have this man!'

Well, whatever your priorities, it was always nice to have a neighbour admire your lovely house and possessions; and she did not need Tom to tell her she was lucky. She felt it every day in a familiar surge of love and surprise. How could she, ordinary Polly Walsh, the one plain sister of four (as she thought of herself), have managed to catch wonderful, brilliant Seth? It was a question she always asked herself when she got that warm feeling in the pit of her stomach from looking at him. It was a question, alas, that she often saw mirrored in Sophie's cool and appraising eyes. But Polly comforted herself with the thought that no one would have been good enough for him in his mother's opinion. And however difficult he sometimes was (and there was that business a while back – but it was over and done with, and she dismissed it impatiently from her mind) the fact remained that he *had* chosen her, so it must mean that he loved her and no one else. Let Sophie suck the pips out of *that*!

She padded towards the bathroom across the broad boards of silky blonde wood. All the floors, except in the kitchen (which was slate), were of polished Portuguese eucalyptus. Seth did not approve of carpets, which he said not only harboured dirt and caused allergies (to which he was prone), but were spiritually and aesthetically clogging. Everything in their house was bare, minimalist and hypoallergenic. And from sustainable sources. Seth took great care and trouble over sourcing materials. It was one of the things that made him so much in demand from the new millionaires of Notting Hill, Chelsea and Islington, fashionistas for whom pure Egyptian cotton was now as laughably passé as pine kitchens. Seth was always at least one obscure, third-world, fair-trade source ahead of the game – which was why, incidentally, a certain prominent politician's wife, who was keen on that sort of thing, had booked him to buff up the central London house they were going to live in when her husband left office. It was also one of the reasons he won so many awards. He was going to collect one on Friday in Paris. Polly had a photographic memory and could see the entry in the diary, in her neat block letters with two exclamation marks because it was so important. Well, she thought so. She had been much more excited about it than Seth, who had only given a funny little shrug and said it was good for business.

She went into the bathroom and sat down on the loo, and had her usual difficulty in relaxing. There was no door to the bathroom, and although Seth could not have seen her from the bed, she always hated the idea that he might *hear* her. He had no inhibitions about bathroom things: he could have performed in a room full of strangers. But she had always liked – no, *needed* – to be private. He laughed at her about it and called her hopelessly bourgeois, so she had stopped complaining. Seth had a thing about doors, saying they blocked the flow of chi energy through a house. It was a feng-shui sort of thing. But if he had grown up, as she had, in a small house with father, mother and three sisters, to say nothing of friends and relatives dropping in, he might have understood. The downstairs loo, she noted, *did* have a door – for the sake of their hopelessly bourgeois friends and visitors, she supposed!

Apart from the open doorway, she loved the bathroom, with its Lagoa Claro marble walls and the black granite bath. Just inside the doorway, there was a glass table (Seth's design) on which stood a slim, blue glass vase, a perfect foil to the black-and-whiteness. She always had either blue or white flowers in it. Today it was blue hydrangea heads. She'd had to order them specially from Floral Dance – the florist on the Green – because the soil round here was acid, so all the hydrangeas in people's gardens were pink. But it was worth it – they looked gorgeous. The only thing about hydrangea flowers was that they were practically indestructible, and she hated to throw flowers away while they were still alive. Life was something *she* was sensitive about. But Seth liked the flowers changed frequently, so she sometimes sneaked them into a vase in a spare room if they were still fresh, and apologized to them – she knew *that* was ridiculous, but no one heard her so what harm? – in case they felt slighted.

A low, dull pain griped her, interrupting her thoughts. It was faint and fleeting, but she knew what it was. *Oh damn, damn, damn!* It was the Early Warning System. Later today, or possibly tomorrow morning, the flags would be out. There was no mistaking it. Her mouth bowed with disappointment. She had so hoped that this time it really would happen. It had been a lovely night and

10

bang on the right date. Seth had been wonderful, really gentle, loving and affectionate. She had always hoped that their child would be conceived on such an occasion. Of course, she reminded herself, she was in no position to be picky. She wouldn't *much* care by this point if it was one of his frivolous, bed-bouncing, wham-bam-thank-you-ma'am sessions that did the trick, as long as she got pregnant.

Well, not this time, anyway. Sadness overwhelmed her. Her inhospitable womb was about to shed its lining, and another month had passed without result. She thought about the child of that egg that would never be born. Tears prickled the back of her nose and she had to gulp them back, but even so one escaped, and the feeling of it, wet against her skin, made her feel even sadder. It was stupid to be sentimental about an egg, she told herself, as firmly as she could in the circumstances, and blew her nose. Much better to think positively about next month, because according to Seth negative thoughts could hang around on the aether and blight your chances. Oh, but it was hard to be cheery in the face of renewed disappointment. She was now thirty-two years and seven months old, instead of thirty-two and six months: one more missed month, and thirty-one days further down the road to being too old ever to have a child.

Of course you read all the time about

people having difficulty conceiving, but she had never thought it would happen to her. She was one of four, plus three stepbrothers (her father had married twice but they were much older and had left home by the time she was born), and everyone in her family was tremendously fertile. Polly had a million cousins. She had always assumed that once she stopped taking the pill it would be like falling off a log. Ginnie next door had helpfully suggested she ought to stop a few months *before* she wanted to conceive, to give her system time to clear, but Polly had laughed and said all the women in *her* family got pregnant simply sitting in a chair a man had just got out of.

She flushed the loo and walked over to the window to stare out at the gardens. The window was Seth's latest addition. It was enormous, one sheet of glass unbroken by glazing bars. He said it allowed the outside energy to flow in, removing the barriers between the domestic space and the natural world. She was never *absolutely* sure when he said that sort of thing whether he meant it one hundred per cent, or whether it was a leftover bit of his sales pitch that had got stuck between his conversational teeth. Sometimes she half hoped he *didn't* mean it, because there was a rebellious bit of her that thought all this intenseness about interior design was a bit – well – daft. But she didn't often allow herself to think that way. It was obviously a good and laudable thing for someone to be passionate and dedicated about their career; and the passion and dedication had made Seth supremely successful in his. And it *was* marvellous to have such an unimpeded view (even if it was only over everyone's back gardens – though there were some wonderful old trees, too). It was just that she sometimes felt horribly like a *voyeur*. No, not *voyeur*, the other thing. The opposite. Exhibitionist? That was it. And really, she was the last person who'd ever expose herself in public.

All the windows at the back were going to be like this when he'd finished. And Seth hated curtains even more than he hated carpets and doors, so though there were going to be plain unbleached blinds for decency's sake, Polly was ready to bet Seth would never pull them down. He often walked around with no clothes on, and *he* wouldn't have minded who saw him. Would even probably have enjoyed it. There was quite a bit of the exhibitionist in Seth. But perhaps being so hairy, he didn't really *feel* naked.

They couldn't touch the windows at the front, of course, because although Albemarle Terrace – of which their house was at the centre – wasn't listed, the council had become very fussy lately about architectural integrity. It was probably prompted by the consideration that these fine early Victorian houses were exchanging hands for upwards of two million now, since Notting Hill had gone through the roof. People who paid that sort of money weren't just buying their one house, they were buying the look of the whole terrace, and there was no doubt that horrors had been perpetrated in other terraces all over London. One idiot putting up stone cladding or painting their bricks could ruin it for everyone. Not that that sort of naff thing was likely to happen in *this* price bracket. But there had been bitter complaints from some of the neighbours about their bathroom window, even though they could only see it by deliberately going down their gardens and looking back, and even then only by craning around the various lilacs, laburnums, pergolas and trellises that had been put up, in most cases, deliberately to prevent this.

Still, Ginnie next door had said she was amazed Seth had got planning permission. But Seth always managed to get his way. His degree had been in architecture – though he had taken a sideways path into interior design which was *far* more lucrative these days – and he knew just about every planning officer in the south east. He lunched the important ones regularly, and had chummy phone conversations with the rest in which he asked after their wives and children *by name*. He needed to have them eating out of his hand, given the wild and wonderful things he was always doing to his clients' houses. Anyone who could afford a Seth Muller design had to have cast aside all inhibitions – along with several elements formerly thought essential to houses, like walls and ceilings. His ideas were so far ahead of the cutting edge they were practically having to *invent* awards for him to win.

It was odd, given his talent for getting what he wanted, that they had not been able to get her pregnant yet. The doctor said it was too early to worry and wouldn't even recommend them for tests until they had been trying for two years. Dr Farleigh was very calm and reassuring, and kept saying there was nothing unusual in this failure to conceive. 'You're both young and healthy, and there's no reason to think there's anything wrong. I have dozens of patients who've taken time to get started, and then pop them out like shelling peas. Just relax and try not to think about it.'

That was all very well, but not thinking about it was like that old cure for warts, walking round a donkey and not thinking of its tail. Impossible to do. And it was nearly two years now. Everyone in her family had children. Only two more failed months, and she would be officially allowed to worry – or at least officially allowed to take the tests. She hadn't dared raise the subject with Seth again, after that time at the end of the first year. He had got really riled. He had said there was nothing wrong with *him* and that was that. He wouldn't be treated like a Hereford bull, tested to see if he was good enough to inseminate cows. Marriage was a meeting of minds and spirits, and to reduce it to the level of animal husbandry would block the flow of energy between them, destroy their marriage and probably destroy his creativity into the bargain. So she knew he would not take any tests, and that if she did – *when* she did, let's be honest – she would have to do it secretly. If only it should turn out not to be necessary! She still tried to pin her faith on Dr Farleigh, because the thought that it might be her fault, and that it might be permanent, was too hard to bear. Every month when the sadness came, it seemed to sink deeper into her, like a stain. She was afraid that eventually other people would be able to see it on her.

She turned away from the window, went back into the bedroom, and slipped on her robe. Seth still slept, his dark eyelashes making long crescents on his brown cheeks. She padded downstairs to the kitchen and made herself a cup of rooibos tea, sipping it while she ground Namibian beans for Seth's coffee and put it on. It was a gorgeous day outside, and she went and opened the back door to let in the sunshine, feeling suddenly more cheerful and determined. Even if she had lost out this month, there was always next month. She and Seth were young and healthy and they *would* have children. Positive thinking, that was the thing! She must *not* allow it to colour her whole life. New month, new chance. She began to plan what they would do on the next Baby Night – perhaps a small dinner party, just two other couples. She loved to cook. She thought about menus. Something baby-friendly, but nothing obvious like oysters, which would have Seth raising his eyebrow in that mocking way that made her feel like an idiot. Limpets, perhaps, though she'd have to go to Fish Collective in Notting Hill to get them. There was a definite need in Shepherd's Bush for a good fishmonger. Limpets and pink langoustes, and maybe tiny noisettes of baby lamb, cooked very pink, which would be an excuse to have pink champagne...

Ginnie's cat, Mr Big, a handsome, slim, marmalade tabby, appeared in the doorway and gave a questioning chirrup. Polly would have liked a cat, but Seth didn't approve of animals inside houses. He had driven Big away from the door on so many occasions (with the tip of his boot, sometimes) that the cat was naturally wary, but Polly invited him in whenever there was no chance of them being caught. She bent now and held out her hand. 'Come on, then, Biggie. It's all right.' Big walked in with that superb feline confidence that made him look like the classier sort of gangster, and came to duck his head under her palm. She let her hand linger down his spine and up his tail, and he circled

17

for a repeat, then gave a suggestive 'proop' and stalked towards their brushed-steel Smeg 500 series larder fridge, where he stood looking up at her expectantly.

'Oh, Biggles, that's just cupboard love,' she said, but she opened it anyway to see what she could find for him. They were not really leftover people, but there was a seared tarragon chicken breast from Fare Earth that she had been intending to have with salad for her lunch. She opened the packaging and broke off a piece for the cat. 'I could get into real trouble for this,' she said as Big took the chunks from her hand and engulfed them with those sideways smacking chomps as if he had been on the brink of starvation. She would have to dispose of the rest now, in some way, because Seth would want to know why it had been opened and part was missing. So she wouldn't be lunching off it after all. She tore off another piece for Mr Big. 'But I won't tell Uncle Seth if you don't – OK, Biggle-baby?'

She was aware that this was a very silly way to talk to an animal, but she didn't care. Seth was upstairs asleep, and Mr Big probably couldn't hear her over the noise he was making eating.

# Two

On his return home, Mr Big found the door to his own kitchen also standing open that fine morning. Inside the usual morning bedlam reigned so he sat down in the doorway out of the way of it to clean his whiskers. Polly's chicken had been cooked in tarragon and lemon juice, but he was a cat of sophisticated tastes. He actually quite liked garlic now.

All five of the Addingtons were around the kitchen table, though Ginnie's tenure of her seat was intermittent. She jumped up every few minutes to fetch refills or search for clothes and mislaid homework, while she answered questions and directed comments at all three children at once. Flora, nine, was talking seamlessly about ponies while Jasper, eight, shovelled in mini Oatibix like the fireman on a steam train and roared out derision of things equine, while pressing his own counter-passion for rugby, a tame version of which they were to be allowed to play at school from September. Benedict, six, was angsting about his class assembly on Friday when he would have to say three lines about

Africa. He couldn't remember his lines, couldn't pronounce them when he remembered them, and didn't understand them anyway.

Julian sat like a monument of calm with his half-moon glasses slipping to the end of his nose, reading the *Telegraph* business section and simultaneously listening to the *Today* programme on his Roberts radio – an original, *mirabile dictu*, not the new retro digital version. All his treasured possessions seemed to last for ever. He'd been wearing the same suit to work for ten years. It had been made for him by some old fossil at Henry Poole's in Savile Row and was intended to last for a lifetime: he could be buried in it one day and it wouldn't be any more out of style than it was now. Sometimes Ginnie feverishly planned to cut it up into shreds behind his back in the hope of getting him into something Boss or Armani. He was eating organic three-grain toast and marmalade (home-made, but not by Ginnie – Polly next door made pounds every January when the Seville oranges came in, and always gave some to the Addingtons because she knew of Julian's dislike of what he called 'boughten preserves'). Despite mouth, eyes and ears all being occupied with different inputs, he still managed to listen to Ben intelligently. It infuriated Ginnie. Multitasking was supposed to be a woman thing; about the only thing they ever got credit for these days.

'That's all nonsense anyway,' he told Ben. 'They're just peddling the politically-correct, soft-left line. Ethiopia's troubles are about equally caused by war and international aid. Bloody chancellor!' (The last directed at the radio.)

'Don't tell him he's being taught rubbish,' Ginnie said.

'I didn't say "rubbish", I said "nonsense",' Julian corrected maddeningly. He had a reverence for words that Ginnie reserved for handbags.

'It's the same thing! Suppose he repeats what you've said? Jasper, you're spraying milk everywhere! Don't talk with your mouth full.'

'Flora does, and you don't tell her.'

'If the teachers talk nonsense – or rubbish – they ought to be told.'

'Flora does it daintily. Your bit of the table looks like the Okefenokee Swamp. Yes, but if he upsets the teachers they'll take it out on him in other ways.'

'What's the Oaky-folky swamp?' Flora asked.

'What a deplorable attitude! Do you want your children taught lies for the sake of getting meaningless good grades?'

'It's in America. Yes, if that's what it takes. Do you want them to get meaningless *bad* grades?'

'Where in America? Mum?'

'Education is not about grades.'

21

'Mum?'

'Maybe, but grades are what get university places and jobs. All very well for you to be grand, you went through school in a different age. We are where we are, and we have to get on with it.'

'Mum?'

'If we accept bad standards without protest we'll never be anywhere else.'

*'Mum!'*

Ginnie whirled on her daughter. 'Don't shout at the table!'

Flora burst into tears.

'Now her nose will bleed,' Jasper said with satisfaction, and the weeping increased a notch.

Julian reached behind him for the tissue-box on the dresser and handed it to his daughter, then went back to his newspaper, with Ben trying to read the back of it out loud, labouring over the long words letter by letter. 'Fer-iss-cah-ler-ler-yer. What does that mean? Daddy, what's fer-iss-cah-ler-ler-yer?'

Ginnie finished comforting Flora (her nose hadn't bled, thank God!) and poured herself another cup of coffee from the tarnished Georgian silver pot. It didn't keep the coffee hot and always needed cleaning, but Julian liked it to be used – an Addington heirloom, of course, so it was sacrosanct, or she'd have sneaked it out into the nearest skip. Not long now and she would have the place to herself. Heaven! Julian was taking them to school this morning because he was going to meet an agent in Kensington before going to the office and had to drive right past the door. The first thing she was going to do was have a long, undisturbed bath. She longed and longed to have a bathroom of her own, and it was absurd in a house this size that they didn't have their own suite. There was the whole attic unused except for storing Julian's old rubbish, and Seth Muller next door could have made them a glorious bedroom/dressing-room/wet-room suite up there with a balcony overlooking the gardens. He'd sketched it out for her once on the back of an envelope when the four of them were out to dinner. If only Julian weren't so bloody tight with the money.

It wasn't only tightness with money, of course. He hated change as well. And he thought the whole concept of interior design ludicrous. His idea was that you got the house the way you liked it – which to him mostly meant comfortable rather than attractive in any way – and then left it alone for the rest of your life. The suggestion that it should have a 'look' or follow (let alone *lead*) a fashion made him snort with derision. It was all right, he supposed, for the sort of people who bought their own furniture: he had said that to her once, and she had not quite dared to ask him what was wrong with buying your own furniture. Many of his strictures were incomprehensible to her. If you bought your own furniture at least it would be stuff you liked, not musty old walnut and mahogany monstrosities dumped on you by the in-laws. And you could change it when you got tired of it. But Julian never got tired of things. She supposed that was something that ought to have comforted *her*, but oddly enough didn't.

This kitchen, for instance: Julian had bought the house back in the eighties when it was dirt cheap and he had just started working at his father's firm. He had wanted to live somewhere on the Central Line because the office in those days was at Chancery Lane. He had lived upstairs and had let out the basement as a separate flat. Then, when he and Ginnie had married, he had got rid of the tenants so they could live in the whole house, and they had redone the basement as a kitchen–breakfast room. At that time, pine was the thing, and Ginnie had chosen the best kitchen Smallbone could provide and adored the result. But that was then. Now it made her want to scream. Polly had told her in an unguarded moment that Seth had laughed so much about the Addingtons' pine kitchen once he had *hurt* himself. The Mullers' kitchen was all steel and chrome, black and white, and high tech; so stark and hygienic you could have done heart surgery in it. Why wouldn't Julian let her do something like that here? The space was good and she had already done the research on the Internet, browsing through Gaggenau, Philippe Starke, Miele, Alpes Inox ... Julian had just about heard of Aga and that was it. He was immune to brand names, blast him.

'What are you doing today?' he asked her now, interrupting her dream.

'Oh, this and that,' she replied vaguely, coming back to earth; and then, realizing she had to keep her end up. 'I've loads to do, with Marta not coming.'

'Well, I'd be grateful if you could find time to take my dinner suit into the cleaners,' he said with impeccable politeness. He had beautiful manners towards everyone and never snapped even at the worst bungler at work – which meant everyone adored him – but Ginnie always felt when he was polite like that to her that he was laughing at her. She couldn't help it but it always sounded ironic to her.

'You could drop it in at Sketchley on your way,' she said, though she knew the answer to that. He insisted on having all his clothes cleaned at Jeeves – and not just any old Jeeves, but the specific Jeeves on Pont Street where he had always had his things done, as if, she thought, it could make any difference. Dry cleaning was dry cleaning, for Pete's sake! But he said it did make a difference, and that you had to treat good cloth properly. And it meant a special trip for her all the way to bloody Knightsbridge which would use up practically all the time she had before having to pick up the kids again. Her whole day wasted! Though she could, a little devil whispered to her, pop into Harvey Nicks while she was up that way. She dismissed the devil. Better a good grievance than looking at clothes she oughtn't to buy because she was over her budget.

Julian said, still politely, 'Never mind, I'll see if Fiona can do it in her lunch hour.' Fiona was his secretary, whom Ginnie hated. She was one of those tall immaculate Sloanes who held their glossy hair back with an Alice band and probably wore pearls in bed, and had been photographed once for the totty-spot in the front of *Country Life*: *Fiona Fforbes-Cotteson, only daughter of Lieutenant-Colonel Gerald Fforbes-Cotteson of Calcot St Denis, Glos…*

'Can't it wait until tomorrow? I can take it in tomorrow,' Ginnie said.

'Don't worry,' he said. 'I'll see to it.' And he smiled, and she was certain he was mocking her. She found herself grinding her teeth and made herself stop. She'd had them expensively capped last year and grinding cost about a hundred quid a minute.

Of course, before she could go and run a bath, she had to clear up the kitchen and load the dishwasher, because it wasn't Marta's day to come in. Julian was so mean about money, and would not let her have

Marta more than three times a week, as if Ginnie had nothing better to do with her time than be a domestic drudge, cleaning up after four people who thought the floor the correct place to hang clothes and wet towels.

Marta had come to them on recommendation from Cora Summers, one of the editors at Julian's firm. She was having a baby and moving out of London, and couldn't keep Marta on because Chesham was too far for Marta to travel. Cora had said Marta was fabulous, a wonderfully hard worker, and great with kids – she'd helped Cora give a birthday party for her twin nieces and apparently had the whole boiling eating out of her hand – so Ginnie had immediately imagined a nice, round-faced, motherly Polish woman of about fifty who would have marvellous ethnic recipes for cheesecake and pierogi and golabki, and a wonderful way with hand-washing, and who would scrub the bath and loos properly without being told and know not to use Mr Sheen on Julian's antique furniture.

But when Marta turned up, she had proved to be in her twenties, slim and gorgeous, with very white skin, blue eyes, a glamorous smile and an even more glamorous accent. Ginnie had immediately suspected Cora Summers of pulling a fast one on her (and Greg Summers of having pulled an even faster one, presumably necessitating the Sacking of the Maid). But Marta had turned out to be the stated hard worker, and she did clean the bathroom properly – not to mention the skirting boards and picture rails, which Ginnie had never before succeeded in getting a cleaner to acknowledge the existence of. She dusted Julian's books, of which he had a million, and buffed up his antique furniture in the approved way, with nothing but a soft cloth and elbow grease. She cleaned the silver, too, and admired it, which made Julian smile on her. And, yes, she hand-washed delicate fabrics with a masterly touch. She ironed exquisitely, and made golabki and bigos to die for: the very smell of the latter cooking slowly in the cool oven seemed to make Ginnie's waist expand. She had made zakuski for their last party which had the neighbours twittering and begging to 'borrow' her. And when she babysat for them while they went out she had the children clean and in bed in a brace of shakes as if it was the easiest thing in the world.

All round she was indeed pretty wonderful, and Ginnie would have liked to have hated her, but Marta was a pleasant, sunny, cheery person that it was very hard to hate, even when she was zooming round at top speed, singing while she cleaned as though it was the nicest job in the world. Ginnie also watched Julian carefully for signs of Greg Summeritis, and it was a worry for several weeks because he was not only obviously impressed with Marta's industriousness, but delighted with her appreciation of his musty old antiques and dreary old watercolours. In addition, it turned out that Marta was very intelligent and had a degree in economics from the University of Gdansk, and was only doing domestic cleaning to enable her to live in London while she studied for a second degree in Fine Art in her spare time. Which accounted for her appreciating Julian's watercolours, which were eighteenth and early nineteenth century (and a complete wash-out as far as Ginnie was concerned) and also, since she had visited the Wallace Collection several times, enabled her to understand Julian's joke about Gdansk to the Music of Time and *laugh* at it.

Fortunately, Julian's interest in Marta turned out to be entirely cerebral, and while Ginnie was glad about that, it also irritated her, because she felt any proper, red-blooded male *ought* to have fancied the pants off such a delectable girl. Julian's obvious and utter sexual indifference to the maid seemed to Ginnie a symptom of a deeper problem, that he had no interest in sex *at all*. He was, of course, a good deal older than Ginnie, but, my God, that shouldn't matter, and Ginnie had always been the sort of girl to appeal to older men. She'd had pleasant trouble that way many times during her career, both before and after marriage. Anyway, Julian wasn't *old*, he had just become dull and set in his ways (or, she should say, *more* set in his ways, because he had already been pretty set in them when she first met him.) So while she was grateful that he didn't seem to notice that Marta was a woman, it simultaneously annoyed her. They didn't have sex much any more – The Silence of the Springs, Ginnie called it – because he was always too tired by the time he went to bed, and tended to drop off to sleep while she was still reading. She supposed she *could* have put her book down sooner and caught him before he passed out, but she didn't see why she should have to, especially as in bed at night was the only time she had to *do* any reading. Anyway, she got the feeling the only reason he'd ever had sex was for procreational purposes, and now they had three children and she didn't want any more, there was no reason in his view to do it again. He ought to have married Polly next door, Ginnie thought grumpily as she shoved cereal-cemented dishes into the dishwasher. The would-be Earth Mother. It was such a waste, Polly wanting babies so much, when Seth had so much money and Polly had such a great collection of shoes...

By the time she had finished cleaning up, and put down some dried food for Mr Big, who couldn't fancy it, but made it clear he couldn't be sure about that until she had got a new packet down from the high dry-store cupboard, cut it open and filled his dish (it smelled like school gravy), she had gone off the idea of the bath, and had a quick shower instead. Then she dressed in faded Levis and her adored old Biba tee shirt – a carefully treasured antique which she only wore when she needed cheering up and was the closest she ever got to understanding Julian's obsession with all things old – and telephoned Polly to see if she'd like to meet up for lunch.

# Three

Shepherd's Bush had been a respectable working-class area in the fifties, had sunk to near-slumhood in the seventies, and partially revived to a mixed status in the eighties. In the nineties it had begun to take off, as the fashionable money which could not get a foothold in overcrowded Notting Hill had discovered there were beautiful big houses going for practically *nothing*. It was the last westward reach of Old London: beyond it everything was 1930s semis and worse, until you got to Ealing which was OK but too far out. Now in the noughties, known to locals as The Bush – which signified quite a tightly-defined area around the Green itself – it had been thoroughly colonized by the young, rich and beautiful. It had been profiled in the glossies as the New Notting Hill, house prices were in the stratosphere – you could not get so much as a maisonette for less than a million – and, best of all for the residents, gorgeous shops and restaurants, niche traders and elite services had followed the fashionable money. Now you could get anything you wanted in The Bush, as long as you were prepared to pay for it.

Polly and Ginnie met for lunch in Fare Trade, Ginnie's absolutely favourite place, which combined coffee shop, restaurant and delicatessen. At the coffee counter you could choose from twenty-six coffees in a hundred and thirty combinations, and either carry it out in tall insulated containers that immediately proclaimed your status to passers-by as one of the world's movers and shakers, or sit down with it in deep armchairs around low tables in the window and let them enviously watch you drink it. In the restaurant you could eat the very latest, cutting-edge cuisine, all of it organic, fair trade and dietetically balanced for a holistic mind-and-body experience. And in the delicatessen you could buy all the same things, either prepared for take-out or raw to cook for yourself at home.

Consequently, Fare Trade was always heaving, particularly at lunchtime, when the queue to the deli counter stretched out of the door and it could take you half an hour to purchase one of their delectable salads (complete with recyclable *wooden* fork – no plastic cutlery at Fare Trade!) or a heated carton of beetroot linguini with seared tuna carpaccio.

To be completely honest – which she only ever was with herself, inside her mind, where no one was listening – Polly wasn't *that* mad about the food, which was so cutting edge it sometimes tasted very weird indeed, and so conscientious it generally left her feeling hungrier than before she began. She liked the atmosphere, but sometimes thought the place could do with an injection of common sense, not to say roast beef, Yorkshire and three veg, just to bring it back to Planet Earth and stop it levitating up its own Buddhist temple bells.

But Ginnie adored it all. It made her feel virtuous, given her tendency to put on weight, to eat so little and pay so much for it: on the principle that, as with exercise, it only worked if it hurt, it provided a doubly exquisite pleasure to pay twenty quid for a tiny bowl of transparent soup with a few scraps of bok choy floating in it, or a seaweed and tofu wrap the size of a spectacles-case. She loved the décor, the pale panelled walls with the ebony-framed eighteenth-century botanical drawings, the black marble floor, the steel and glass tables and the deep purple chairs. And she loved the people – rich, fashionable, important, rich, rake thin, fabulously dressed, rich, and frequently famous. It was not unusual to find the likes of Richard E Grant, Kate Moss, Andrea Galer, Allegra McEvedy or Toby Stephens at the next table. Polly swore she had once, on a very crowded day, shared a table with Cavolo Nero and Belle de Fontenay. The names had sounded annoyingly familiar to Ginnie so she hadn't admitted that she couldn't think who they were.

Polly was already seated when Ginnie arrived. She had got a good table in the middle at the back, against the wall, under the drawing of the paeony, where they could look outwards and see everything. Not that there were any obviously famous people there at the moment, as Ginnie noted while she wove her way slowly on a circuitous route between the tables for the purpose. The waiter was hovering impatiently so they ordered their food quickly. Polly chose one of the more substantial things on the lunch menu, the red Thai chicken with risotto-stuffed tomatoes and a rocket salad, and Ginnie went for the prawn miso macaroni with enoki mushrooms.

'Pasta?' Polly said teasingly, raising an eyebrow – a facial gesture she had caught from Seth. 'To smithereens with the diet, eh?'

'Can't help it,' Ginnie said. 'I must have carbs. It's that sort of day. I don't care if I blow up like a balloon.'

'I was only joking,' Polly said hastily, because Ginnie fretted constantly over her weight, and what she had chosen was pretty meagre anyway. Besides, Fare Trade portions wouldn't blow anyone up. 'You've got a lovely figure. I wish I had proper boobs like you.'

Ginnie was wearing a tight V-necked Malo cashmere sweater that emphasized her breasts sensationally.

35

'Are you kidding me?' Ginnie said. 'You're so lucky to be flat. Everything looks better when you're flat down the front. I bet you're not even wearing a bra under that.'

Polly was wearing a loose brown raglan over a sleeveless white silk vest. She looked down at herself. 'What would be the point?' She sighed. 'Do you think I'd get proper boobs if I had a baby?'

Ginnie picked up quickly on the subjunctive. 'Don't tell me?'

Polly nodded. 'This morning, damn it.'

'Oh, Pol, I'm sorry. But chin up, there's always next month.'

'That's what you said last month.' Polly tried hard to smile, but it was an obvious effort.

'Look, I think we both need a glass of wine,' Ginnie said. She looked around but the waiters were all elsewhere. 'I'll go up to the counter and order them. It'll be quicker. Pouilly Fumé?'

Polly nodded. 'Lovely.'

When she got back with the tall, chilled glasses, Polly took a deep sip of the delicious, perfumed wine and then, being a good friend, said, 'So tell me, why do you need carbs?'

Ginnie sat with a sudden, flouncing sort of movement, jammed her elbow on the table and her chin in her hand, and said, 'Oh God, Pol, I'm just so *bored*! Nothing ever seems to happen. Julian goes off to his boring old job every day – which of course isn't boring to him, which shows how boring *he* is – and I stay home and keep house like some 1950s vacuum-cleaner advert. He's so mean about not letting me have Marta every day. I'm tied to the bloody place. And nobody clears up after themselves. I practically had to muck out the kitchen this morning when they'd all gone. I mean, what have *you* done today?'

Polly felt a little uncomfortable. 'Well, I cycled down to Hammersmith Town Hall for some papers for Seth, did a bit of shopping while I was there, went to my Pilates class, showered and came here.'

Ginnie pounced, as Polly knew she would, on the bit that mattered to her. 'Shopping? What did you buy?'

'Food for tonight. Sashimi from Miso en Place, and some roasted butternut squash with chilli oil.'

'From the new Ottolenghi in King Street? I love that place! It's so nice not having to go to Notting Bloody Hill for everything. What else?'

'I was going to griddle some steak. Seth loves it.'

'The carnivore! But I didn't mean what else are you having for dinner, I meant what else did you buy? As you very well know.'

Polly knew, but she didn't really want to get into it. Shopping was Ginnie's passion, far more than it was hers – she would sooner have something useful to do on the days when she wasn't at work. And she didn't want to stir Ginnie up more than she was already stirred about the contrast in their lives. But Ginnie would be answered, and she said reluctantly, 'Just something I spotted.'

'What sort of something?'Ginnie leaned forward eagerly. 'Wait! Not shoes? Come on, don't give me that look. I know when you're holding out on me. You know how I feel about shoes.'

Polly, sighed, and extended her foot out from under the table so that Ginnie could see they were metallic green strappy sandals.

Ginnie practically drooled. 'Gorgeous! Simply Gorgeous! Oh, you are so lucky! I never have anything nice like that.'

'Oh, come on, Ginnie, you know that's not true,' Polly protested. 'You had those Emilio Pucci wedges a couple of weeks ago.'

'Nearly *four* weeks ago,' Ginnie corrected. 'And Julian made such a fuss about them. He said he could buy a second home on what I spend on clothes. He made me promise not to buy anything else this month – while you can have whatever you want, whenever you want it.'

'But you've got three lovely children,' Polly said. 'That's something I don't seem to be able to have.'

'Oh,' said Ginnie impatiently, 'that's not the same thing.'

'Of course not,' Polly said. 'It's much,

much better. There's no comparison.'

'But you wouldn't want to be me.'

'For the three lovely children I would.'

'No, seriously, you'd want children *and* all the nice things you have. Why should a person have to choose one or the other? Your house is so gorgeous, while ours is practically *suppurating*, and you have clothes and shoes and bags to die for, and Leela six times a week so you never have to clean anything and you can go where you like and do what you like.'

'But I'd give that all up to have a baby!' Polly cried passionately.

'You wouldn't,' Ginnie said flatly.

Suddenly Polly saw the ridiculous side of the conversation. 'Well, maybe not the shoes,' she said to make Ginnie laugh – and failed. She looked at her companion's stormy face. Ginnie's boredom was a formidable thing that raised its head every few months, and generally led either to a new fad (reiki, crystals, a personal nutritionist) or a spending spree that set poor Julian reeling. Polly thought he had been looking worried lately. She suspected privately that Julian was not quite as rich as Ginnie seemed to think he was, and three children (especially three lots of school fees and all the etcetera that went with them – uniforms and kit and musical instruments and God knew what these days) must take a lot out of even a rich man's pocket. Julian bore with it all so patiently: he

39

was the kindest man, and sometimes Polly envied Ginnie him as well as the children. Seth was brilliant but could be demanding and ultra selfish, as geniuses were allowed to be. This Paris trip for instance – it never seemed to occur to him that she might like to go along. They could have made a nice weekend break of it. Even if he had to work, she could have done the galleries and shopping by day and they could have had the evenings together. But he had not only not asked her, he had made it very clear that he expected and intended to go alone. He hadn't even enquired as to what she would do with the time while he was away. Julian, she was sure, would at least have found *that* out, even if it was only because of his extremely good manners. And there was something to be said after all for good manners in a marriage – they could smooth over a hell of a lot of the natural bumps that were bound to occur.

The waiter brought their food. Ginnie's came in a plain, thick white bowl – like sanitary ware, Polly thought without enthusiasm. The glutinous curls of miso macaroni, the greyish slippery mushrooms and the fragments of colourless raw prawn combined with the thin, shiny sauce to look like – it had to be said – snot. Slightly fishy snot. Like something a penguin would regurgitate for its chick – a penguin with bronchitis, perhaps. But Ginnie seized her chopsticks and

dug in with apparent relish, and Polly avert-
ed her eyes to her own more cheery plate,
and addressed herself to Ginnie's problem.

'If you're so bored,' she said, 'why don't
you get a job? That would give you some
money, too, so you could buy shoes without
asking Julian every time.'

'How can I get a job? Once I've dropped
the kids at school, it's only a couple of hours
before I have to pick them up again. I'd
never get to work and back in that time, let
alone do anything when I was there.'

'I wasn't thinking about an office job,'
Polly said. 'Why not go back to what you
used to do?'

Ginnie had been a photographer, mostly of
grand houses and interiors, selling to
magazines like *Playfair*, *Giles*, *Country Life*,
*Vogue* and so on. It had been reasonably well
paid, as far as Polly could gather, and had
also given her wonderful opportunities for
mixing with rich people.

'I don't have the contacts any more,'
Ginnie said.

'You'd soon work them up again.'

'You don't understand. It's an incredibly
competitive market. And I'm out of the loop
now. You can't get editors even to look at
portfolios these days. I'd have to have a
terrific splash piece to offer just to get them
to remember who I was. Some amazing
scoop with really wicked visuals. Where the
hell would I get that?'

'Well,' Polly began thoughtfully, but Ginnie cut her off.

'Anyway, I still wouldn't have time, with the kids.'

'It is possible to use children as an excuse not to do anything,' Polly suggested as mildly as she could.

Not mildly enough.

Ginnie snorted. 'What do you know about it? You people who don't have children just don't understand how incredibly time-consuming they are. They take up your whole life. You don't have a moment to call your own any more, what with school runs, homework, music lessons, cub scouts, speech therapists, special tutors, plus illnesses and doctors and dentists, plus making costumes for school plays and bloody mediaeval castles out of egg-boxes for their bloody projects! All of it *times three*. And that doesn't even take into account the fact that I only have Marta three days a week, so I have to skivvy as well. It makes me want to cry just thinking about it.' Her eyes were sparkling, but it looked more like anger to Polly than sorrow.

'How about another glass of wine?' she said soothingly.

Ginnie sighed. 'Better not,' she said. 'I've got to get my legs waxed at two thirty and I'd better not turn up at the school gates reeking of booze or all those Filipina nannies and yummy mummies from Holland Park will

42

look down their noses at me even more than they already do.'

The scowl was still prominent so Polly had one more try. 'You know, if you worked again you'd probably make enough to hire a nanny, so she could do the school run.'

Ginnie's scowl segued rapidly into a grin, and Polly thought how tremendously attractive she was when she smiled. 'Ah, but you see, I'd have to have the job before I could hire the nanny, and I'd have to have the nanny before I could do the job.'

A while later Ginnie got up to leave, saying, 'Sorry, but I'll have to dash. You know what they're like at Zippy's – two seconds late and they give your slot to someone else. It's like getting a wax at Heathrow Airport.'

'Shame,' said Polly. 'It feels as if we've only just got here.' She hadn't had the chance to talk about her own woes yet – it had all been Ginnie's.

'I know,' said Ginnie, feeling a little guilty for the same reason. 'Look, are you and Seth eating alone tonight? Then why don't you come over after dinner for drinks and coffee? About nine thirty, so the kids'll be in bed? We can have a good natter then. And it'll put Julian in a good mood. He's got a soft spot for you.'

'Has he?' Polly asked, and to her annoyance felt herself blushing.

Ginnie didn't seem to notice. She hauled

43

her oversized Lulu Guinness bag on to her shoulder, shook her curly auburn mane back, said, 'See you later, then,' and began sidling her way out. She had to squeeze past Nita Ranjani and Nick Ellis *tête à tête* at a table to one side, which cheered her up and gave her something to wonder about. It made her think that it might have been fun to take up the old camera again. Not that she had ever been a pap, but when you were in the profession you always had your camera with you just in case, and a good frame of the young ballet dancer – who was currently appearing in a modern two-hander (two-footer? Or four-footer even?) at the Bush Theatre – and the grizzled arts critic together might have earned a few bob in the right place. Especially as he was married to a formidable producer and yet seemed to be holding one of Nita's hands under the table. My God, she *was* skinny! Her elbows were thicker than her arms, she wouldn't want to be *that* thin, Ginnie thought. She swung out into the dusty warm street with something of her normal swagger.

# Four

Julian was tired when he got home and not best pleased to be having people in, but he accepted it in his usual way, with bland politeness, which normally would have made Ginnie want to scream, but today didn't bother her because on the way from Zippy's to the school she had passed Velveteen and had popped in – just to look, because she needed cheering up – and found a pair of aubergine Marc Jacobs cords which fitted her like a glove. She was going to wear them tonight, and although it was not the end of the month she thought she looked so good in them Julian would relent, if he even noticed they were new. She had managed, while the children were rampaging about performing their usual just-home-from-school jungle-gym routine, to make some canapés (shop puff pastry, but who was going to notice?) to go with the drinks, because she had invited the Wentworths from three doors down as well as the Mullers. *He* was a stockbroker and mega-rich, but he had grown up in the country and knew a number of the same families Julian had in his boyhood, which would keep Julian happy. *She* was of Japanese blood, though she had been born in London, and designed a frighteningly smart line of children's clothes called Mesodo, which were sold, among other places, at Wilde Child on the Green – for Bush dwellers the Mecca of fashion for Little People, as they tended to be called in those circles. Ginnie had once had a Mesodo frock given her for Flora when she was two, and since it hadn't quite fitted – and was the wrong shade of pink for Flora's then gingery hair – she had taken it back to Wilde Child to see if she could exchange it, and discovered that it had retailed originally for close to £300. And that was *then*. But the other thing about Tammy Wentworth (her name was Tamiko) was that – ironically, given her business – she and Sam hadn't been able to have children, which ought to make Polly feel better. Ginnie liked to be a good hostess – and if anyone was going to have to listen to Polly's disappointment about missing for another month, it might as well be someone who had gone through it. She felt bad about having harangued Polly at lunch about childless people not understanding the problems of having children, which although true had been pretty tactless considering the circumstances, though of course she had not meant to hurt her feelings – Polly was her best friend. And in any case, she didn't think Polly had noticed or minded because she hadn't said anything or even looked miffed so Ginnie thought she had got away with it. Still, it might do Polly good to be able to have a heart-to-heart with a fellow sufferer. And that would leave her, Ginnie, to take care of Seth.

When the children were finally settled in bed – Ben with Wabbit (actually a toy dog, but who was counting?), the other two with books ('half an hour only, and then lights out, I mean it, it's school tomorrow!') – Ginnie went to the bedroom to get changed. Julian was in the shower – she could hear the grinding of the power unit along the passage – which was a big concession as he liked a bath in the evenings when he had time to lie and soak and read an old favourite like Tristram Shandy (what was all *that* about?) or Gulliver. He came in wrapped in a towel just as she was shrugging herself into the Marcs, and she allowed herself a moment to think how he wasn't half bad for his age. He had one of those lean figures that would never be any different, and though the towel had slipped down to pubic level there wasn't a hint of a pot belly or love handles. A rasher, her Irish granny had described him, short for 'a rasher of wind' which was what she called thin people (though he was not skinny at all, just fat-free and not over-muscled) but always made Ginnie think of streaky bacon. Not inappropriately, since he was straight and narrow and really quite tasty. He had a longish, smooth Rupert Brooke sort of face, and the light brown, smooth hair that breaks into little curls at the nape of the neck, that went with it. Altogether the image of the English aristocrat. He was going grey now, but because he was fair the grey blended in so you didn't really notice it.

He didn't look at her as he came in so she thought she had got away with the new cords. But as he stood with his back to her and rummaged in his drawer for a clean pair of underpants, he said, 'Is that a new pair of trousers?'

His voice was so neutral it would have taken an expert to guess his mood from one short sentence, but of course she was an expert. She went straight into defensive mode.

'I haven't bought anything since the sandals! And it's nearly the end of the month!'

He turned and looked at her.

'Wait, wait, don't say anything until you've seen it with the top,' she said hastily, grabbing the Malo cashmere from the bed and struggling into it.

'I don't think—' he began as she thrashed out of the neck hole.

'*Please*! Wait to see it all together!'

'It doesn't matter—'

'It *does*. You can't judge. Wait, wait, wait! The shoes!' She dashed to the wardrobe, stubbing her toe on the bed leg on the way and, hopping the last few steps saying, *'Fuck-fuck-fuck!'* under her breath, scrabbled for the Emilio Puccis which were the cause of the last altercation, climbed on to them (the wedges were four inches high) and buckled the straps, then strutted round the bed into the open space so he could see all of her and flung her hair back and her chest out in a half joking pose. She had actually been intending to wear a white top with the Marcs, but the pink went all right and she'd needed to be quick.

'Now,' she said. 'Aren't they sensational?'

He was looking at her oddly, his head slightly tilted and a quizzical look to his mouth, but it was not disapproval. She wasn't sure what it was, but she saw he wasn't about to bawl her out. She gave him her best impish grin. 'You see how I couldn't have resisted? Now do admit! And it is *almost* the end of the month.'

'Almost,' he agreed neutrally.

'Don't you think?' she appealed, giving him a half-turn of the shoulders and another shake of the hair.

'I think,' he said, and came to her, put his arms round her and kissed her softly on the mouth. It made her shiver, because it was not like him, not something he tended to do, and she couldn't read him. He was perfectly capable of being angry and not showing it until some more convenient time, and they *were* expecting people and this wouldn't be

49

the time to have a row. But he didn't *feel* angry to her. One of his hands, which had been splayed against her back for balance while he kissed her, crept upwards to the back of her neck as he looked down at her. He wasn't particularly tall – five foot nine – but she was only five foot three, so she had to tilt her head to see his face. His fingers played with her nape and made her shiver again, and he said, 'I don't mind about the trousers. They look nice on you.'

'Thanks,' she said. But she still couldn't read him. He looked sad, or – or *something*. She couldn't pin it down. Then he let her go quite abruptly and went back to dressing, which he did with the rapid efficiency of movement of men who have lived communally, like soldiers or public school boys.

Seth didn't want to go, and was cross with her for accepting without checking it with him. 'But it's only drinks next door,' Polly said. 'I don't usually check with you for that. We needn't stay long if you don't like.'

'I just don't feel like going out,' he said. 'I thought we were going to have a nice, intimate dinner together.'

'We are. I mean, we'll still have the dinner. We don't have to be there until nine thirty.'

'*The Sopranos* is on. We could watch that and then have an early night. Our last before the weekend,' he offered seductively.

It fell flat for her. 'My period started today.

This afternoon.'

'Oh,' he said. And then, 'I'm sorry.'

Tears leapt to her eyes at the words, but the first thing she wanted to say was, '*Are* you?' Because if he wanted a baby as much as she did, he shouldn't be apologizing to her. It ought to be his sorrow as much as hers. But she controlled herself, pushed the tears down because she knew it would only annoy him if she cried (he was not one of the world's great comforters), and told herself that men never felt exactly the same way about it as women. And they didn't have the same sense of urgency. Charlie Chaplin was eighty or something when he fathered a child. So one month's failure didn't strike them the same way, because there was always another month for them, and another. Polly felt them all stacking up against her, like snow against the door of an Alpine shelter, walling her in with her failure and barrenness.

Then she told herself briskly to stop being melodramatic and reached for the most ordinary, everyday thing she could, something not only so sensible as to convince him of her not-going-to-cryness, but so dry as to make it true. 'We can tape it and watch it later,' she said, and felt her tear-ducts shrivel miraculously. 'Why isn't there a nice short word for DVD-ing?' she went on, interested in her own physiological reactions. She couldn't have cried now if you'd shown her *that* bit in Old Yeller. '"Taping" was all right when we had videos, but you'd never say "disc-ing".'

'You could say "recording",' Seth suggested, proving she had been right about his feelings.

'But it's not short and convenient. Are you going to change now or have supper first?'

'Oh, change now, I think,' he said. 'I might not feel like it afterwards.'

'All right. Starter in ten minutes,' she said, turning away.

'Make it fifteen. I want to have a shower. Hey!' She turned back enquiringly. 'I love you.'

'I love you too,' she said.

She went downstairs, thinking that she didn't really want to go out either. They could have had their meal (though it would not have been intimate and romantic, not now she had the curse – Seth would never do anything while she was menstruating, didn't really even like to touch her in bed, and she had never known whether it was for fear of staining their beautiful white sheets, or an animal squeamishness. On the whole she rather hoped the former.) Then they could have put on slobs and curled up together in a corner of their huge sofa with large brandies (Armagnac for him, Calvados for her, which would help with her cramps), and watched a bit of what Julian next door called MTV – mindless television. She wasn't wild

52

about *The Sopranos* (she preferred *The West Wing* and *Gray's Anatomy*) but Seth adored it and it took no effort on her part to watch it. Then she'd have made some hot chocolate with almond biscotti and made him watch *Grand Designs* with her, which she enjoyed for the sheer, touching doggedness of the subjects, and which made Seth-the-architect shout with laughter, so they'd have gone to bed in a good mood and maybe for once he would have cuddled her a little bit before they went to sleep. She really felt she needed to be held.

Instead they were going to have to get dressed again and go and have drinks next door and she was feeling just a little bit peeved with Ginnie. It wasn't just the monstrous tactlessness of telling her, as people so often did, that she didn't understand because she didn't have children – Ginnie obviously hadn't even twigged to what she was saying and who she was saying it to, and Polly had forced herself not to react because you can't spend your life being sensitive to that sort of thing even if you felt your best friend ought to be a bit more thoughtful.

But it always did and always had exasperated her, how people with children made such a huge *thing* of it. They went on and on about how they had no time to themselves, how their social life was ruined, moaned that bedlam reigned at home, the children broke things and left fingermarks on things and were rude to them, that they spent their lives picking up after them, that they cost a fortune and childless people didn't know how lucky they were. Why did they have children if they hated them so much? Polly found herself wanting to yell. And as often as not they said all this stuff *in front of the children*, as if they were idiots or foreigners who couldn't understand English. They made martyrs of themselves as if there was nothing they could do about any of it, but she had been brought up with three sisters and bedlam most certainly had not reigned, nor had they broken things or been rude – the thought would never have crossed their minds. Her parents simply wouldn't have tolerated bad behaviour. But if she ever even hinted to the parents she knew now, that any of the things they complained about were their own fault and that they should bring their children up better, they would only sigh and roll their eyes and say things were different nowadays and *she didn't understand because she didn't have children*!

So she was glad when she and Seth went round next door and found that they were not to be alone with the Addingtons after all, because Ginnie had invited the Wentworths from number 7 as well. From a look and a nod Ginnie gave her she suspected she and Tammy Wentworth were supposed to spend the evening commiserating with each other – and she *had* had some heart-to-hearts in the past in Tammy's kitchen – but Polly knew her well enough to know Ginnie was mistaken and that Tammy would never mention that subject unless they were *à deux*. Which suited Polly, because she wanted an evening off from her thoughts, and if it wasn't to be thanks to MTV it had better be through civilized conversation and a few drinks.

They had gone to the front door, which was up a flight of steps over the semi-basement where the kitchen was. The basement was knocked right through, as theirs was, and since all the lights were on they could see that there was no one in there, except for Mr Big who was making hay by sitting on the lid of the cool plate on the Aga, something normally forbidden him. Julian opened the door and escorted them into the drawing room which was the first room on the right, with the bay window on to the street. The heavy velvet drapes were drawn though it was still light outside, and the lamps in the corners were lit, which made it cosy and intimate, though more like winter than summer. Polly felt there ought to have been a fire in the fireplace, and kept catching herself glancing at the paper fan that Marta – from some early training or other – put there instead.

Julian had very nobly broken out a couple of bottles of good claret. The '83 Chateau Margaux was wasted on at least three of those present, but Polly had heard Julian say on other occasions that he would sooner waste good wine on people who didn't appreciate it than give them poor wine and have to drink it himself. After the greetings and the provision of drinks Polly let herself be annexed by Sam Wentworth. He was evidently still hyper from work because he kept talking non-stop about the market while simultaneously inhaling nuts from the priceless Qing teabowl at his elbow. She didn't mind accommodating him. It was only a matter of listening and nodding now and then, and since she didn't understand most of what he said and he didn't require any response it wasn't taxing at all, and allowed her to enjoy the wine and the surroundings. She loved this room. It was the match of their own, of course, but theirs had been changed out of all recognition, whereas the original owner of this one, time-travelling from 1840-ish, would probably have felt quite at home. The cornice and picture rails and the elaborate rose in the centre of the high ceiling were still there, and the tall chimneypiece was the original. The wallpaper was dark red and there was a Turkish carpet on the floor and big old chairs and antique side-tables and a walnut chiffonier from which Julian produced glasses and bottles. It was hopelessly old-fashioned, of course, but it was nice now and then to see what a house had used to look like in its heyday. Because there was no heating on, there was a dampish smell, which Polly found rather romantic though she wouldn't have liked to live with it. She knew Ginnie hated the old-fashionedness and longed to get Seth in, but Julian would not hear of it, and on an evening like this Polly was quite glad.

Ginnie and Seth were talking together, heads close, laughing a lot, and Polly, nodding away dutifully for Sam, supposed they were rubbishing the drawing room and Julian's taste as they sometimes did when they got together – they really weren't good for each other. Ginnie seemed in an odd mood. She kept looking at Julian with a sort of guarded, quizzical expression. When Sam stopped talking to take a drink, Polly was able to look at her friend directly and saw at once that she was wearing a new pair of cord jeans that looked expensive, along with her Emilio wedge sandals, and wondered if she had bought them today and whether there had been a row with Julian about it, which would explain the looks. Ginnie looked fabulous in them, she thought – amazingly slim, which made all the more of her terrific boobs. Her hair, a mass of dark red curls, was held back from her face by two sparkly clips, and she had lots of smudgy navy mascara on, which made her eyes look alluring and mysterious, and very dark glossy lipstick. *The Bad Girl look*, Polly thought; the look that men found so irresistible, and which Polly could never hope to emulate. Ginnie was doing a lot of shaking her hair back and gazing up at Seth, but it was probably only to get Julian to notice her. He was talking quietly and calmly to Tammy and not paying Ginnie any attention at all. Polly could have told her that Seth could not be more indifferent, since he liked smart, severe good looks along the same lines as the interiors he designed – he had said more than once that he *supposed* Ginnie was attractive *in her way* but she was just not his type.

Finally Ginnie gave up her attempts at fascination and went down to the kitchen to fetch canapés. Polly was interested to note that she had made them herself, some on puff pastry and some on ciabatta toast, so she was evidently trying to please Julian, and Polly wondered again about the trousers.

People had changed their seats while she was out of the room – Julian got up to pour more wine, Tammy went to look at the porcelain in the glazed cupboard and then asked Sam if one of the pieces wasn't like something her parents had at home, making him get up to look too, and then they sat down in different places, Tammy next to Seth, Sam on the sofa and Julian in the chair next to Polly. So when Ginnie had been round with the plate the conversation became general.

After a bit Tammy said she thought she had seen Ginnie coming out of Fare Trade that afternoon and Ginnie said yes, she had been having lunch with Polly.

'See any celebs?' Seth asked.

Ginnie started to tell about Nita Ranjani and Nick Ellis, and seeing that she was amusing him, began to spin the story out and embellish it.

Tammy's rather immobile, pale face, framed by its bell of heavy, black silk hair, was turned attentively to her, and she said, 'My God, what can she see in that horrible old man? He smokes *cigars*!'

This seemed to pique Julian for some reason, because he said to Ginnie, quite severely, 'You know I disapprove of this sort of gossip. Before you know where you are, it spreads and someone gets hurt. You're jumping to conclusions from the simple fact of two people having lunch together.'

'But they were holding hands!' Ginnie said indignantly, turning to him with a faint appearance of surprise.

'Maybe she was confiding in him and he was comforting her,' Polly found herself saying, though she really had no desire to side with Julian against Ginnie.

Julian did not look at her. He said to Ginnie, 'We shouldn't be talking like that about people we don't know.'

But Seth laughed at Polly. 'Of course he wasn't just comforting her! They're having an affair – s'obvious. Everyone does it these days! Nobody minds about that sort of thing any more. As to not talking about people we don't know – my God, we'd all be sitting about in silence at social gatherings if we followed those rules!'

He only meant it jokingly, and was trying to lighten the atmosphere, but Polly could see Julian didn't like it. Presumably Tammy saw the same thing as well, because she intervened in her calm, level voice that never showed any emotion, one way or another, and said, 'We can talk about houses instead. Have you heard they're moving into that big one on the corner at last?'

'You mean number one?' Julian said. 'The sold notice came down weeks ago.'

'How do you know someone's moving in?' Ginnie asked

'Because I saw the van from that specialist house-cleaning firm, Maxiclean, outside, when I was coming home today. The people were just coming out so I stopped and asked them, and they said the new owner is arriving tomorrow. Then I rang up the estate agents and they confirmed it.' Tammy was nothing if not thorough.

'Did they say how much it went for in the end?' Seth asked.

Julian gave him a look. 'Of course they wouldn't say that.'

'I heard it was five million,' Sam said. Then he wrinkled his brow. 'Can't remember who said that.'

'It needs doing up,' Ginnie said. 'Old Mrs

Tennison hadn't done anything to it since her husband died – and not much while he was alive, either.'

'Job for you, Seth,' Sam said.

'Oh, I've got too much on my plate already,' Seth said. 'Couldn't take on a new client for six months at least. I wonder who the new owner is, though?'

'The Maxiclean man said he was American,' said Tammy. 'Something important in global media.'

'Rich, obviously,' said Ginnie.

'But could still be reasonably young, if he's talented,' said Seth.

'I don't know if he's young,' Tammy said, 'but the Maxiclean man said he was single – or at least, it's just him coming, not his wife, if he has one.'

Julian said, not sounding angry, only bored, 'You see, we're doing it again, talking about someone we don't know.'

'But we're not gossiping about him,' Seth countered.

'Just being good neighbours,' Tammy said. 'We ought to call on him, welcome him to the Terrace, that sort of thing.'

Ginnie lit up. 'We could have a party for him. How about this weekend? He'll probably be feeling a bit lost, moving into a strange place in a strange country.'

'I'm not going to be here this weekend,' Seth reminded her.

'Oh, of course.'

'Well, I'm in, anyway,' Polly said. 'It's been ages since anyone had a party.'

'We'll come, won't we, darling?' Tammy said.

Polly caught Julian's eye and guessed a second before he said it what he was going to say. She didn't know what made her psychic in this instance, but she was right.

'I'm afraid this weekend's out for me,' he said with his usual calm politeness. 'I shan't be here either.'

And Ginnie didn't know. Her head swung round fast in a blur of eyes and hair. 'What do you mean?'

'I'm going in the other direction. I have to go to New York.'

'You didn't tell me!'

'It was only decided today. I was going to tell you later.'

'But why are you going? And why can't I go with you?' Ginnie wailed. 'I've never been to New York!'

'We'll talk about it later,' Julian said with deadly firmness. For a moment Polly thought there was going to be a scene, and suspected that, if there was, she would be the person who minded it most. Ginnie's eyes were very bright, but she must have seen something in Julian's face because she shut her mouth with a snap, though words were obviously seething behind her teeth, trying to get out.

Into the slightly awkward silence, Seth

spoke in an easy, laughing tone. 'How can anyone possibly get to your age and be able to say they've never been to New York? Now, if it was Vladivostok—'

'*I've* been to Vladivostok,' Tammy said.

'Well, I suppose that's not so surprising in your case,' Seth said.

'It's in China, not Japan,' she said.

'Same part of the world,' Seth said largely. 'All right, let's say Anchorage, Alaska.'

'I've been to Fairbanks,' Sam said. 'Not Anchorage, though.'

'You haven't really, have you?' Seth said, laughing. 'Whatever for?'

'Business, of course,' Sam said imperturbably. 'I've been to Archangel, too.'

'He likes cold places,' Tammy remarked. 'Colder the better. Me, I like to be warm.'

'Talking of cold places, are you skiing at all this year?' Sam asked the room in general, and so the awkward moment passed and conversation became general again.

# Five

Ginnie could hardly wait for everyone to go so she could have a row with Julian, and she ended up drinking too much, whereat Julian gave her *A Look* and deliberately and insultingly (or so it seemed to her at the time) opened a bottle of something cheap (Languedoc, she thought it was) implying that it was pearls before swine to give her twenty-year-old claret – as if she wasn't just as capable of appreciating fine wine as *he* was.

And then when everyone was gone, he refused even to have a proper row at all.

'Why didn't you *tell* me?' She rounded on him virtually as soon as the door closed on Seth Muller's heels.

'As I said, it was only arranged at work today,' Julian said calmly, walking back into the drawing room and starting to collect up glasses. 'I was going to tell you when I got home, but then you sprang this drinks thing on me, so I decided to wait until it was over. But of course Tammy's party idea flushed it out.'

'Flushed it out?' Ginnie said, angered by the phrase, though she couldn't have said exactly why. Perhaps it was because of the shooting connotation. She didn't like to be reminded of Julian's aristocratic origins, *especially* since he never mentioned them directly himself and always behaved as though they didn't matter. 'And I suppose if it hadn't been *flushed out* I'd have heard about it just as you walked out of the door with your suitcase in your hand?'

He looked at her quizzically. 'What are you so mad about?'

'*I* want to go!' she wailed, betrayed by alcohol into sounding like a thwarted child.

'It's business,' he said firmly and reasonably. 'I don't particularly want to go myself, but I have to.'

'Oh, you have to, do you?'

She saw him suppress a smile. He was trying not to laugh at her, damn him!

'Yes, I have to. Mark Stephens had a fit of temperament and he's threatening to take his next book to someone else, and you know how much our balance sheet depends on a new Mark Stephens every year. We can't afford to lose him.'

'I thought you always had an option on a writer's next book?' Ginnie said suspiciously.

'No, my sweet. Not at that level of fame and remuneration. The agents won't let them be tied down.'

*Agents! That was it!* Ginnie almost snapped her fingers as the weak point in the story hit her. 'Yes, and this is agent's business, not yours. Why on earth should you get mixed up in it?'

Julian rubbed a hand over his face, looking tired. 'Mark likes me because I gave him his first break, when all the other publishers turned him down. Angela thinks I'm the only person who can talk him round.'

'Who's Angela?'

'Angela Demarco at Day Valentine – they do the US hardback. Mark's agent wants him to go elsewhere for more signature money, as agents always do, but Angela thinks I can talk him into seeing that there are other values that he'd sacrifice if he left us. He's agreed to see me, but it has to be tomorrow because they're lining him up to sign with Transglobal on Monday. And now that you have all the facts, can we please go to bed and sleep, because I have a horribly early start? I have to be at Heathrow for the seven fifty-five plane.'

She was too drunk to assemble her arguments at once, and followed him in silence through the processes of taking the glasses to the kitchen, locking doors and turning off lights. Big, already settled in his basket in the corner of the kitchen, gave her a cynical smirk before she switched off the light.

It was only when they were in their bedroom that she had defuddled enough to confront him again.

'I still don't see why I couldn't have gone,' she said. 'If you'd 'phoned me as soon as you

66

knew, I could have made arrangements. You know I've always wanted to go to New York.'

'And who would have looked after the children?' he asked wearily.

'We could have dumped them on my mother.'

'They have to go to school tomorrow.'

'They could miss one day. You always say they're not learning anything useful there anyway. Or Marta could have taken them and picked them up and Mummy could have come for them.'

'But Marta's away this weekend as well,' Julian pointed out. 'And it's too much for your mother, looking after three children, if we're not there.'

'All right, your mother could have them, then.' She knew she was not being rational now.

'In that tiny house?'

'She could always take them to your brother's. God knows there are enough servants there to take the strain.'

'You can't play fast and loose with other people's hospitality,' he said. 'Particularly at short notice.' He started jerking off his clothes in a way that told her he was angry but not choosing to express it. It made her feel even more hard done by. Why should *he* be angry? *She* was the victim here! 'There's no point in talking about it any more. I have to go, and you can't, and that's all there is to it.'

Ginnie felt very strongly that that *wasn't*, but she couldn't think of any more arguments. *Damn you, fine claret! You'll pay for this!*

'When are you coming back?' she asked at last, in what she hoped was a civilized, neutral voice, but which even to her ears sounded merely sulky.

He didn't answer until he was in his pyjama bottoms, the only thing he usually slept in. 'I don't know,' he said. 'I'm meeting Mark and Angela for lunch in Manhattan, and I dare say the talks will go on all afternoon and into the evening. I'd be surprised if Wolf – his agent – didn't try to crash in on us. And depending on what happens tomorrow, I might have to be around for further talks over the weekend. As soon as I know, I'll telephone you and let you know. But for better or worse, it will all be over by Monday and I can fly back then.'

For better or worse, she thought. Now where had she heard those words before? He came round the bed to her, and looked down at her with that expression she had seen earlier which she couldn't quite fathom – was it tenderness, or sadness, or a bit of both?

'Don't look so forlorn,' he said. 'It would not have been any fun for you. We'll go to New York together one day and do it properly.' He took hold of her chin and tilted her face up to kiss her, rather paternally she thought, but on the lips. 'And while I'm

68

away, try not to spend any more large sums of money?'

She jerked away, scowling. 'One pair of trousers!'

He left her then, and got into bed without another word.

Going to bed drunk and in a temper, Ginnie slept heavily, but her sleep didn't refresh her. When the alarm went off, she jerked awake violently with a thudding heart and a thumping headache. Julian's arm snaked out and stopped the noise, and Ginnie groaned. He leaned over her. 'Go back to sleep,' he said. 'I'll get breakfast at the airport. I'll reset the alarm for you.'

But though he moved quietly, the sounds he made opening and closing drawers and doors as he packed, and the cranky roar of their old power shower, woke her fully, and in the end she got up and went downstairs to make him a cup of tea. Mr Big looked up in surprise from his basket, and then stepped daintily out, stretched luxuriously fore and aft, ending with the usual extended arabesque of the left hind, and came across to circle her bare ankles and make suggestions about breakfast. Ginnie took two aspirin and drank two glasses of water while managing to ignore him, but in the end she found him a dab of pâté on a saucer covered in clingfilm which she had doubts about. He found this acceptable as a pre-prowl snack, polished it off, and sauntered out through the cat flap to face his world.

Julian was grateful for the tea, and when the car arrived they parted in better humour than the previous night might have suggested. It was still hideously early so Ginnie went back to bed, but she couldn't get to sleep again, so she put the *Today* programme on, which always acted as an instant soporific. She woke in a second, thudding panic when Flora burst into her room to ask why she wasn't up and tell her, with a certain pleasure-in-catastrophe, that her school blouse needed ironing.

Ginnie laid her forearm across her eyes and moaned. 'Ask Marta to do it.'

'Marta's not here,' Flora said in the tone of one stating the obvious. 'She went home for the weekend, to Poland.'

'Oh God, I forgot again,' Ginnie said. 'Why does everyone go away for the weekend except me?'

'Has Daddy gone away for the weekend too?' Flora asked, suddenly putting together the empty half of the bed and the lack of activity in the bathroom. 'I wonder if he's gone to Poland too?'

'He's gone to New York, on business. Flora, go and get dressed. Yes, I know, your blouse needs ironing. Get everything else on and I'll go and do it now.'

Ginnie staggered out of bed, dragged on her dressing gown and headed heavily towards the stairs, with Flora prancing behind, chanting, 'Poland, Poo-land, how are you-land? Monkey in the zoo-land!' She could hear the boys having a raucous argument about something in Jasper's bedroom, while behind her John Humphrys interviewed the Education Secretary about A-level grade inflation yet again, and a full ironing basket awaited her in the kitchen. She felt that Mr Big had had the right idea, and wished she had slipped out with him into the cool, sweet morning.

Seth was departing at a more civilized hour for Paris, and Polly left him in the bedroom packing his usual enormous quantity of clothes (he changed more often than any woman she knew, and their annual dry-cleaning bill ran easily into four figures) when she left for work. He kissed her rather brusquely and she wondered if he was still cross about the drinks party last night, but when she got to the front door he reappeared at the top of the stairs to call down to her that he'd bring her back some Geneva. 'Love you, honeybunch!' he concluded.

'Love you too,' she said, and felt a warm surge of it. Her view of him was foreshortened by his being at the top of the stairs, but he was not ultra-tall anyway, and was so muscular (he worked out religiously every day at the Riverside gym, and was planning his own weights room in the next round of alterations to the house) that it made him look shorter still. With his intense swarthiness and hairiness, he was like a troll looking down at her – her own, darling, brilliant, dangerous, exciting troll!

Polly worked at the Esterhazy Gallery in Bond Street three days a week. The pay was only reasonable, but the commission if she sold anything was terrific, which made it very much worthwhile. Not that the money was everything. Frankly, Seth earned so much that they could have afforded to live on his income alone: they had bought the house on Albemarle Terrace *for cash*. But she liked to feel she made her own contribution; and she simply loved going to work and being part of the art world.

She was going through the card file on Friday morning, checking clients' listed preferences against the new acquisitions, so that Nigel could call them up later and ask if they would like 'a private viewing before the painting goes into the showroom, because I just know it's right up your particular boulevard, my dear duchess, and I wanted you to have first refusal. This one isn't going to last ten minutes in the window, it's *gorgeous*!'

Nigel Leominster, Polly's boss, was as gay as a striped parrot, and knew absolutely everyone. He was a small, neat man, given to exquisite three-piece suits and handmade Lobb shoes, who always wore a white gardenia in his buttonhole – he had a standing order at House of Flowers and a fresh one was delivered every day by courier. He had thick black hair with a startling white streak in it, neither colour natural – 'From my Diaghilev period, darling,' he once told Polly – and a small, but thick black moustache to complete the resemblance. These affectations made him instantly recognizable while simultaneously making it difficult ever to remember what his face actually looked like. 'Which is a good thing,' as he also once told Polly, 'because it's necessary for people to like me, but I actually have rather cruel eyes.' His knowledge of art was encyclopaedic and his business sense was formidable, though he liked to cultivate the persona of an over-sensitive aesthete. He lived with Sir Trevor Beddoes, a retired heart surgeon much older than himself, in a large and rather dark flat behind the Albert Hall which Trevor had inherited from his mother, and they had a cottage in Surrey which they hardly ever visited, though Nigel talked fondly about it all the time. 'I *need* the country – I stifle in the city,' he said. Polly had decided this was just another pose: the city, *au contraire*, stimulated him, and he would have pined without the shops and people and black taxis and all the other flowers of civilization around him. Besides, he had once confided to her in an unguarded moment that Surrey these days wasn't country at all any more, just one enormous *banlieue*.

He claimed that Trevor was the real brains behind the business, but Polly had met him once or twice when he came in to lunch with Nigel or to see a picture that had just come in, and doubted it. He was a tall, shapeless, rather shambling man, vaguely kind, harmlessly forgetful. Nigel bullied him about taking care of himself and not forgetting his pills – ironically, the heart surgeon had been grounded by a heart complaint. When he came to the gallery, Nigel would scold him for being underfoot and send him off to wander round Fortnums until lunchtime; and Trevor would look mournfully at Polly and say, 'You see how I'm treated? I was a knight of the theatre once, and now I'm dismissed like a housemaid!' But he and Nigel adored each other, and they both seemed very fond of Polly, who Trevor said was 'a find' and Nigel said 'had potential'.

The gallery dealt solely in non-representational art, heavy on the Abstract Impressionists – de Kooning, Kline, Philip Guston, Clyfford Still and so on – and on promoting and discovering modern abstract artists, though it drew the line at anything installationist, anything that didn't use paint and canvas, in fact. But despite all the aggressive modernity, Nigel's real love (his Diaghilev period had never really ended) was for Degas ballet girls. He had a formidable collection of valuable Degas drawings and paintings at home, along with two priceless

74

Degas horse-racing oils. He and Trevor loved racing, had Royal Enclosure vouchers for Ascot, and never missed the Derby and Newmarket. Nigel always said when he retired they would buy a racehorse, just for the fun of it, but Polly couldn't see that he would ever retire. He loved the thrill of the chase too much, closing a sale, discovering a new talent, hunting out a particular work, making boodles of money.

In the window at the moment, as Polly sat bent over the card index, there was a Harold Cohen, which looked like a mass of semi-transparent creamy-grey bubbles with darker spots in them, and reminded Polly irresistibly of frogspawn. Its title was 'Untitled, 1968', which was not much help, though Polly had long known better than to wonder what paintings 'meant' or 'were about', which would have called forth Seth's most powerful scorn for being 'hopelessly bourgeois', not to mention a brisk tut from Nigel. And there were two enormous canvases by new artists, one David Pullman and the other Philip Sawyer. Nigel, in one of his less precious moments, had told Polly that there was more profit to be made in the long run with the newcomers. It felt good to sell a painting for two million, but you probably had to pay one-point-nine to buy it, which was a lot of capital tied up in one place, and if it got stolen or damaged, where were you? Whereas if you had a good eye and a well-earned reputation, you could pick out a new talent, buy him up for next to nothing, and build him up until you could name your own price. The David Pullman had cost two hundred and fifty pounds – practically the price of the materials – but Nigel had put a reserve price on it of twenty-five thousand, and he had told Polly that it ought to go for a lot more. And he had twenty more Pullman canvases in store. He had early works from all sorts of people hidden away until the price was right. Philip Sawyer, for instance, was now fetching close to six figures, and Nigel had spotted him twelve years ago doing a free exhibition in Burgh House in Hampstead when he'd never sold a thing before and was living off the earnings of his wife who worked in an employment agency.

Polly knew her stuff – she wouldn't have been employed by Nigel for a minute if she hadn't – but spending her whole day surrounded by these energetic blobs and streaks of colour with their harsh emotional demands perversely left her with a craving for the polite, delicate English watercolours of the sort that Julian Addington had on his walls – pictures of places and people someone had once loved so much they wanted to immortalize them, paintings whose only request of you was to appreciate their beauty. She understood so well why Nigel liked to go home to his ballet girls, who laced their battered shoes, stretched their aching sinews and wiped their sweating brows in the dusty, size-smelling wings, and then fluttered out like moths into the spotlight to dance on bleeding feet for the uncaring, cigar-puffing Parisian patrons. Degas had known them, their weariness and pain, had known their world, these Paris rats whom the ballet took from the gutters and 'broke in' to the harshest of all artistic disciplines. Degas knew that the price of beauty was suffering, and his pictures showed it without disguise. It was real life. Nothing in this gallery, by contrast, seemed at all real.

A shadow crossed her peripheral vision and she looked up to see that a man had stopped before the window and was examining the paintings with a more-than-casual interest. She noticed his clothes first – a suit so beautiful but so modern she guessed it was Prada or Calvin Kline, which was cut to swooning-point, outlining the body underneath, which she felt sure deserved it. He was tall, around six foot, and well made – athletically lean, nicely muscular – and she could see he had thick dark hair, slightly wavy, and extremely well-styled.

The shadow of the letters of the gallery's name were obscuring his face from her at first, but then he moved along to look at the David Pullman, and she saw that he was extremely – perhaps breathtakingly – handsome. His face was lean, rather dark, with a long, mobile mouth that seemed to quirk up slightly at one corner, and his eyes, in start-ling contrast, were blue. He looked past the canvas and into the shop, and saw her, catching her staring at him in a most un-professional way. He reminded her a little of McDreamy from *Gray's Anatomy*, except that he had more of a sportsman's build – the doctor, after all, was a tad on the under-developed side.

Meeting her eyes, he smiled. His own eyes crinkled as he did, and with that crooked, more-up-one-side-than-the-other tilt to his mouth, it looked rueful, as if he and she shared a secret understanding of the truth denied to a deluded general public. She found herself smiling back as if he were someone she knew.

Behind her, she heard Nigel, in the door of his office, draw an excited breath. 'Who is that *gorgeous* man? I feel I know him. And he's looking properly at the pictures, as if he might want to buy – not like the gruesome tourists who smear the window for no pur-pose. *And* he can afford them. You can tell at a glance.'

You could, Polly thought with amusement. There was just a certain look to rich people that the non-rich could not fake.

Nigel continued to ponder. 'Is he in *buying* mood, that's the thing? Yes, keep looking, Polly dear. Eye contact confers a sense of obligation. If we can just get him inside ... But he's not English.'

'You don't think so?' Polly said.

'That's not English tailoring,' Nigel said with certainty.

'I saw that, but I thought it was something like Prada, and you can get that anywhere.'

'Prada!' Nigel said with a little popping out-breath of his lips. 'It's not *that* sort of suit, dear.'

'What's wrong with Prada?'

'For those that like that sort of thing, that's the sort of thing they like. But our friend there's suit is bespoke, my darling, from the New York equivalent of Savile Row. He's American – God bless him, and his whole bountiful land of plenty! Oh, he likes the look of that Pullman. Come on, come on little fishie,' he breathed enticingly. 'You know you want to.'

Polly glanced back at him in amusement, and even as she did he stiffened and, oddly, drew back, though his expression was one of excitement.

'I do know him! It comes to me now. I saw his photo in *Forbes* magazine. There was a big article on him. Simon Harte's his name. He's something big in Transglobal Media.'

'So he *is* American.'

'Didn't I say so? He's coming over here to start up and run a new division, with head-quarters in London. Not just visiting, you see, but *coming to stay*. That means he'll be setting up home!'

'And he may want something to put on the

walls,' Polly appreciated the point.

'He's fabulously rich – even Forbes was impressed. And single! At least, the article didn't mention a wife, and they always do if there is one.'

'Is he gay?' Polly said doubtfully. For a second she felt disappointed at the idea, then brushed the thought aside.

'One can hope, can't one?' Nigel said with dignity. Then he clasped his hands together and whispered, 'Come in, come in. Oh, please-please-please!'

McDreamy (she mustn't let herself start calling him that!) looked up again and met her eye, and then turned. His hand went to the door handle.

'He's coming!' Nigel almost squealed, flapping his fingers; and then as the door began to open he made one of his instant business judgements. 'You have him,' he said quickly to Polly. 'I shall disappear, but call me out if you need me.' And he whisked himself into his room as the tall dark stranger entered the shop, the spider's parlour, Polly's life.

# Six

'Hi,' he said.

Unusually, he grew even more handsome the closer he got: most people's features benefited from a little distance. And he was not really much like McDreamy, beyond the general air of darkness and handsomeness. This man was bigger in every way, solid, powerful, real, with good shoulders under the tailoring and a grown-upness in his face that made Polly's breath catch. No hint of trailer-rat about *him*. This was a man whose approval would be worth having. There was a gravitas under the charming lightness of the smile: this was a man who thought, who made decisions, who carried responsibility.

Polly stood up.

'Hello,' she said.

She came round the desk and stood before him, and then they just looked at each other in silence for a noticeable moment. Oddly enough, this did not feel awkward. The sensation she had had when she first smiled at him, of already knowing him, persisted. His eyes, she noticed, were the true, bright blue of a Siamese cat, most unusual. She wondered if he wore tinted contacts. But could you get contacts that colour?

'Does this place belong to you?' he asked at last.

'Sadly, not,' she replied. He *was* American, and she was aware of how ultra-cool and English her own voice sounded. It was odd: when you watched American series, like *The West Wing*, on television, you quickly stopped noticing that they had American accents, until an English actor came in, and then the difference was shocking. 'Is there something I can show you? I saw you were looking at the Pullman in the window.'

'Which one was that? The purple one, or the one that looks like a giant zit?'

'The purple one,' Polly said, suppressing a grin. The Sawyer painting had, against a streaky background, a large, angry-looking red blob near the top, and a creamy-whitish blob near the bottom, and she had always thought it looked unfortunately like a burst boil. 'It's called "Dark Materials II". One of his earlier works, but already fully informed with his later themes, and indicative of the direction of development of his style.'

'Is it a good investment?' he asked, and went down just a notch in her estimation. If he was just buying as an investment it took most of the fun out of it. She'd certainly hike the price up, if he went for the painting, to punish him for disappointing her.

'Of course,' she said coolly. 'My principal, Mr Leominster, has been responsible for the careers of many of our leading artists.'

'It's good business to buy ahead of the market,' he said, and he sounded as if he was mocking her.

'Both the Pullman and the Sawyer would be excellent investments,' she said.

'Well, that's a good thing, because I can't imagine anyone buying them for pleasure,' he said; and as his mouth curled into its crooked smile, she couldn't help laughing.

He was examining her face with interest. 'You didn't like it when I asked about investment,' he said. 'Why was that?'

'It's my job to sell pictures, but it's nicer to sell them to people who really like them,' she said. 'But if you're going to read my thoughts, it's going to make it rather awkward for me to conduct business with you.'

'I can see that,' he said. 'It would interfere with the old smoke and mirrors, wouldn't it?'

She put on a shocked look. 'There's no smoke and mirrors here, Mr—?'

'Harte,' he said – little knowing how he could have destroyed Nigel's reputation for omniscience at a stroke. 'With an "e" at the end. Simon Harte.' And he held out his hand in that frank, compelling American way, so that she had no choice but to offer her own. His hand was large and engulfed hers in a warm, dry, capable grip, and just for a moment her knees went weak as she thought what it would be like to be capably engulfed by the rest of him, too.

'Polly Muller,' she said, and got her hand back before someone got hurt. 'There's no smoke and mirrors here, Mr Harte. Esterhazy Gallery prides itself on service and value. Every provenance is guaranteed, and we will always buy back anything we sell, because we have every confidence in the work we handle.'

'That was a nice speech,' he said, still smiling at her.

'It's true.'

'I know.'

'How do you know?'

'Oh, I've heard of the Esterhazy Gallery. First rule of business – always do your research.'

She began to doubt his seriousness. 'So,' she said, 'were you looking for anything in particular?'

'I have an empty new house with a lot of bare walls,' he said. 'I need to put something on them. I'm a businessman, so it has to be something that will appreciate in value, but it needs to be something I want to look at as well.'

Polly almost felt Nigel sighing with relief through the wall. 'So, no giant zits,' she said and, turning towards the rear display wall, obliged Mr Harte to turn with her.

'No zits at all,' he said. 'Now, *that*'s better, though a little sentimental for my taste.'

'It's a Patrick Heron, dating from 1950.

84

There's a similar one in the Tate from the same period.'

'He's a British artist, is he? I don't know his work. But this – ' he moved on to a very bright four-foot-square canvas – 'looks like an Eberhart.'

'It is,' Polly said, pleased. 'I love his colours, don't you?'

'How much is it?' he asked. Music to her ears.

'Three hundred and fifty thousand,' she said. He nodded, still looking at the painting, but he hadn't flinched. Of course, that was small change to the new rich: some city types got *bonuses* of seven or eight million.

He moved on, and then drew a breath. 'My God, that isn't a Rothko, is it?'

'Yes, it is,' Polly said, impressed. He clearly knew his stuff. 'It's quite a late signature period oil from 1957, just before he abandoned red pretty much altogether. Even in this one, you see the reds tend towards brown and purple, showing how he's introducing more blue and green to his palette.'

'How did you get hold of it?'

'It's just come out of a private collection – a Mrs Seagram, who died recently. Apparently she bought it direct from the artist and it's been in her private collection ever since. Quite a rare piece, in that sense.'

He turned to her. 'I must have it. I've seen them in the Whitney, but to have one of my own would be fantastic! How much is it?'

Polly was on the verge of saying she had better call Mr Leominster, when Nigel appeared behind them, having drifted silently up on printless toe, carried on the zephyr of their voices.

'A superb choice,' he said, extending his hand and almost fluttering his eyelashes. 'Nigel Leominster. A very rare chance to own a Rothko, my dear sir, which has virtually never been seen, and it would be my delight to sell it to you, because otherwise it will probably go to the Tate, which has expressed an interest; and, I don't know about you, but I always think it rather sad that pictures that were meant for people's houses and hearts should end up on cold, sterile gallery walls. Don't you agree? Won't you come to my room and we can sit down and talk about it. A cup of coffee, perhaps – or a glass of sherry?'

Simon Harte went with him meekly, but he looked back over his shoulder at Polly and winked in the most reprehensible way.

Polly went back to her desk, tingling pleasantly from the exchange and the thought of the sale. If he bought the Rothko it would mean a nice little bonus for her – even though Nigel was going to close the sale he was never less than fair and would acknowledge her part in it. So, Simon Harte was ready to part with a couple of million for a painting for his new house? She wondered where it was. She imagined a penthouse flat on the river, all open spaces and huge windows, a sunken seating area with a vast sofa, bare white walls with spots trained on the few, fabulous paintings, chrome and glass and leather, and a kitchen so high-tech it not only cooked the food itself, it would eat it for you as well.

Or perhaps he'd buy a gated mansion in Kensington, with its own pool and gym complex and a helipad on the roof? She couldn't quite determine his likely style from the little she had seen of him. She wondered if Julian knew him – like the art world, the publishing world was quite chummy, and people at the same level tended to know each other. Though, of course, Transglobal Media was vastly more than simply book publishing, so perhaps Simon Harte wouldn't really be on the same level as the chairman of Addington & Lyon.

It was some time before they came out, though Simon Harte had refused both coffee and sherry, and when they did, Polly looked round and saw that he was looking pleased with himself, and that Nigel was looking just faintly baffled, which wasn't at all like him. Once the fly got into his parlour he usually wrapped them in silk and ate them without breaking, as the saying was, a sweat.

'Darling, I've got a teensy favour to ask of you,' Nigel said, approaching her desk. 'Mr Harte—'

'Simon, please,' said Harte. 'I'm sure we're

going to be good friends.'

'Oh! I feel that we are already,' Nigel beamed, but his cruel eyes were watchful. He suspected, Polly thought, that he was being sent up. 'Simon is going to buy our lovely Rothko, *and* the Eberhart you so cleverly picked out for him, dear.'

Extra bonus for her on that one, then, Polly thought, pleased, and saw Simon smiling at her over Nigel's shoulder as if he knew all about it and had intended it.

'And,' Nigel went on, 'he's interested in some more lovely things, because he's got a simply *huge* house to fill, so would you be an angel and take him out to lunch and take the photographs along with you so he can have a look at them? And then,' he looked at Simon again, 'if he likes them we can arrange to have them sent over to his house on approval.'

'Of course,' she said, trying to sound businesslike but feeling fluttery, 'it would be a pleasure.' I'm sure it would, dear, said Nigel's narrowed eyes. 'Which paintings is he interested in?'

'All the Paul Edelsteins and the two late Herons,' Nigel said. 'Just pop and sort out the photographs, dear, and I'll organize a taxi.'

Polly did as she was told, though there was no reason he couldn't look at the photographs right here and now. There was something going on, and from Nigel's demeanour it hadn't been his idea. Could it be that Simon Harte had just wanted an excuse to have lunch with her? If so it was rather cruel to make poor Nigel pay for it – though of course, business was business and he'd make a good deal on the Rothko and the Eberhart.

She came back with the folder and collected her handbag from her desk. Simon Harte thanked Nigel and shook his hand again, and Nigel said, 'Oh, don't thank me, it's a great, great pleasure to know the lovely Rothko will go to someone who appreciates it. I'm delighted to do business with you. And I'm so thrilled you are going to be staying in London, because we may be able to be of help to you again, and you know *nothing* would make me happier.'

'I'm sure we shall do business again,' Simon said. 'And in recognition of that fact, and of your generosity in loaning me Mrs Muller for a couple of hours, I just want you to know that *I* shall be paying for our lunch.'

The taxi was waiting, ticking, at the kerb and already clogging up the traffic, so Polly cut short any further politenesses by heading out. She looked back once, and saw that Nigel definitely felt he had been outmanoeuvred in some way, and she felt rather puzzled herself. But lunch out, and with a companion both handsome and promising to be amusing, was not to be sneezed at, even if it did not result in more sales.

But how did he know she was Mrs Muller, and not Miss or Ms?

'So what was all that about?' Polly asked when they were settled in the taxi and it had removed its cork from the bottle of the narrow street.

He didn't pretend not to know what she meant. 'I made having lunch with you a condition of buying the paintings.'

'Why?' she said.

'Because I thought it would be more fun to have lunch with you than with him.'

'How does lunch come into it at all?' she asked severely. 'If you have to lunch the proprietor every time you buy something, it must make shopping a very time-consuming business for you.'

He laughed. 'All right, I just wanted to have lunch with you. Is that better?'

'More honest, anyway, I hope.'

'Your boss didn't like it?' he hazarded.

'Well, it did rather put him in the position of pander, didn't it?'

He raised his eyebrows. 'Harsh words, Mrs Muller. What *are* you suggesting?'

'Hadn't we better make it Polly, as we've got this far?'

'Polly, then. And if it eases your conscience, I really do want more pictures.'

'Then I shall make very sure you look at the photos,' she said severely.

'Yes, ma'am.'

90

'Where are we going?'

'I'm taking you to one of my favourite restaurants.'

'I thought you'd only just arrived in London.'

'I've been here before, of course. Many times.' He turned his head to look down at her. 'If you know I've only just arrived in London, evidently the cat, as they say, is out of the bag. You know who I am.'

'The gaffe, as they say, was blown by Nigel. He recognized you from the article in *Forbes*. He said you're setting up a new operation for Transglobal in London.'

'Just the book publishing side. We haven't got a hardcover outlet here, and we've been doing our paperbacks through Macmillan. We thought it was time to do the whole thing ourselves, vertically, and I was chosen to be point man.' He smiled. 'Well, I volunteered so hard they'd have had a struggle not to choose me.'

'So does that mean you'll be settling in London?' she asked, and felt herself blushing as she realized how eager the question sounded. What does it matter to you, girl? You're a married woman. Yes, but he's likely to be a good customer, she hastened to answer herself.

'For a while, anyway,' he said. 'I'm not just going to take Global's titles, I want to build up a list of my own, with its own distinctive character, and that takes time. We'll have

Global's backing and finance behind us, but we'll be a completely separate imprint with our own editorial policy. I want to make it an energetic, independent publishing house that will bring in fresh ideas and new blood and blow the boring consensus publishing world apart.'

She laughed. 'I'm sure you'll be successful. And as soon as you are, you'll be bought out by a soulless conglomerate and disappear for ever into corporate blandness.'

'How do you know so much about publishing?'

'My next-door neighbour is top bod at Addington and Lyon.'

'Julian Addington? I've met him. Nice guy. So he—?' He stopped himself and went on. 'Anyway, you seem to forget – we're already part of a soulless conglomerate, so we can't be bought out any more than we already have been.'

It obviously wasn't what he had been going to say, but she didn't pursue it.

# Seven

She had suspected he might take her somewhere to impress like the Dorchester or the Savoy, or somewhere English like The Ivy or Simpsons, but the taxi pulled up outside the almost hysterically understated façade of The Square, a sleek, modern, minimalist sort of restaurant, with excellent food. She added this choice to what she knew of his taste. It looked as though it would be the riverside penthouse for him, then, rather than the gated Kensington mansion.

They went in, and even as the girl at the desk was still smilingly running her finger down the bookings, the maitre d' hurried up to them and was shaking hands with Simon saying, 'Good to see you again, Mr Harte.' He smiled civilly at Polly.

'It's good to be here again, François,' Simon said.

'I have your usual table for you,' said François, leading the way. 'A little bird told me you were going to be settling in London this time?'

'For a few years, anyway.'

'I'm delighted to hear it. Madam?' He

93

stopped at a table and pulled out a chair for Polly. Another waiter came up silently to seat Simon. 'Something to drink?' François said, offering menus. 'Would madam perhaps care for a glass of champagne?'

Polly looked up at Simon and saw him smiling, relaxed. 'Do you know, I think I would?'

'The eighty-five, then,' Simon said. 'And a Pernod for me.'

The drinks came and they ordered, and then they were free to talk.

'I'm wondering,' Polly said, 'why someone as senior as you obviously are in a powerful multimedia company would want to be head of a mere book publishing division. Isn't it rather a step down? I mean, there's not a great deal to be made in book publishing these days, is there?'

'Money isn't everything,' he said.

She did not take it as a rebuke. 'No, but it's the marker for power and influence, and I wouldn't have thought there was much of either in books any more. Not the billet for one of life's movers and shakers.'

He grinned. 'And you take me for a mover and shaker? Thank you, Mrs Muller, for those kind words.'

'I thought we'd agreed on Polly?'

'So we had. Well – Polly – you're not entirely wrong. But it was something I wanted to do – set up a new imprint, create my own list, perhaps create a new force in publishing

94

that will make other houses wake up and stop being so lazy. Books *can* be influential. And – in case you're worried about my career within Transglobal – I should say that I have other things to do while I'm here which will be less personally enjoyable but more lucrative to the mother ship. Contacts to make, lines of communication to lay down, research to be done, contracts to secure. So don't worry about me being underused. When I go back I shall still have a place waiting for me.'

'So you *will* go back?' She felt obscurely disappointed.

'It's possible,' he said, sipping his Pernod. 'It's also possible that I'll stay. They're giving me five years to get the new imprint on its feet, but by that time my other seeds will have sprung, and there will be other operations they may want me to take charge of. Powerful and influential ones, thank you for caring!'

She smiled. 'You like London?'

'Of course. I thought that was established – otherwise I wouldn't be here. It's the second greatest city in the world.'

'The second?'

'I'm a New Yorker,' he said with a grin, 'so you couldn't expect me to put it first. But just at the moment.' The smile faded a notch. 'I'd sooner be here than New York.'

The waiter brought their first course – she had chosen lasagne of Cornish crab with a cappuccino of shellfish and champagne foam, and he'd gone for the mousseline of smoked eel with horseradish. Polly tasted and praised – it was delicious.

Then she said, 'Tell me, you obviously know a lot about paintings and like them. Why don't you have any? You said you had a lot of empty walls to fill.'

'I've been living in rented for five years, since my divorce,' he said with easy frankness. 'I'm starting all over again, and while it's daunting, it's also a great challenge. You've probably gathered by now, I like a challenge.'

She laughed. 'I had got that impression.'

'I've bought a completely empty house,' he went on, 'and I'm going to have fun doing it up and buying stuff and having it exactly the way I want it.'

'But didn't you bring *anything* with you?' Polly said in surprise. She had thought American divorces divided things equally down the middle. 'I mean, when you split up, didn't you share things out?'

'I let my wife have everything,' he said coolly. 'Ex-wife, I should say. Not my taste. Anyway, I wanted a clean break.'

'I'm sorry,' said Polly. 'It was rude of me to ask.'

'Not rude at all,' he said. 'I love your cool English manners. Americans at home ask much more probing questions with far less justification.'

'You don't mind talking about it?'

'Not if you're interested – and I'm flattered that you are.'

'I am,' Polly said, though the critical voice that lived at the back of her mind was asking her why that should be so. But I'm interested in *people*, she told the voice crossly, so you can just shut up.

'Well, Robyn, my wife – my ex-wife, I should say – was a lawyer, and a damn good one. Sharp as a whip, and shooting up the career ladder. But you have to be hard to get on in the law, and it's not easy to keep the inside of you soft while the outside grows a shell. The shell is all too apt to thicken inwards until there's nothing left.' He shook himself back into light mode. 'And there's nothing brings out the beast in a lawyer so much as a divorce. There wasn't anything in our home by then that I had such a sentimental attachment to that I was willing to fight over it. So I told her to take everything, including the apartment, in return for a completely clean break and no future claims of any sort.'

'That sounds sensible,' Polly said cautiously. She couldn't be sure from his words how much he was still hurting.

'It would have been sensible,' he said, smiling, 'not to have got together in the first place. Lawyers always prefer the company of other lawyers. Hanging around with publishers ranks as intellectual slumming for them.

We just don't have the smarts. Robyn was in a different league from me and we both knew it. She could think me under the table with one hand tied behind her back.'

'You seem intelligent to me,' Polly said.

'Thank you, pretty lady. But trust me, she was a giant to a pygmy, brainwise.' He laughed. 'At the beginning when we were trying to get along with each other's sets, we used to have these agonizing dinner parties when the lawyers set the conversation at table. My poor arts and business friends didn't understand one word in three. We'd end up standing in the kitchen gossiping about authors and who was sleeping with who.' He grinned across the table. 'Lawyers don't gossip, did you know that?'

'That's unnatural,' she said, laughing.

The waiters came to clear, while a second team (the service really was superb) arrived with the second course – roast saddle of hare with a celeriac and pear tart for her, calves sweetbreads with savoy cabbage for him – which they served with despatch from little folding tables they had brought with them under their arms. In a twinkling the food and wine were there and the waiters weren't, and it felt as if conversation had barely paused.

'So how did you come to get married in the first place if you were so different?' Polly asked

'Sexual attraction. We were both young and hungry for love and I guess we hoped it would work out. We both had demanding schedules so it wasn't easy to find anyone in the first place. We had to give it a chance. And of course, having demanding schedules also meant that we never had enough time together to discover how unsuited we were. Not until one day we woke up as strangers, and Robyn told me she was leaving me for another lawyer – a hot-shot district attorney in California.'

'That must have been tough for you,' Polly said. The voice-at-the-back-of-the-mind worried that this was all being too easy, that she had only just met him and he was telling her his life story. But she *felt* easy with him, as if she had known him for years, so why shouldn't he feel the same about her? 'Did you have any children?'

'No, which I suppose was a blessing in the circumstances. Robyn wanted to have children, but we just didn't manage it, though we had all the tests and they said there was nothing wrong with either of us. I guess it just wasn't meant to be,' he concluded. 'Maybe some people just don't go with some other people. Maybe if we'd been able to have kids things would have worked out. Anyway, she left me for this DA and they set up a practice together, and before you know it she had three kids, bam-bam-bam. Three daughters. Now as well as the practice she and Dennis have this swanky horse ranch up in the north of the state selling jumpers and hunters and equitation horses, and the three daughters compete in posh horse shows all over the States and win sackloads of cups and prizes. Happy ending.'

'Oh, I'm so sorry,' Polly said, feeling an urge to put her hand over his across the table. All her sympathy circuits were engaged. In the back of her mind she was aware that there was something about the story that was puzzling, but she hadn't time to track it down just then. 'That must be hard for you.'

'No, I'm happy for her. She's got what she wanted, and that can't be bad, can it? Increasing the sum of human happiness, that's what it's all about. How is your hare?'

'Delectable. How are your sweetbreads? I didn't think Americans ever ate them.'

'Americans aren't big on offal as a rule. But once you get the wrong idea about them out of your head (you know the one I mean), sweetbreads are a real English find. Hare, though, I'm not sure about. They're wild creatures. Should we be eating wild creatures? And is it jugged? I can't get it out of my head that "jugging" is some horribly cruel way of killing the poor things, like a mediaeval torture.'

'It's not jugged, it's roasted,' she said. 'And it was almost certainly not wild, but raised in a pen in China.' She had a fit of conscience. 'You know, we really ought to be looking at these photographs.'

'Later,' he said. 'Really, I'm not sure the photographs will help much. I need to see the pictures themselves against the walls to know if I'll like living with them.'

'Well, we can arrange that,' she said.

'I know. I mean to have you do it, too.'

The way he was looking at her made her feel a little uncomfortable, and she looked down at her plate and said, 'So where is this new, empty house of yours? Is it modern? Is it by the river?'

'No, it's a crumby old place that needs completely renovating, but it's going to be great because it's really big and it has high ceilings and a great yard – garden – out back. And it's not by the river, it's in Shepherd's Bush, and before you laugh—'

'I wouldn't laugh,' she said. 'I live in Shepherd's Bush. It's nice.'

'Well, all my work colleagues back home laughed like anything because it sounds so bucolic. They wondered why I wasn't settling in Mayfair or Chelsea or Kensington or Notting Hill – they were wild for Notting Hill, after the movie – or even Islington. Somewhere they'd heard of, at any rate.'

'Well, why *did* you choose Shepherd's Bush? I must say it isn't what I would have expected.'

'You get so much more for your money there. And didn't I say, it's good business to buy ahead of the market? If anyone's going to make a big profit out of that house, I want it to be me. Doesn't that make sense?'

'A lot of sense. I'm just a bit surprised you happened to light on Shepherd's Bush, though. I thought it was rather a Londoners' secret.'

'I told you, I always do my research.' He looked at her with an expression of suppressed amusement that was very attractive.

'So whereabouts in Shepherd's Bush?' she asked. 'We might be neighbours.' She doubted it, though. It was a big territory.

'It's a place called Albemarle Terrace,' he said. 'Do you know it?'

Polly put down her fork. 'How absolutely extraordinary. I live in Albemarle Terrace!' And at the same moment she twigged, and wondered why she hadn't before. 'You're the person who's bought the corner house, number one.' And Tammy hadn't said – or the Maxiclean man hadn't said to Tammy – that he was something big in global media, he was something big in *Global* media. 'What an amazing coincidence.'

'Isn't it? But a delightful one. I'm glad to hear I shall know someone in the neighbourhood. It can be a bummer being the new boy in Britain. It's not like in the States where as soon as you move in all your neighbours knock on your door with home-baked pies.'

'Oh, we're very friendly people along the Terrace. We all tend to know each other, and visit and have parties and things. In fact, some of our neighbours wanted to give a party for you this weekend. Not that we knew it was *you*, you understand, but we heard the new owner was moving in and we thought it would be nice to welcome him, or them.'

'That sounds like a great idea. I'd love to come along and meet the neighbours. When is it?'

'Oh, we haven't set it all up yet. My friend Ginnie – Julian Addington's wife—'

'God, yes, I'd forgotten. He's going to be a neighbour too! What a great place!'

'We like to think so. Anyway, Ginnie wanted to hold the party at her place, but Julian's away this weekend so I don't know whether she'll feel like doing it alone. But there are plenty of us, so I'm sure we can work something out.'

'Your house, maybe?' he asked.

'My husband's away for the weekend too. In Paris. On business.'

'Oho! The plot thickens,' he said, grinning.

She felt herself blushing. 'It does no such thing! I'm a happily married woman.'

His face straightened. 'I'm sorry. I didn't mean to offend you. I was just kidding around. I'm a great kidder, but sometimes I don't know when to keep my mouth shut. Forgive?'

'Of course. I'm sorry. I'm not usually without a sense of humour myself.'

'I can tell that,' he said. 'I like the way your eyes crinkle. Look, I'm really up for this party idea.'

'When do you move in?'

'I've ordered some basic furniture to keep me going, which is coming tomorrow morning, so there's no reason not to sleep there tomorrow night. I want to do the whole house out from top to bottom but it'll take time so I guess I'll just take it a room at a time and move myself about. The company has paid for the apartment I'm renting until the end of the quarter so if it gets too uncomfortable I can beat a retreat. Hey,' he said as he thought of something, 'here's an idea. If no one else wants to host it, we could have the party at my house. While the place is nearly empty and it won't matter if anything gets spilled.'

'You won't have enough chairs for people to sit on,' she said. 'Or glasses.'

'Caterers,' he suggested.

'You've hardly time to arrange anything like that.'

'Well, I'm determined to meet my neighbours this weekend one way or another.'

'Leave it to me. I'll ring round and find out who wants to be host. Believe me, there won't be a problem. They'll all be dying to meet you when they find out who you are.'

'What a practical lady you are. Will you ring me, then?' He passed over his card. 'Here are all my numbers, but my cell is the best bet.'

She dug out a card of her own. 'And we

have to think about these pictures some time,' she said severely, putting the folder on the table again.

'Maybe we can do it this weekend. If you bring the folder to my house, at least we can hold the photographs up against the wall.'

'If you think it will help,' she said. She wondered whether he was trying to wriggle out of the purchase now, and how Nigel would feel about her failure to nail him down. But you couldn't rush the purchase of paintings, after all. Nigel understood that. And at least she could report she would have him just a few doors down from her, and therefore within her sphere of influence. It wasn't as if he was going anywhere.

# Eight

It was Ginnie's misfortune that she had been born a girl into a diplomatic dynasty. Her grandfather, Sir William Fawcett, had ended up representing His Majesty in Paris, one of the plum jobs (Paris and Washington were considered the best ambassadorial billets because of the pleasantness of the surroundings: good shops, restaurants and parties, and easy transport in and out) and her great-grandfather had actually been ambassador to the Court of St Petersburg, around the turn of the previous century.

Her father, Edward, despite, Eton, The House and a couple of years in the Guards before joining the diplomatic service, and the best suits money could buy, had not reached ambassadorial rank. It was essential to him therefore, when he married rather late, in 1963, that he should have a son to carry on the family tradition, regain the heights he had failed to conquer and restore the family honour. He must have a boy. Females did not cut much ice in those circles, and could certainly never be ambassadors.

He chose a wife with care, with her career as a breeder of fine sons in view. He was, though in his forties, a reasonably attractive man, distinguished-looking and extremely well off, so he was not lacking in choice among those who would have been debs in an earlier age (Court Presentation had been halted in 1958 and the Season was falling to pieces without it). He asked around, scanned the pages of *Tatler*, consulted colleagues, and his eye fell in due course on Veronica Glenulick, a tall, good-looking girl with an athletic figure that impressed him as strong and healthy, clear, pale skin and a mass of auburn, curly hair. She was twenty-two, and the daughter of an Irish baronet. She was his superior in rank, and he hers in fortune, so it was all fair enough.

They married and he settled her in the house he had inherited from his father in Horn Hill, just outside Denham, a solid Edwardian building of eight bedrooms in grounds of four acres, originally built for his grandfather in 1905. Because of the existence of 'the Pile' as it became known in the family, Edward did not oblige his wife to travel around with him to his postings. In truth, he had got rather used to his bachelor life and found it comfortable (if it had not been for his dynastic obligations, he might have settled happily to a modest, donnish life at Oxford, living in college, looked after by a scout and eating at High Table). His wife, he reasoned, would soon be pregnant and would be better off staying safely in England, with proper medical facilities and all home comforts. It would only need the occasional visit home from him to top up the family and make decisions about the boys' schooling and so on.

From one reason or another – possibly the infrequency of their marital intercourse – it took Veronica five years to conceive, but when at last she did give birth, in 1968, at least it was a boy, whom they named William after his grandfather. Edward was keen that there should be 'a spare', but it was another five years before Eugenia came along. The disappointment of her being a girl, after all that waiting, took the heart out of both parents (Veronica, whose father's title was one of the earliest creations, as her mother was fond of telling people, was quite as keen on male babies as her husband) and they simply couldn't be bothered to try again.

So Ginnie grew up in the shadow of her brother, and in full awareness of her uselessness. With their father absent in body and their mother even more absent in spirit, Bill and Ginnie had only each other to love. Having fulfilled her duty, their mother abandoned her children to nannies and servants and spent as much of her life as possible in the homes of friends in London or the better shires – for she never forgot whose daughter she was. Fortunately for Ginnie, Bill adored and protected her, while she thought the sun rose and set by him. It broke her heart when he went away to school, and she lived for holidays when he would come back like Odysseus from exotic lands to tell her stories of his adventures and create new ones for her. The Pile at least had excellent grounds for children to romp in unsupervised, and open countryside nearby for walking and biking.

One day in the summer holidays, when Ginnie was eight and Bill thirteen, they had been playing at the far end of the Pile's four acres. Bill had been showing off to her, climbing trees and performing daredevil acts of swinging and jumping which he described as 'commando'. He had joined OTC in the previous half. Ginnie had watched him from below, starry-eyed, with complete confidence that anything Bill wanted to do, he could do. If he had said he could fly, she would not have disbelieved him.

'Watch this!' he had shouted exuberantly, drunk with her admiration. He hurled himself from the branch he was standing on towards the next tree, an old oak, catching a protruding branch with his hands, intending to swing himself further in. The branch was not strong enough. It broke with a sickening crack and he fell like a stone to earth, knocking himself out.

He came to a few moments later to find his little sister, white faced, shaking him frantically and shrieking, 'Don't die! You mustn't die! Please don't die, Billie, please don't!'

As he sat up groggily, holding his head, she stared at him wildly as though her eyes would fall out of her head. Then she turned away and was sick, with the simple ease of an animal, and burst into tears.

Miraculously, he had not broken anything, only sustained some interesting bruises, a mild concussion and an anything-but-mild headache. The instinct of children, particularly such close children, made them conceal the incident from the grown-ups. When Ginnie had stopped crying they helped each other back to the house and kept out of the way for the rest of the day. Bill slept, curled up on the nursery sofa, for an hour or two, with Ginnie watching him as though she feared he might be snatched away any moment. But by teatime his headache had gone, her swollen eyes were back to normal, and they both had huge appetites. There happened to be Victoria sponge for tea, and in the immediate pleasure of the treat they forgot the whole thing. Except that Ginnie was subject to nightmares from time to time, from which she woke screaming but with no memory of what she had been dreaming about. And she and Bill loved each other more than ever.

When there was nowhere else to send them, Veronica was in the habit of dumping them on her mother in County Wicklow.

Lady Glenulick – 'Irish Granny' – lived in the only sound wing of the family seat, which was still pretty ramshackle and comfortless. The rest of the house had been partly destroyed by fire and as no one had bothered to repair it, it had thereafter simply fallen down bit by bit. Her son, the baronet, had wisely moved to a flat in Dublin which at least had hot and cold running water, and divided his time between there and London. But Lady Glenulick spent too little time indoors anyway to care about the state of the house. Her passions were hunting, eventing and horse shows, and her life revolved around the stables which were, by comparison, palaces of luxury. Bill enjoyed their visits, because he loved horses and was never happier than when riding. Ginnie enjoyed them at first – she liked anything if it meant she was with Bill – but when she was eleven she had an unfortunate experience. The three of them were preparing to go out riding, Ginnie on a borrowed pony, Lady Glenulick on her chestnut hunter mare, and Bill on a bay youngster being brought on for the next season. Irish Granny had told Ginnie to hold the chestnut while she tightened the girths, and the mare, who didn't like the process, whipped her head round, sunk her teeth into Ginnie's skinny little arm and hung on like a bulldog. Irish Granny had to beat the creature across the eyes with the man's brown trilby she always wore when riding before it finally let go; and then told Ginnie she had made things worse by screaming.

'You frightened her, that's why she hung on to you. How many times have I told you always to be gentle and quiet around horses? They're sensitive creatures. You must never, never scream like that.' She then proposed to carry on as if nothing had happened. It was left to Bill, coming to comfort his sobbing little sister, to see how nasty the wound was and to insist on driving her in Lady Glenulick's battered ex-army jeep to the hospital for treatment and a tetanus shot. He'd been driving the jeep around the estate since *he* was eleven, and though he was under age for a driving licence, the Gards all knew him and turned a blind eye to his occasional forays on to public roads.

Since then, Ginnie had hated and feared horses, and by extension hated everything to do with Ireland, country houses and anything old, antique, dusty, mouldy or crumbling. She much preferred visits to her father's mother, known for convenience between the children as Paris Granny. To her face they called her Iris, as she said being called Granny made her feel too hideously old. Iris had never been happier than when she was the ambassador's wife in Paris before the war: it seemed to her a golden age of unsurpassed pleasure. So in widowhood she had returned, and lived in a flat in a modern block, with a balcony that faced south and west over the Bois de Boulogne. At least, it was modern to her, having been built in 1935 and furbished in what was then the most avant-garde style. Purchasing it in the 1950s she had restored it to its glory and never altered a thing again, simply cleaning, repainting and repairing as necessary. It was an art deco time warp.

Ginnie adored it too. Everything was plain and clean, lots of chrome and glass, and everything in shades of mushroom, peach and cream. The sitting room had huge glass doors on to a balcony that slid back into the wall so that the day flooded in. The flat was on a level with the treetops and Ginnie sometimes thought it was like being by the sea. The trees rolled away like a deep green ocean as far as the eye could see, and they whispered when the wind stirred them like waves breaking on a shore.

Iris was a pleasant, vague guardian, a little at a loss with small children – her own had been brought up by nannies at Horn Hill – so she tended to treat them exactly like adults.

'Now, have you everything you need?' she would enquire when they arrived. 'Have you a book?' It was the worst fate she could think of, to be stuck anywhere without a book to read. Thereafter she would leave them a good deal to their own devices, remembering her duties as hostess from time to time by sweeping down on them and taking them out to delicious lunches at restaurants, to sumptuous teas in hotels, to galleries to look at paintings, or to shop for clothes and shoes in heavenly-smelling stores full of black-clad Parisian assistants and customers who wore furs no matter what the weather. It all seemed to Ginnie the apogee of civilized pleasure, and she vowed inwardly that when she grew up and got married, she would have a house like Paris Granny's, with everything shiny clean, modern and new, and she would live in a city, and never, *never* in the country.

She knew, of course, that what she had to do in life was get married. That had been drummed into her from earliest childhood. It was the result of being born to a diplomatic family: sons followed in the service; daughters got married so as to breed more sons to go into the service. That was the way it had always been, and the way it always would be. The changes to women's status of the sixties and seventies had passed that world (like that of old military families) largely untouched. Girls might, at a pinch, take on some slight, decorative job when they left school, just to keep them out of mischief or in pocket money, but it was only ever a pastime until their real career of wife and motherhood began.

And Ginnie knew she could not marry just anyone: she had to marry *well*. She had no objection to that. She wanted to be rich, to have the comforts and luxuries that money could provide, and because of the closed nature of her family's connections she was largely unaware of the new ways people became rich in the 1980s – or rather, she knew about them vaguely, but never saw them as having any relevance to her. Her mother was anxious for her to marry into the aristocracy (*back* into the aristocracy was how Veronica thought of it to herself) and Ginnie had no objection to that, either. A title of some sort might be agreeable. She was not a heartless fortune hunter, however. She expected to fall in love before accepting a proposal – could not have imagined marrying without love. It was just that she expected to fall in love with a rich, preferably titled man, that was all.

In the mean time, while she waited to find him (or rather for him to find her) she had to do something to keep herself occupied. Her father had by now retired and money was, if not exactly short, at least to be looked after, so Ginnie was encouraged to stay on at school into the sixth form, which was cheaper than a finishing school abroad. She was not academic, but her private school in Buckinghamshire, unwilling to allow her to bring down their averages, steered her in the direction of A levels she had a chance of passing. She emerged at eighteen with two, in geography and art, and on the strength of the latter went on to Art School, living at home and travelling up by train to London every day.

Bill was by now away, serving the Crown in far-flung places, and home held no great comfort for her, but she loved being in London, which seemed to her the delicious antithesis to the horrible countryside. She still mixed with a very limited circle, but she was *there*, in the great capital, with noise and people and possibilities all around her, and she knew she had found her heart's place. Paris was lovely, but it wasn't home. She never wanted to live anywhere else as long as she lived.

At art school she discovered that while she had a lively mind and a good eye, she had no real skill in drawing or painting, so she turned to photography, and found a small but real talent there. Meanwhile, she was doing the late eighties' version of the Season – going to cocktail parties, dances, group visits to leading race meetings, weekends on people's boats, and country-house visits and balls. Most of the girls she knew and the houses she visited belonged like her to the upper middle classes. But the diplomatic set, while distinct and separate from it, did overlap with the upper class in places: younger sons, and even cadets while they waited for their title, often went into the diplomatic service, or were appointed military attachés during their time in the Guards. Her mother's birth gave her an entrée, and her parents evidently hoped that she would benefit from that and marry someone at least *connected* to the upper classes, if not actually titled himself.

She first met Julian in London, at a party in a flat in Cadogan Square. She didn't notice him at first: he was older than her set; he was quiet – not having noisy fun, flirting and dancing, but sitting in a corner with some other slightly older people, talking. Her eye passed over the group and dismissed them as being dull. But as the evening wore on she noticed that he kept looking at her. Not continuously, but every now and then he would look around as if to discover where in the room she was, and having discovered her go back to his conversation with an appearance of satisfaction, as though his contentment depended on knowing she was there. Intrigued, she began to watch him for these moments, and having him under scrutiny discovered two things: one, that he was reasonably good-looking; and two, that the quiet conversational group in the corner appeared to be having a better time than everyone else. At least, they seemed quite satisfied with their own company, completely at ease, and thoroughly absorbed in their talk.

Her hostess, Emily Watts, came past, and she caught her arm and asked who the fair-haired man in the corner was. Emily looked. 'Oh, that's Julian Addington – Addington and Lyon, you know.' Ginnie didn't. She assumed it was something industrial like Procter and Gamble. 'Are you smitten, darling? Do you want to me introduce you?'

'It's not that,' she said quickly. 'He keeps looking at me.'

'Well, you are looking rather delicious tonight,' Emily said without great warmth. 'He *is* single, if you're interested. Been too busy rescuing his father's publishing company for the past yonks to get married. But he came with Adela Partington – I don't know if there's anything going on there. You might need to hurry if you want to get in with a bid.'

'I think he's a bit old for me,' Ginnie said. 'I just wondered who he was, that's all.' The fact of Addington & Lyon being a publishing company made him slightly more interesting – her photography put her generally on the arts side and therefore more kindly disposed to anything else arty. However, the 'rescuing' bit wasn't enticing – it sounded as if the family firm was in trouble – and he didn't look terribly rich. His clothes were neither new nor fashionable and his haircut was distinctly old-fashioned. She found Henry Maude at her elbow asking her to dance. He was a tall, fattish young man with meaty cheeks who was something in the City, and while she didn't particularly like him it was better to dance than not to dance, so she accepted and forgot about Julian Addington.

Later that evening a group of the noisier ones decided to go on to Annabel's. Ginnie wasn't wild about joining them, because she didn't particularly want to get stuck with Henry. But she had arranged to stay the night with a girlfriend, and the girlfriend was going so she didn't have much choice. At the last minute, as the party clattered down the stairs to the street, she saw that Julian had attached himself to it, with Adela Partington in tow. As she caught his eye he smiled at her, which made her wonder whether he was coming for her sake, because she wouldn't have thought he'd be the Annabel's type.

He wasn't in her taxi, and she lost sight of him; but later at Annabel's she saw him in a group of very smart young people, much smarter than those at Emily's parents' flat, and evidently he was well-known to all of them. Her interest waxed a little. She liked the whole idea of connections, and someone who had more and better connections than her was an object worth considering. After a while he came over and asked her to dance, removing her in the nick of time from Henry's sticky grasp – he had been drinking far too much and was getting frisky.

'I'm Julian Addington,' he said as they swayed with a decorous six-inch gap between their bodies in the midst of the heaving throng.

'I know,' she said. 'I'm Ginnie Fawcett.'

'I know,' he said.

She wondered if he was mocking her. 'How do you know?'

'I asked,' he said. There was a silence – or at least a gap in their conversation. The music and cigarette smoke swirled round them. Then he said, 'Do you come here often?'

She opened her eyes wide. 'That's a very old-fashioned question.'

'Perhaps I'm a very old-fashioned man,' he said, as if he wasn't at all. 'It just struck me that this doesn't seem your sort of place.'

'Why not?' she asked suspiciously. Did he think her not rich enough or well-born enough?

'You look to me the more thoughtful type. I didn't think you were enjoying the attentions of that oaf Henry Maude.'

'I wasn't,' she said. She noticed that while Henry had smelled quite strongly of sweat – fresh sweat, but even so – under his powerful aftershave, Julian didn't seem to have any smell at all. He was cool and detached, an observer of their folly, not part of it, and it intrigued and annoyed her in about equal proportions, especially as he evidently knew so many people here, which made it *his* sort of place – didn't it? 'Do *you* come here often?' she countered.

He smiled, and it changed his rather ordinary face remarkably. She thought he looked more different when he smiled than when he didn't, than any other person she'd ever met.

'Hardly at all,' he said. 'This is the first time this year.'

She was going to ask him why he had come tonight, and then was afraid of the answer, both that it would be because of her, and that it would not. Instead she said, 'What do you think *is* my sort of place?'

'I see you rather in the quiet green of the countryside,' he said.

'Well, you're dead wrong, then,' she said triumphantly. 'I *hate* the country.'

It sounded rude even to her, and she had had no intention of being rude. She saw him withdraw a little into himself. 'I'm sorry,' he said politely, and they talked no more until the music changed, when he thanked her formally for the dance and left her to go back to the smarter group.

She did not see him again until the following year, after she had left college and was trying, for want of anything better to do, to get together a portfolio and sell some photographs. She was still going to parties and dances, and at the end of January was persuaded by her mother to accept an invitation to the last shooting weekend at Bureton Hall, a 'stately' in Berkshire where there would be a large party of young people. Ginnie was not keen – she hated shooting parties even more than hunting parties. Walking through damp fields on freezing foggy mornings to stand behind the guns and be deafened while defenceless birds got blasted out of the sky appealed to her even less than having to explain yet again to entirely sceptical people that she didn't *like* horses.

But the invitation had come through her mother, Lord Bureton being a distant connection of Irish Granny, and Veronica was determined she should go. Ginnie was almost twenty-two and unmarried, and Veronica was anxious to get her off her hands before she slipped into old-maidhood. The fact that young people most frequently didn't marry until their thirties these days had entirely passed her by. There would be more men than women at Bureton, a state of affairs that did not often prevail, and being the last shoot of the season the party would be extra lively.

Ginnie agreed to go in the end, not expecting any enjoyment but as a preferable alternative to staying at home and being nagged. Bureton wasn't as bad as some of the houses she had visited, there being at least some form of central heating, albeit inadequate, and hot water in the bathrooms if you got in first. The first person she met as she came down the stairs before dinner on the Friday night was Julian. He had just reached the foot of the staircase and stopped to wait for her.

'Hello,' he said. 'How nice to see you here.'
She looked at him suspiciously. He smiled

up at her politely, but there was laughter in his eyes. She was reminded of that moment in *Gone With the Wind* when Scarlet and Cathleen Calvert look down and see Rhett Butler leaning on the newel post. '*Who is that nasty man?*' She was afraid he was going to make fun of her. 'Is it?' she said warily.

'I must say I'm surprised,' he said, as she reached him and he turned with her towards the drawing room. 'After you told me so forcefully that you hate the country.'

'I do. My mother made me come. I hate shooting parties worst of all.'

'How so?'

*How so?* He was very grand, wasn't he? Then she remembered the publishing company. Probably he was used to mixing with tremendous intellectuals. And she was not intellectual at all! She went on to the defensive. 'What's there to like about them? Do you *like* slaughtering poor defenceless birds?'

'Oh dear, you aren't a vegetarian, are you?' he asked in an amused way.

'I don't see what that's got to do with it,' she said crossly.

'Well, if you like eating meat, you have to live with the knowledge that animals are slaughtered. At least the pheasant has a good life until it's shot, unlike some wretched battery chicken, rotting in its own mess in a cage too small to turn round in.'

She couldn't think of a riposte to this, and walked on in silence.

In the drawing room over drinks, he asked her why she hated the country. She found herself telling him about Ireland and Granny and the horse incident, and he listened to her as she had never been listened to before – not even by Bill, because he had always been the leader of the two of them, and it was she who had listened to him. And the other girls and men she met at parties mostly wanted to talk about themselves, and did not so much listen to you as wait until you finished so they could start. Julian seemed really interested, and when she finished he asked her something else – something connected which proved he'd actually been listening properly – which made her talk again. She began to warm to him, and was disappointed when they went in to dinner to be seated at the far end from him. Her dinner companions both wanted to impress her, and talked about themselves and their prowess with the gun, and since her indifference became at last impossible to ignore they ended up talking to each other over her head. But at least, she was glad to note, Adela Partington was not there (though horrible Henry Maude was). She assumed that meant she and Julian were not engaged or close to being.

After dinner there was dancing in one half of the drawing room while people stood and sat around talking in the other. The party tended to divide itself with the young people dancing and the older people, of Lord and Lady Bureton's age, talking. Ginnie danced with a number of young men, listened to their nonsense, found them dull. They were the sort of upper-class boys her mother wanted her to choose from, but they talked about shooting, hunting and, endlessly, about other people of their set. Did you go to so-and-so's party? Were you at the thingummies' last month? Will you be at what's-name's next week?

Then there were anecdotes about their friends, with stares of surprise when they found that she didn't know them. 'You don't know Tom Walsingham? I thought everyone knew old Tommy. We were at school together/played in the nursery together/he married my cousin.' The worst thing was that the anecdotes weren't even interesting. They tended to end in tremendous laughter for no reason, or to peter out into nothing. 'You had to be there. It was a riot, simply a riot.' She hated the country set. She began to feel very bored.

And while she danced and was bored, she watched Julian, who was in the other half of the room talking with serious attention and even animation to the older people. Why did he *do* that? And why did he seem to be having a better time talking to people the age of his parents than all the young people down this end put together? And how was it that everyone seemed to know him? She knew how difficult it was to be really accepted by the titled upper classes, especially for a man. A girl might get in through marriage if she were pretty and innocuous enough, but a male outsider would always be an object of suspicion. He must have some magic about him, she thought, watching for the moments when his rare smile would change his face from ordinary to extraordinary in that way she had noted before.

She hoped all evening that he would change ends and ask her to dance, but he didn't. He disappeared early, too, leaving her feeling disappointed, and that the evening had been a complete waste of time. In bed that night she decided two things: one, that he was an intellectual snob (if not some other kind) and he thought too much of himself; he had thought himself too good to dance with her, or indeed at all. And two, she decided that she would jolly well make him notice her, if she had to vamp him all weekend. She would use all her wiles on him, and when he did finally give in, she would dump him flat. That would show him!

Show him what? She didn't know. She didn't like him, that was all. That was one thing she was sure of.

# Nine

In the morning Ginnie went down to breakfast and found most of the party already assembled. Practically everybody, it seemed, was going out, only one or two of the older wives staying at home. Julian was there at the sideboard helping himself to a selection of the delicacies in the chafing-dishes – bacon, kidneys, sausages, mushrooms and so on. She shuddered at the thought: she had drunk too much last night to compensate for her disappointment. She took coffee and toast only, and went and sat down without looking at him; but when he had loaded his plate he came and sat down beside her.

'Is that all you're having?' he asked. 'Oh, but I suppose you're not coming out this morning, so you won't need stoking up. Pity. They do a good breakfast here.'

'You've stayed here before?' she asked.

'You sound surprised,' he said.

'I suppose I was thinking of you as a London person.'

'I live in London,' he said, 'but I grew up in the country. Do you live in London?'

'I wish I did,' she sighed. 'I live near Denham.'

He laughed. 'That is London, to all intents and purposes. At least, that's what any of *them* would tell you.' And he gestured discreetly towards the rest of the company. Then he told her some amusing anecdotes about the old Denham Studios, so different from the sort of talk she had been bored with by men all her life. He struck her as being so much more sophisticated and blessedly *urbane* than the others, that she wondered again what he was doing here and how he could fit in so well with this completely rural crowd. She realized she was liking him again and was cross with herself. But when the party began to move she had another rapid change of mind and decided to go out with the guns after all. Better than sitting with Lady Bureton and her generation all morning.

Or was it? It was a raw day, with a sort of dripping mist that froze your nose and fingers and a clammy cold in the wet grass that froze your feet right through your wellingtons. The calls of the beaters and the strange gutteral clucks of the pheasants echoed on the chilly air, the shots sounded horribly loud and sudden, and talking near the stands was discouraged by the men actually shooting, who seemed to take it very seriously. The birds were driven past in waves and they banged away with scowling intensity. It all seemed terribly industrial. The spare men, wives and the women who weren't actively pursuing one of the shooters hung around the Range Rovers chatting, smoking and drinking rather self-consciously from hip flasks. Ginnie was annexed by a young man called Jeremy who seemed all nose, who gave her a detailed account of every retriever he'd ever owned, and its pedigree on both sides going in both directions. The pain was alleviated only when the soup and pasties arrived and everyone broke off for refreshment.

During the break, Julian was annexed by one of the married couples and didn't so much as look at her, but when the drive resumed, he came straight to her with a friendly smile and said, 'Would you like to come and stand with me for a bit? Or would it upset your sensibilities? I hardly ever hit anything, if it helps.'

So she went with him to his numbered stand. He said, 'Are you having a nice time?'

'Not very,' she said. She gestured behind her. 'They all just talk about people they know and I don't.'

'Yes, that can be tiresome.'

'And when you say you don't know them they look at you as if you come from an alien planet.'

'It's a very small, closed world,' he said, and paused, while a bird came over, to fire. He missed. 'There's no harm in them really. It's just a self-defence mechanism.'

'Well, at least you're different,' she said

crossly. 'You live in London and you've got a proper job. At least,' she added doubtfully, 'I presume it's a proper job. I mean, it's your father's company, isn't it?'

'My grandfather started it,' he said. 'Back in the twenties, which was a good time for starting up new publishing companies. He made quite a go of it.'

'Who was Lyon?' she asked.

'He was a sort of sleeping partner – a friend of my grandfather's from the war. They were in the same regiment. He put up a lot of the money, but it was grandfather who did the work. He turned out to have a talent for picking the right authors and the company flourished.'

'Emily Watts said you were having to rescue the company.'

He gave her an odd smile. 'You don't pull your punches, do you?'

'Oh, sorry, was that rude? I didn't mean it to be. I was just interested.'

'God forbid I should ever be the one to suppress interest. There's little enough of it going around these days.'

'What do you mean?'

'Never mind. To answer your question, I haven't been precisely rescuing the company, but it had got a little dusty and moribund. I've been – modernizing it, if you like. My father took it over from Grandpa when he died, but I don't think his heart was greatly in it. It was the source of his income, that's all. Things went on being done in the same way they always had, even though times had changed. So profits were down – if you don't mind the mention of something as gross as money – and it needed an injection of energy and innovation.'

'And will you inherit it from your father?'

'I already have. My father died two years ago.'

'Oh! I'm sorry.'

He looked at her carefully, as if to see if, indeed, she really was, and she blushed.

'It's the natural course of things,' he said. Another bird came over and he fired, missed, and handed the gun to the loader who came up – they were sharing one between two.

'Do you have any brothers or sisters?' she asked when they were alone again.

'Just one brother.'

'Doesn't he get to share the family firm?' she asked.

He gave her that odd look again, as if amused at her frankness. 'No, he's already provided for elsewhere. The company is all mine, for better or worse. I hope, from the company's point of view, it will be better. It would be nice to be able to pass it on intact to my son.'

'When you have one.'

'When I have one.'

'But not your daughter, of course,' she added.

'Oh, I'm not so hidebound as you think. There's no reason a woman shouldn't run the company. There are lots of women in publishing.'

'But you'd prefer to leave it to a boy.'

'If I had both, I'd choose the boy, unless he really didn't want it and the girl did. Boys need more providing for than girls. Girls can always get married.'

'That's all they're good for, you mean,' she said.

'Not at all. They have more options, that's all. For a boy, marriage is not a possible alternative to earning a living, it's an addition to it. Don't you want to get married?'

'Of course,' she said, and scuffed her boot in the grass restlessly. 'It's just...' She hadn't the words to describe how she felt set aside and unvalued by her parents' attitude. But bit-by-bit he encouraged her to talk and drew it out of her, while occasionally breaking off to fire as a bird came over. He didn't hit anything, and she was glad, while being at the same time slightly disappointed that he should be so bad at it, which seemed somehow to make him less manly. She would have liked to think he was good at everything he attempted. Later she discovered he was, in fact, a very good shot. Whether he missed that day deliberately or because she distracted him she didn't know, but either answer was flattering.

The whistle blew and the drive was over,

and they walked back to the Range Rovers to go home for tea. Julian was immediately annexed again, and Ginnie endured half an hour of name-exchanging conversation while she warmed her frozen body externally at the grand open fire and internally with tea and muffins, and then went off to try to get a bath in before everyone else used up the water.

Julian was late down and was at once taken over by his dinner partner, a very tall, thin, blonde girl who crooked her fingers over his arm like half a handcuff as if to make sure he didn't get away. Ginnie was taken in by Jeremy, and sat between him and Henry Maude. They soon both established their lack of common ground with her and conversation struggled, but at least Jeremy knew who Irish Granny was and thought he had met her son, the baronet, once, so he tried to be kind and kept remembering the names of other Irish peers and asking if she knew or was related to them. Henry, when she had to face his way, entertained her by talking about the Market and various deals he had done, never quite meeting her eyes, so she felt as though he was praying aloud to his personal god and she ought not to listen.

After dinner she was beckoned by Lady Bureton, who was sitting on a hard upholstered settle by the fire, and made to sit next to her. A series of questions followed, while Lady Bureton seemed to examine her minutely. Ginnie felt she was being tested and graded to see if she was good enough – though for what she did not know. Fortunately her boredom and disappointment, as well as the long day in the fresh air, had taken the edge off her, and she answered as docilely as her mother would have wished. Gradually she became aware of a slight softening in her interlocutor. Lady Bureton was not exactly warm, but at least she was not frosty. It happened that she had a weakness for red hair, and she preferred girls to be small and slight so that she could tower over them. Tall girls always had to work extra hard to please her.

'Of course, I met your dear grandmother only once,' she said after some time, 'but Bureton's father knew her quite well. She was a famous beauty in her day, did you know that? There is a portrait of her by Harrison in the National Portrait Gallery. You have the colouring, though I don't know if you resemble her in any other way. It is to be hoped that you do not share her character. She's quite an eccentric now, by all accounts. Bureton has met Glenulick several times when he's been in London – your grandfather, I mean, not the present baronet. The title is quite an early creation, I believe – quite respectable.'

Ginnie simply looked blank to all of this. She was trying to see, without appearing to, where Julian was and who he was talking to.

Her previous night's resolution to hate and punish him was quite forgotten. She now saw him as the only island of comfort in an alien world.

'I see you've been talking to Julian Addington,' Lady Bureton went on, leaping so completely into Ginnie's thoughts that she blushed helplessly. 'He's a pleasant boy. We've known the family for generations, of course.' She examined Ginnie's face, and then said, 'You know that he's the second son?'

She seemed to want an answer – heaven knew why – so Ginnie said, 'He did say he had a brother. I didn't know which was the elder.'

'Hmm,' said Lady Bureton, still minutely observing Ginnie's face. 'It's a pity in some ways, because he would make a better job of things than Rupert. I understand some firm management is needed to get things back on an even keel, and Rupert is not a friend to seriousness and hard work.'

Ginnie looked her bewilderment. 'But I thought – excuse me, but I thought Julian had already inherited the publishing company.'

'So he has,' said Lady Bureton, looking puzzled back. And then she said, 'You don't know Rupert? Or the family?'

'No,' said Ginnie. 'I only met Julian once before, at a party in London. I don't know anything about his family.'

Lady Bureton smiled, and then patted Ginnie's hand. 'Go and join the other young people,' she said. 'I expect you'd like to dance.'

Ginnie accepted her dismissal and got up. On reaching the other end of the room, she was met by Julian, who asked if she would like to dance.

'You were having a very serious conversation with our hostess,' he said.

'She was grilling me. I don't know why. She asked me if I knew your brother. I said I didn't and she seemed to lose interest – thank God.'

Julian smiled down at her, and said, 'Thank God indeed,' and then changed the subject and talked about the forthcoming exhibition of French impressionists at the Royal Academy. It was an acceptable choice of subject to Ginnie. At least she had studied art and knew the names.

It was only when she got home and spoke to her mother that she learned what Lady Bureton's conversation had been about. It turned out that Julian's great-grandfather had not been any old Mr Addington but the second Earl Addington – 'A nineteenth century political creation, quite acceptable,' her mother said. Julian's grandfather had been the younger son, and since the entire estate was entailed he had had, in the manner which is the strength of the English aristocracy, to make a living for himself, hence the publishing company. But Julian's great-uncle, the third earl, had had only one son, and that son, the present (fourth) earl, had no children at all. When he died, the title and estate, which would have passed to Julian's father if he had lived, would pass to his brother Rupert.

Now so many things were explained. That was why Julian fitted in with the set, despite being so different from them. And that was why Lady Bureton had warned her that Julian was the second son – she assumed Ginnie had been making up to him for the title. And why she was first puzzled and then pleased that Ginnie didn't know about the family – Ginnie had been cleared of crass fortune hunting.

By why had Julian not told her? There had been plenty of opportunities but he had allowed her to think he was nothing but a publisher. She felt he had played her for a fool, and felt angry, remembering so many of his odd looks and knowing smiles. She was an ignorant little outsider, despite the Glenulick connection, and they had probably all been laughing at her.

Her mother was saying, 'It's a pity it wasn't Rupert you met. But of course, these things are never certain. There are always accidents. Or he may not marry or have children, or they may be girls. Julian might still be worth cultivating.'

Ginnie rounded on her angrily. 'If he was, it would be for who he is, not in the hope that his brother will die and leave him the title. But in any case he has no interest in me at all, and I certainly have no interest in him. So you can stop hoping for car crashes, Mummy.'

'I didn't mean that at all,' said Veronica indignantly.

'You did, and it's ghoulish.'

Veronica tossed her head. 'If you say there's nothing between you then the point is academic. But really, Ginnie, you will have to start being more agreeable to the young men, because from what you say you made nothing of your opportunity at Bureton Hall, and I don't know how many more invitations like that you think there'll be. If you go on objecting to everyone you'll never get married. Perhaps Julian Addington wouldn't be too bad a choice after all. At least the company he owns is in publishing, not something industrial. Perhaps we ought to invite him to something.'

'He wouldn't come,' said Ginnie, close to tears though she didn't really know why. 'And I wouldn't speak to him if he did. He's the last person in the world I'd want to marry.'

# Ten

Julian telephoned early the following week and asked if he could take her out to dinner and she accepted with her heart bounding with happiness. A month later he came to meet her parents, and charmed them so utterly they entirely forgave him for being a younger son (though Veronica probably never gave up hope of the surgical car crash removing Rupert neatly from the scene). He could talk politics and foreign affairs intelligently to Edward Fawcett, and gossip knowledgeably with Veronica about the families she had known and would have liked to know; and Ginnie felt if he had met Bill he would have charmed him, too, by having a subject ready that was close to his heart. He seemed to know something about everything, and to be able to talk about it fluently. Perhaps it was something to do with being in publishing – perhaps he read acres of books and remembered what he read.

After that the Fawcetts accepted him as their daughter's settled suitor, and while she had not yet made up her mind to marry him, and he had not yet asked her, she couldn't now imagine her life without him in it. Already he would leave such a huge hole. It was the first time in her life she had had someone dedicated to her comfort and happiness, someone who thought her the most important member of her family.

He took her to meet Rupert one evening at a champagne bar in the City. Rupert was not married then, had a flat in Docklands and was messing about in a merchant bank while he waited for the title. They disliked each other on sight. Rupert thought her a provincial nobody trying to trap his brother in the hope of the reversion: the Glenulick connection cut no ice with him, and he had no opinion of the diplomatic set, being as entirely apolitical as it was possible for a grown man to be. He made it clear in as many ways as possible in one short evening that she was not 'one of them'.

She thought him arrogant and stupid, desperately uneducated beside Julian, interested in nothing but himself, and on the verge of being a drunk; they had three bottles of champagne between them and Rupert must have accounted for two of them. He was quite like Julian to look at, only taller, nearly six feet, and more conventionally good-looking, and with fairer hair, almost blonde. But there was something she didn't like about his mouth. He looked *unreliable*, she decided. She found herself agreeing with Lady Bureton that it was a shame Julian wasn't the elder son, though she immediately crossed her mental fingers and cancelled the thought as being perilously close to the wishing-for-a-car-crash mentality of her mother, which she despised. She could not think of any field of endeavour where she would have bet that Rupert could perform better than Julian.

He took her to meet his mother, who had sold the family home at Barton Stacey when her husband died (Ginnie was sorry in a way not to see where Julian had grown up) and moved to a tiny house in Winchester, near the cathedral. It was a narrow slice of mediaeval with a false Georgian front, all smooth stucco outside and terrifyingly ancient beams inside. Here Mrs Addington lived within the sound of the cathedral bells, surrounded by beautiful pieces of furniture and priceless paintings of the sort Ginnie was later to recognize in Julian's possession: the props of rank and family background, the comforting proof that one came of a set that did not have to 'buy its own furniture'. She was small, exquisitely turned out, with the honed clarity of speech of a lifelong addresser of meetings, and she did her best to be kind to Ginnie, which only made her more daunting. She gave them luncheon (she would never have called it 'lunch') at a Georgian mahogany gateleg table, off a hundred-and-fifty-year-old Limoges service, and tried honourably to find something to chat to Ginnie about. In the end she fell back on that trusted standby, stories of Julian's childhood, and since Julian was in fact the only thing they had in common, he bore it nobly, and things went off better than expected. Ginnie was neither enraged nor made to feel really uncomfortable, but she left with the sense, more than ever, that a greater gulf divided the upper classes from the upper-middle than any of the gulfs below.

By far the worst ordeal was the visit to Addington Hall to meet the earl, which happened in the summer, after Julian had proposed and been accepted. The earl's permission was theoretically needed for Julian to marry, since he conceivably might one day take the title. 'You don't mean to say if he didn't like me you'd chuck me?' Ginnie said when he dropped something about this into the conversation on the journey down.

'Of course not. But it's polite to introduce you. He's a nice old boy and I wouldn't want to hurt his feelings. Don't worry, you'll like him.'

Addington Hall turned out to be everything Ginnie hated about the country. The house was Georgian red-brick, barrack-like in its plainness – much admired for the purity of its architecture, Julian told her, but since that purity was severely aesthetic and unadorned it took the eye of understanding or of love to see it, and Ginnie had neither.

She thought it downright ugly. And comfortless. It needed money spending on it. The roof leaked, the plaster was coming off the walls in many places, and the kitchen was a subterranean hell-hole of mould and black beetles. The central heating had been installed in Edwardian times and, despite a boiler that could have served the Queen Mary and consumed coke by the ton, it was as cold as death inside, even in summer – Ginnie dreaded to think what it would be like in winter – and the bathroom taps yielded nothing but a dribble of cold, rusty water. The sash windows of the bedroom Ginnie was assigned (they were to stay for dinner and the night) were warped and immoveable, stuck open about two inches at top and bottom; the mattress seemed to have been stuffed with rocks and had a deep, body-shaped hollow in the middle, the pillows were hard and lumpy, the blankets were worn so thin she could have read through them, the bedside lamp didn't work ('stuck without a book to read!' Paris Granny would have died!) and there was a hole in the carpet that she stumbled over every time she crossed the room. Everything looked and smelled dirty, and she kept everything she had brought with her in the overnight bag rather than risk contamination by unpacking it.

The earl was vague, shambling and ash-strewn, with dirty hair, and he smelt – well, how would you bathe in that house? He seemed to be very fond of Julian (who did his usual charm trick) but did not seem to grasp who Ginnie was. He asked her who she hunted with, and when she said she didn't ride he lost interest in her entirely and talked to Julian non-stop about horses, estate management and which paintings he ought to sell to pay for repairs. Ginnie might have been able to say something intelligent on the latter subject, but when she ventured a question, the earl looked at her for a moment and then asked Julian quite audibly, 'Who *is* that?' as if she'd just wandered in off the street.

The earl lived with his long-term mistress Mrs Simmons (his wife had died twenty years ago), a woman whose size hinted at an amplitude of delights in earlier years which had spread in all directions with age. She smelt too, but of mothballs, which mostly overpowered any other odours. She chain-smoked, as did the earl, but she did it with a sort of conscious archness as though she were doing something rather racy and *fast*. She questioned Ginnie about her family and forebears, got as far as the Glenulicks, found there was nowhere else much to go, and lapsed into silence.

Dinner was meagre, though served with great flourish in the vast dining room with a great deal of fine china, crystal and ancient silver that needed cleaning. The room was as cold as a morgue and smelled of damp, and the food, having to come from such a distance, was no better than tepid when it arrived. They had tinned soup, shepherd's pie with frozen vegetable medley (peas, carrots, beans and sweetcorn), a savoury of cheese on toast, and then a cold (shop-bought) apple pie with cream. The cream was off, as Mrs Simmons herself mentioned, but the earl said (and it was clear that this was something he'd said many times before) that he didn't care for milk or cream until it was 'ripe'.

They drank hock with the soup and claret with the rest, and even to Ginnie's untutored palate they were excellent. At some point during the meal Julian managed to get through to the earl that he wanted to marry Ginnie, and when they retired to the drawing room he called for champagne, which was also excellent, and drank her health, only spoiling it by referring to her as Angela. There was some weak, muddy coffee and some more silence for Ginnie while Julian carried on talking to the earl and Mrs Simmons carried on smoking, and then they were able to take a blessedly early night. On the way upstairs Julian said, 'They liked you,' and she gave him a withering look.

The following morning, after a restless night on the rock bed, they abandoned Mrs Simmons at home and were taken round the estate by the earl, which was at least better than staying in the house, though it was clear he had forgotten who she was again, and looked reproachfully at Julian when he tried to include her in the conversation as though he were fraternizing too much with the peasantry. The talk between the earl and Julian was all about the estate and much of it was technical and boring to Ginnie. She sat in the back, being bumped over the ruts in the springless Land Rover (1960s vintage) until her backside felt like tenderized steak, and looked out at the scenery. The tour ended at the stables, where there were still four horses and an ancient groom. The three men discussed the bloody animals lovingly and endlessly. They examined their teeth and feet (all the dangerous bits; are you *mad*? she wanted to shout) and petted them, and Ginnie kept well out of the way and breathed through her mouth to keep the hated smell out. Eventually they came away, and the earl clapped Julian on the back and said, 'By God, I wish you were my son! You're a real horseman, my boy, you know that?' He almost bumped into Ginnie, standing by the Land Rover, and said, 'Oh! Ah! Yes! Angela, isn't it? Having a good time, m'dear?' and then forgot her entirely again.

Julian helped her into the back, and she discovered she had a big gob of greenish manure on her shoe. She took a mild pleasure in surreptitiously wiping it off on the edge of the earl's jacket which, being open and too big for him, was trailing beside his seat. He'd never notice the difference, anyway.

They were offered lunch but Julian, thank God, refused and said they had to be getting back. When, as they turned out of the gates he said, 'What about a pub lunch somewhere?' she almost fainted with gratitude.

'Was it a terrible ordeal?' he asked as they drove through green lanes decked with moon-daisies and Queen Anne's lace. Ginnie thought it wiser not to answer that. 'Dinner was pretty vile, wasn't it? I thought you'd prefer not to eat another meal there.'

'You thought right,' she said shortly.

After a moment he went on. 'It's a damn' shame the place is in such bad order. It needs money spending on it, but the land's good, and there's a lot he could do with it, if he weren't so old. I just hope Rupert doesn't take one look and give up – or worse, sell off the land.'

'Why would that be worse?' she asked. It was just a lot of pointless muddy fields smelling of animal shit as far as she was concerned. What was the big deal? She felt no family attachment to 'the pile' and its four acres: in her circle houses were things to be bought and sold as convenience dictated.

But he looked faintly shocked. 'The title without the land would be worthless. The land *is* the earldom, surely you can see that? Otherwise it would be like being one of

Blair's placemen.'

She did not pursue the point, seeing one of the gulfs between them opening up. Instead she said, 'But if there's no money, how will Rupert do things to the estate even if he wants to?'

'He'll have to marry an heiress,' Julian said matter-of-factly.

'Then it's a good job you aren't the eldest son,' Ginnie said, and then wished she hadn't, in case it made him think. But Julian only gave one of his sidelong smiles and touched her hand in between changing gears.

Over lunch she said suddenly, 'We *are* going to live in London, aren't we?'

'Of course,' he said. 'Most of the time.'

'All of the time,' she stipulated firmly. 'I hate the country.'

'Still?' he asked, with that faint, strange smile.

'More than ever,' she said. And then, for several reasons defiantly, she said, 'I'm jolly glad you aren't the eldest son. If I ever had to live at that awful place I'd die. Literally die.'

Julian digested this quietly, with a serious look, but all he said was, *'Elder* son, as there are only two of us.'

They were married eighteen months after their first meeting – which was not bad going – and moved into the house Julian had already bought in Shepherd's Bush. With his contacts in the publishing world he was able to help her to put her photographs around and she built up quite a successful career until the children started coming along. She worked through her pregnancy with Flora and did a bit between Flora and Jasper, but she didn't really go back to it after that, and gradually she lost her contacts.

She loved London, and seized on to the new people of the late nineties and early noughties with delight, making her life among them. They were the antithesis of the landed set, whom she still disliked – they bored her, and they never quite accepted her as one of them, even when she was married to Julian. They had all played with each other in the nursery, or were cousins, or their parents had played together or been to Eton together. They all knew each other and they couldn't quite get over their suspicion of anyone who didn't know the same people.

But the new rich, the smart London set, had no families, no traditions, no customs, no weird social rules and taboos, no barriers except the simple one of wealth. They didn't care where the money came from as long as one had it. And Julian had enough, it seemed, to give her what she wanted and needed.

But though she adored modernity and newness and fashion and designer restaurants and ostentatious consumption, and grabbed them and held them to her to keep the other world out, she could never quite wean Julian from his old life. He had his bespoke suits, made to last a lifetime, and his inherited furniture, and his valuable paintings and old silver, and his amused contempt for the idea of 'doing up the house' and of 'fashion' in general, whatever field it was applied to. He still saw his old friends and she had to go with him sometimes, and remember things like never to knock on a sitting-room door, never to cut an egg with a knife, never to call pudding 'dessert' or the chimneypiece the 'mantelpiece'; to remember that London was simply Town, and that it was always *up* to Town and *down* to the country regardless of what direction on the atlas you were travelling in.

Julian liked shooting and he liked hunting (he missed riding most of all, living in Town) and when he went for a country-house weekend to do those things, he liked her to go with him. Then she would be the odd one out all weekend, not riding, not liking shooting, and not joining in the conversations about old so-and-so, even when, by now, she actually did know the person concerned. And of course the children, as they grew up, loved all that kind of thing: they adored going to big country houses, they loved company, and Flora was horse mad while Jasper was longing to be able to shoot. They much preferred visits to houses like Bureton and Addington, to visiting Horn Hill, which they saw as small, shabby and dull by comparison. Ginnie was left to feel in a minority of one amongst them.

She envied Polly her house and her clothes and her shoes, and she even envied her Seth, for though he wasn't at all handsome, he was utterly modern and cared nothing for antiques or old masters or classical music or any of those 'superior' things. He sneered at them. And he adored Polly – he was always saying he loved her, according to Polly, often bought her flowers and took her out to expensive restaurants, and always brought her presents when he came back from his trips abroad.

Julian, of course, had given Ginnie the first and best proof of love in marrying her and agreeing to live all the time in London which was not what he would have wanted. But he hardly ever *said* he loved her, and they didn't make love much any more (she turned her mind away from the thought that that was as much her fault as his). Worst of all, because she did not share his tastes and values she felt that he was always laughing at her. That amused, closed smile of his that had intrigued and then enchanted her now unnerved her. She was afraid that he didn't love her much any more: he couldn't even be bothered to have rows with her.

It was Ginnie's tragedy that she didn't understand – or perhaps had forgotten – that Julian's unshakable politeness stemmed from good manners, not from indifference. He never bellowed, which she saw as a sign that he didn't care enough. Her father had bellowed, when there was only her and her mother to hear. Perhaps for him bellowing was the antidote to having to be diplomatic at work all day.

# Eleven

Polly telephoned Ginnie as soon as Nigel was out of earshot.

'I've met our new neighbour.'

'What new neighbour?' Ginnie didn't sound that interested.

'The one who's moving into the big corner house.'

'No-o-o!' she growled excitedly. That caught her attention. 'How? Where?'

'He came into the shop this morning looking for paintings for his new, bare walls.'

'What a coincidence!

'Isn't it!'

'It shows he's one of us, though.'

'One of us, as in...?'

'Liking modern paintings instead of dopey old nineteenth-century watercolours.'

'Why are you so mean about Julian?' Polly asked mildly.

'Today, mostly because he wouldn't take me to New York. But tell about the new neighbour. Who is he, what's he like?'

'His name's Simon Harte, he's a bigwig in Transglobal Media, and he's come to London to set up a new book publishing house for them. He's heard of Julian, by the way.'

'Amazing. Transglobal's huge, and he's still heard of Addington and Lyon? Go on.'

'He'll be staying for at least five years, but he says he loves London so he may stay permanently. He must be very rich because he bought our Rothko and didn't even blink at the price.'

'Well, we knew he must be rich to be buying the corner house. Did he pay five million for it?'

'I didn't ask him *that*,' Polly said, laughing. 'What do you take me for?'

'And what's he like? Old and ugly and boring?'

'He's in his mid-forties, I should say, well-built, intelligent, nice, and absolutely *gorgeous*.'

'George Cloony gorgeous, or someone in real life you might spot on a train gorgeous?'

'He leaves George Cloony standing,' said Polly, who had never found him particularly attractive anyway. 'And he's single. Divorced, that is, but not recently. It was a very sad tale. His wife left him.'

'Nasty habits at home, then, probably,' said Ginnie, but not as though she believed it.

'Nonsense. He's not the type. Robyn had no taste, that's all.'

'Robin?'

'With a "y". His wife. Ex-wife.'

'How do you know so much about him?' Ginnie said suspiciously.

Polly paused a beat, and there was a, perhaps justifiable, hint of smugness in her voice as she said, 'We had lunch.'

'*Polly!*'

'It's true. He was sort of – not exactly flirting with me in the shop, but we just got on like a house on fire, and when he came out after closing the deal with Nigel, he said he'd made having lunch with me part of it. The excuse was that he wants to buy more pictures, and I was to take the photos along with me to show him.'

'How did Nigel take to that?'

'Oh, he was all right with it.'

'But why did he really want to lunch you? Is he smitten?'

'No, nothing like that. He knows I'm married.'

'When did that ever stop a determined man?'

'But he wasn't being determined. I think maybe he just – wanted the company. It must be a bit daunting relocating to a new city.'

'Divorced and lonely? He sounds dangerous,' Ginnie said with relish. 'I must meet him.'

'Well, you'll get your chance. He's really up for the welcome party this weekend.'

'We'll have to try and impress him. Better not have it at my tip,' said Ginnie. 'What about yours?'

Polly had thought of that and, given how

almost-flirty they had been over lunch, she somehow felt it might send the wrong signals to invite him to her home while Seth was away. She didn't want to try to explain this to Ginnie, however, because she felt Ginnie would think her being silly and over-sensitive – or alternatively assume she was up to something. She said, 'I'd rather not. Seth would kill me if anything got spilt, or some-one made a mark on his walls. Better for a couple to host it, anyway. It looks more – well, it'd be better.' Ginnie did not object to this idea. 'I'm going to ring round the neigh-bours,' Polly went on, 'and see what they think. I suppose it had better be Saturday night – or Sunday lunchtime maybe. I said I'd ring him later today and tell him what we'd arranged.'

'Well, ring me as soon as you know,' said Ginnie, and changed the subject abruptly. 'Do you think Julian's having an affair?'

Polly was startled. 'What? Of course not! What makes you think that?'

'Oh, I don't know that I actually think it. Yet. I was just wondering. This trip to New York, for instance. It was awfully sudden, and then he didn't tell me about it until it was too late for me to arrange to go.'

'But he said he didn't know about it before,' Polly reminded her.

'Yes, but he asked me to take his dinner suit in to the cleaners yesterday. He got his secretary to take it in the end, but he had the express service done on it, and picked it up on the way home. He *never* normally does that. He thinks the express service isn't good enough. So that suggests that he knew *yesterday morning* that he was going, while he told me he only learnt about it *during the day*.'

'You're not being logical. If he'd planned the trip beforehand, why wouldn't he get his suit cleaned much earlier? Why leave it to the last minute? It's much more likely that he was going to get it cleaned the usual way, then this trip came up and he had to switch to express service. Doesn't that make more sense?'

'I suppose so, damn you,' Ginnie said moodily. 'But I still don't think he actually *wanted* me to go. So I thought – maybe there's a woman.'

It reminded Polly of her own thoughts about Seth, that he didn't actually want *her* to go, either. 'That's rubbish,' she said. 'Men don't like women hanging around when they're on business, that's all.'

'They don't like *wives* hanging around,' Ginnie corrected.

'Look, Julian is not having an affair,' Polly said firmly.

'Yeah, you're right. Who'd want an affair with him? Boring, tweedy old Julian?'

'I didn't *mean* that—'

'So then you think he *might* have one?'

'Any man *might*, but they don't. He just wouldn't do something like that.'

'That's where you're wrong. The upper classes do it all the time. It's only us middle-class types who think it's dodgy.'

'But Julian's not like that. Look, Ginnie, I know you're not really serious, but I wish you wouldn't talk like that. Who on earth do you think he'd be having an affair with anyway? Does he know anyone in New York?'

'There's this editor at Day Valentine – Angela Demarco. He's always talking about her and how *wonderful* she is. She sounds like a sultry piece. I bet she's Italian, glossy black hair, tan skin, fabulous shoes.'

Polly laughed. 'You haven't got enough to keep your mind occupied, that's what's wrong with you. Didn't Julian have a good reason for going to New York?'

'Well, yes – on paper.'

'On paper nothing. Work yourself up about something else. Julian is not having an affair – and Nigel's coming back, so I've got to ring off. I'll call you later.'

'OK. Bye.'

Tammy must have been talking to the neighbours, or the word had got about some other way. When Polly rang Sukey Arrosto, at number 8, she already knew all about it.

'I've heard, I've heard,' she said gaily. 'The Bickersons are giving a party for the new man at number one!'

'They are?'

'It's all decided. They've got the biggest

158

house – and besides, Sadie Bickerson practically said she would assassinate anyone who stepped on her toes, so far better let her get on with it, don't you think? At least you can be sure of decent food and enough to drink. They may be rather loud and pushy, but there's nothing mean about them. My God, I just thought – what if he's that way himself, the new man? Loud and pushy. He's American, apparently.'

Polly shook her head at this blinkered racism. 'He isn't. He's charming and *urbane*,' she said, and added mischievously, 'You'd never know if you didn't know.'

'Oh, good,' Sukey said, and then caught up. 'How do you know? Have you met him already?'

'He came into my shop to buy paintings. We had quite a chat.'

'Lucky you! Tammy Wentworth seems to think she's taken out a patent on him. Apparently Sam's spoken to him already, rang him up at work first thing, gave him a rundown on all his new neighbours. He still wants to meet us, though! Tammy got his name from the estate agent. They wouldn't give it to her at first – how mad is that?'

'Data Protection Act, I suppose,' said Polly.

'Someone who's going to live next door to you? It's not exactly a state secret. So I suppose you must know his name, if you actually met him.'

'Simon Harte.'

'That's right. I'd never heard of him – but maybe Peter has. I might give him a tiny tinkle at the office, actually, see if he knows anything. Why let the Wentworths have all the fun? If Sam can ring him cold for a chat, so can I.'

'I've got to go, Sukes. I have to ring Sadie.'

'Oh, yes, go on. Let me know as soon as you've got it all fixed.'

She rang Simon's mobile number, as he'd said it was the preferred one, and he answered at once with, 'Hello, Polly.'

'How did you know it was me?' she asked.

'I've put Esterhazy's number into the memory,' he said. 'And I somehow didn't think it would be Nigel.'

'Lucky for you that you were right.'

'Very lucky. Charming as your boss is, I'd sooner chat to you.'

She felt she ought to nip this in the bud. 'I'm afraid I can't really chat on the firm's time. I was just calling to say that your welcome party is being organized. The Bickersons are hosting it and they want it to be Sunday lunchtime, so that those of us with children can bring them and not worry about sitters. They can all stay in the garden so they won't annoy us.'

'No problem. I like children.'

'Oh, good. Well, is Sunday lunchtime all right for you?'

'Yes, fine. And who are the Bickersons? I

rather thought you'd be organizing it your-self.'

'We thought it would be better for a couple to host. And the Bickersons live in number twelve, the other corner house, which means it's bigger, which is good for holding parties, but also that it's the mirror image of yours. It might be nice for you to see what they've done with it. It might give you some ideas.' She confounded herself with her own words and added hastily, 'Not that you need to be given ideas, of course, or that their taste will necessarily appeal to you. I mean, I'm sure you already know what you want to do. That's to say—'

'Polly, shut up,' he said gently, interrupting her babbling. 'I'm not offended. How could you think it? And I'd love to see what some-one else has done with the same space, and I'm sure it *will* give me ideas – even if only what to avoid!'

She laughed in relief. 'Well, I don't like *everything* they have had done, though I shouldn't say so to anyone but you – and please don't quote me. But they're nice, generous people and they'll lay on a good "do".'

'It'll be great, I'm sure.'

'Everyone's keen to meet you, so there'll be a good turnout. You'll get to meet most of your neighbours – even if they won't be bringing you pies.'

'That's all to the good. What would I do

with a bunch of pies? Listen, now we've got that fixed, I've a favour to ask you.'

'Oh? What is it?' She heard herself sounding cool, and was sorry. It was just her caution, not wanting to give the wrong impression. But there was no need to frost the poor guy. 'I mean, anything I can do to help,' she added, trying for more warmth.

'I really would like to see those photographs, but at the house. And I'd value your opinion about them, whether they'd suit me – and where to hang the two I've bought already. Would you be willing to bring the photos round to me, say, on Saturday?'

'Well,' she said, and then, 'But won't you be busy with moving in?'

'I'm having a few necessities delivered first thing, but it won't take long. It isn't as though I have all my worldly goods and chattels to unpack. If you were to come along around twelve thirty, we could look at the photographs and go round the house, and then I could give you some lunch. It will probably be a bit of a picnic affair – I don't cook much, and I don't know the kitchen, so it will be what I can pick up from the deli. But if you were willing to rough it, we could carry on talking while we eat. I'd really like your advice about a number of things.'

Polly had been making up her mind during this speech, and so was able to say with an appearance of decisiveness, 'Yes, I'd be happy to come. But you don't have to give me lunch.'

'That would be my pleasure,' he said gravely.

*Mine too*, Polly thought. But she did not say it. 'So, twelve thirty, then?'

'I'll look forward to it. Oh, and Polly?'

'Yes?'

'Bring anything you think might interest me. Don't just restrict it to the ones your boss picked out. I have pretty eclectic tastes. I'd like to see the things *you* like as much as anything. Whatever might give me ideas.'

*I suspect you already have ideas*, Polly thought as she rang off, *and probably more of them than are good for either of us.* She thought what a good thing it was that she had the curse, and then blushed to her hair roots at the implication. She always had the fatal ability to embarrass herself with her own mental processes.

She suddenly thought that it would be nice to talk to Seth. But though he had his mobile with him, of course, he didn't like to be interrupted when he was away on business. In fact, he didn't like to be rung up at work even when he was in England. He said it looked fatally naff to be talking to your wife in front of customers or, worse, potential customers, because it was either, 'Yes, dear, I'll pick up a lettuce and the dry cleaning on my way home,' or 'Of course I love you, snookums, but I'm busy right now. I'll see you tonight, sweetie, kiss kiss kiss.' In either case it made you look like a moron. Polly saw his point, and never telephoned him unless it was something to do with his work, and then only if absolutely necessary. Their occasional daytime conversations were when *he* called *her*, which was often just to say he loved her. She loved that, and if it had to be on his terms, so be it. Anyway, she had nothing to say to him now, it was only a case of wanting to hear his voice, and she would die rather than subject him to the snookums routine in front of the pick of the Eurofashionistas, with whom he was no doubt fraternizing right now, making lots of useful contacts for the future and impressing the potential customers, to ensure that the boodles went on boodling in so as to keep her in the style to which he had accustomed her.

# Twelve

On Saturday Ginnie hustled the children off to their various social engagements: Flora to ballet, from which she would be going home with a classmate for lunch and the afternoon, Jasper and Ben to the Leestons', who had three assorted sons and a large garden, not to mention a vigorous and completely unflappable Australian nanny who would organize cricket and join in the building of a den in the shrubbery without actually being forced to. She then took herself up to the bedroom to drag every piece of clothing out of the wardrobe and fling it on the bed in an attempt to decide what to wear to the welcome party tomorrow.

The trouble was that everyone had seen her in everything, and although that didn't apply to the new man, there was nothing here that she wanted to show herself to him in, if he was as *gorgeous* as Polly said. She wondered if she could get away with a shopping trip. After all, if she shopped today, the bill wouldn't come in until next (financial) month anyway, so technically she'd be in the clear. She was shot of the children until about four o'clock, which gave her a couple of hours. Trouble was her credit cards were all about at their limit, so she'd have to draw a cheque on the joint account, which would not only reveal the date of her peccadillo but the *exact amount* she had blown, on the next statement. Still, she thought, that was a long way off, and the party was tomorrow. *Carpe diem*, as Julian's nobby friends so often said, which seemed to mean something like *sod the expense*, a philosophy she could handle.

By the time she had come to this decision it was nearly twelve, and because of the morning rush and the bathroom bottleneck she hadn't showered yet, so she was going to have to hurry. As she was heading into the bathroom, towel in hand, the phone started ringing. She was minded to ignore it when she thought it might be Julian, and it was.

'How are things? Did you get everything sorted out yesterday?' she asked.

'Sadly, not. Mark is being quite difficult. I think he wants to get his pennyworth for his penny.'

'Meaning?'

'Oh, that he likes having everyone rushing round after him, bathing his ego in sunshine. Authors are all paranoid, poor things, and believe no one likes them, so the chance to have everyone telling him how wonderful he is is too good to pass up. He knows once he's signed the contract everyone will walk away and ignore him again.'

'Will you?'

'Well, up to a point. Fortunately we've got until Monday to change his mind, and he's invited us up to his place in New England for the weekend, which must mean he's still flirting with us. I mean, if he'd decided already that he was going to sign with Global, there'd be no point in asking us. So it's a golden opportunity for us to make our case, *and* when he's in his own home, and nice and relaxed. The best of it is that it will get him away from Wolf Saltzman, because he's otherwise engaged, which gives us a chance to work on Mark undisturbed. Wolf was spitting tacks when Mark invited us and he realized he couldn't be there, but he could hardly do anything about it – though I wouldn't be surprised if he didn't find some way to wriggle out of his engagements and suddenly burst in on us unannounced.'

'Who's "we" and "us"?'

'Angela and I,' he said.

Ginnie's radar swung round on instant red alert.

'Oh?'

'She's been marvellous,' he said warmly. 'Anyway, the thing is, darling, that I shan't be back *before* Monday, but I'll let you know as soon as *I* know when I will. Is everything OK there?'

'Yes, fine.'

'It sounds quiet. Where are the kids?'

'All on play dates.'

'So you're alone? I'm sorry, darling. It must be dull for you. I'll make it up to you when I get back.'

'Oh, don't worry, we're having the welcome party tomorrow for the new man.'

'I'd forgotten that. Where's it to be?'

'Not here, don't worry,' she said, anticipating his objections. 'Your precious artefacts will be quite safe. The Bickersons are doing it.'

'That's good. They'll—'

Someone spoke to him in the background and he broke off. The voice was too quiet for Ginnie to hear what was said, but it was a woman's voice. She did a quick work-out in her head. What the hell time was it there? Wasn't it early morning? Was he at the office, and if not, where?

He came back on the line. 'Sorry about that.'

'Who was that, room service?' she asked cunningly.

'No, I didn't go to the hotel. That was Angela. I stayed the night in her apartment in Manhattan.'

'Oh, did you?'

'Yes, she invited me as soon as I arrived, so I was able to cancel the room in time to avoid the charge.'

'How kind.'

'Well, it's much more comfortable for me here, and it meant we were able to get a bit of work done after dinner.'

168

'I'm jolly glad to hear it.'

He seemed to be missing her irony. 'It made sense, anyway, since we've got to make such an early start this morning. She was just saying that we should go if we're to get through the tunnel before the traffic builds up, so I'd better ring off.'

'Yes, you mustn't keep Angela waiting.'

'Are you all right? Your voice sounds funny.'

'I'm fine. Everything's fine. Why shouldn't it be?'

'All right, then. I'll ring you when I can, or anyway when I know what flight I'll be getting.'

'I'll count the hours,' she said.

There was a pause. 'Are you really all right?' he said. 'I've only been gone one day, you can't have got up to anything.'

*Got up to anything?* That was rich, coming from him!

'You'll have to wait till you get home to find out, won't you?' she said, and hung up. At least she'd given him something to think about – she hoped. Unless he was too transported with rapture about being with bloody Angela to care. *Bastard!* Stayed the night to do some work? More comfortable? She betted it was. Early start? Probably meant they hadn't slept a wink all night! And now they were going on a road trip together, a nice leisurely drive through the countryside, maybe stopping at a romantic wayside inn for lunch, and they'd end up by staying in the luxurious mansion of a megastar author – Mark Stephens was probably the most famous writer on the planet. He probably lived in the style of Bill Gates! *And Ginnie wouldn't get to see it!*

A different thought occurred to her: if that's where they were going. Maybe Mark Stephens had made his mind up already and there was no invitation, and this was just an excuse to spend the weekend with Angela she's-been-marvellous Demarco. And there was no way Ginnie could check up on it, because she didn't have Mark Stephens's phone number and a person answering a mobile could be anywhere. How convenient!

A small voice in the back of her mind intervened at that point to ask her if she really believed all this. Did she really think Julian was that devious? The Julian she had lived with for ten years, the father of her three children? But then she remembered her own words to Polly, that the upper classes did it all the time and thought nothing of it. Only last year his brother Rupert had had an affair with some actress, and nobody had turned a hair, because although everyone seemed to know about it *there had been no scandal.* That was the point – the only point, it seemed to be. Rupert's wife (his second, and not that long married, either) hadn't thrown a fit and rushed to a lawyer. And Julian hadn't blown a gasket about it, he'd merely shaken his head afterwards and said he was glad it was all over, and that it hadn't come out. *Hadn't come out!*

The rich were another nation. Who was it had said that? But it wasn't only the rich, it was the upper classes who were another nation yet. And Julian was one of them to his bones, even though they didn't live like Rupert, and didn't see much of him or his set.

Well, she wasn't going to take it lying down. She had to do something. She didn't know what. The first essential was to spill it all out to Polly and hear what she thought. She sat down on the bed and rang her number. It rang for a long time and then was answered by Leela, the Mullers' Turkish help. *Six days a week*, Ginnie's grudge circuit reminded her.

'Hello, Leela, it's Mrs Addington. Is Polly there?'

'No, sorry, she not in. Not know when she coming back.'

*Damn.* 'Do you know where she went?' If it was shopping, she surely wouldn't be long.

'Oh, she not far away,' Leela said blithely. 'She visiting with Mr Harte in house on corner. Maybe you can see her there if it urgent.'

'No, it's all right, it isn't urgent. Thanks, Leela. I'll talk to her later.'

She rang off. The cunning little minx, she thought. Didn't say a word to me about it.

171

Getting in first before anyone else has a chance to meet him. But what was she up to? Surely Polly wasn't ready for a frisk? She and Seth were supposed to be so devoted, and they were trying for a baby – my God, they hardly ever seemed to do anything else! She surely wouldn't be getting up to anything with the new man, even if he was *gorgeous*.

A shocking thought came to her. Had she given up on Seth in the baby department and decided to try to get one elsewhere? No, not Polly! She wouldn't. She just wouldn't. *Would she?* No, definitely not. But maybe she was just smitten and couldn't help herself. The bloke had come on to her, by the sound of it, taking her to lunch when there was no need to. Any girl can have her head turned, get herself into trouble on the whim of a moment without meaning to. And if that were the case, it was up to her best friend to try to rescue her, before she did any damage.

Ginnie grabbed her towel and headed for the bathroom. While she was showering, some of her feverish speculation cooled down and various second and third thoughts came to her on a variety of subjects. But by the time she was out and dried and facing the heaps of clothes on her bed, she had managed to crystallize her resolve into one simple determination that she was not pre-pared to analyse any further. She was going to go round there, knock on the door, and meet the new man face to face. After that she would play it by ear.

First, though, she had to decide what to wear. She began trying things on.

When Simon opened the door to Polly's knock, the first thing she thought was that he didn't fit in with his background. Mrs Tennison's dark, drab wallpaper and the dinginess of the ceiling and paint-clogged mouldings did not accord with his personal beauty. He smiled at her (*be still, my beating heart!*) and said, 'Great minds do think alike. How did I know you would be wearing that?'

She looked down at herself and blushed, stupidly. He was wearing stone-coloured chinos and a Chambray shirt (the colour made his eyes look darker, summer-sky blue); she had put on stone-coloured cargo pants and a mid-blue shirt of Seth's that he had discarded because he didn't like the cut of the sleeves. She had picked the clothes carefully as being practical and non-dressy, what you might wear for looking round an empty, dusty house, and therefore incapable of sending the wrong message. Now dumb luck had them dressed like twins, as though she had some way of spying on him to copy what he was wearing.

'Coincidence,' she mumbled, still looking down.

'You're admiring my shoes, I see,' he said. He was wearing dark-blue suede loafers trimmed with brown leather. 'I call them my

Elvis shoes. Don't you step on them, now.'

He put on a Southern accent for the last sentence and it made her laugh and look up. Awkwardness fled: despite his beauty, he looked familiar and friendly, someone she just wanted to chat to.

'I'd call them Svetlanov shoes. Yvgeny Svetlanov?'

'The conductor?'

'You've heard of him! Thank God. You must like music, then.' Seth only listened to rock and some pop music (and castigated her for calling it pop music and not knowing the different divisions in the genre, but it all sounded the same to her) and all but called her pretentious for liking classical music (even though she didn't castigate him for calling it classical music and not knowing the different etc, etc ... )

'I have catholic tastes,' he said gravely. 'What about Svetlanov? Come in, by the way – there's no reason we should hold our conversation on the doorstep.'

He led her inside, down the bare, dark corridor. Maxiclean had done their job: everything had been dusted and scrubbed, and the air smelled of soap, polish and other cleaning fluids.

'Well, Svetlanov picked up a pair of blue suede shoes when he was on tour in America once,' she narrated, 'and he loved them so much he insisted on wearing them at every concert after that. With his white tie and tails. They were dreadful.'

He laughed. 'I can imagine. One thing I have got in this nearly empty house is a sound system,' he said, 'so we can have some music later.'

'I saw the furniture van this morning,' she said. 'I suppose everyone in the Terrace was peering from behind their curtains, to see what you were having delivered.'

'Just a few essentials.'

'I'm amazed you got them to come so early. Everyone I know has removal men horror stories that would turn your hair white.'

'Ah, but my stuff is all new, not having to be collected from another house. And I paid them something like the National Product of Lesotho to be here and gone by nine. Now, a quick tour before lunch?'

She tried to look stern. 'I'm here for business purposes, you know. Lunch is meant to be an adjunct, not the purpose of the visit.'

He shook his head. 'Lunch is never an adjunct. What a sad way of getting through life, Mrs Muller! Lunch is the highest invention of civilization and the reason we were designed by a beneficent God to walk upright – otherwise we could never have learned to use cutlery.' He opened the door into the drawing room. 'Have a look in here.'

The two rooms on this level were divided by wooden doors that ingeniously slid up into a slot in the ceiling, though the few times Polly had ever been here, in the Tennisons' day, she had never seen the rooms opened up. The door was up now, and she was interested to see the mechanism, which Simon obligingly showed her. Up above, it must slide into a space between bedroom walls. The bottom of the door fitted flush into the ceiling and had a neat hinged brass ring to pull it down with. She was charmed by the ingenuity. 'It makes a good space when it's up, doesn't it?' she said.

'It'll make a better one when this whole wall's taken out,' he said. 'I want one big room here, right the way through.'

He sounded like Seth, and she felt a twinge of disappointment. 'But this way you have the best of both worlds,' she suggested shyly.

'You forget I'm American. We like big rooms. It's one of the reasons I bought this house. And I would never want to live in a room the size these are with the door down, so there's no point in keeping it.'

'I see,' she said. The front room had embossed wallpaper which had been cream and gold, but because of the open fires had turned grey. The rear room had Regency-striped wallpaper that had been green and cream, but was now grey and grey. But the fireplaces were original and lovely, and the mouldings and ceiling roses were intact – a rarity these days – and only needed a hundred-and-sixty years of paint cleaning off them.

'The fireplaces will have to go, of course, and the plaster twirls,' Simon said, treading on her dreams. 'Imagine this completely opened up.' He made a sweeping hand gesture. 'Polished floors, clean, straight walls and ceiling, and I thought maybe French doors of some kind down the garden end.'

'You're not at garden level there, you know,' she warned.

'Yeah, but I was thinking a deck of some kind, and steps down into the yard. Nice for summer parties.'

'You'll make friends all right if you have summer parties. There's nothing Albermarlians like better.'

'What do you think of my domestic arrangements?'

In the centre of the rear room was a thick, blackberry-coloured rug with an enormous glass coffee table on it, and arranged around it a vast black leather sofa and two very modern chairs in chrome and red sailcloth. The promised sound centre was against the wall, along with a 24-inch plasma TV and DVD recorder, and an array of speakers placed, she could see, for the sofa occupier.

'Cosy,' she said. 'Stick a fridge at the side of the sofa and you'd have no reason ever to leave.'

'Oh, I can think of a few things,' he said. 'Let's go downstairs.'

Polly had never seen the basement of the Tennisons' house, and it was a fascinating time warp, because it still had the original layout of kitchen, scullery, larder, servants' 'hall', boiler room, coal-hole (with glass-brick port to the pavement above), and servants' lavatory. They would all have been like this, of course, when they were built (though obviously not as large) – a warren of small rooms divided by purpose. She picked her way, fascinated, from one to another, imagining the scene in 1850.

'Foul, isn't it?' Simon said, mistaking her silence for horror. 'But in actual fact, the space here is good, if you take out all these dividing walls. Imagine it bare, light and bright.'

'I am,' she said, and then pulled herself together. 'You could improve the height of the ceilings by digging down.'

'Hey! Great idea.'

'And you could even extend further into the garden, if you wanted more room. The only thing is, with your deck up above, you'd make it rather dark in here. But there are ways round that. If, instead of a solid deck, you had alternate panels of glass and wood, you'd let in a lot more light down here.'

'You are full of good ideas,' he said admiringly. 'I knew I was right to get you over here. But let's have lunch.' He led her into the kitchen. There had been moderniza-tions, of course, with the installation of an Aga in place of the original coal range, units and a stainless-steel sink – all of them Tennison vintage and pretty horrible, but service-able. But there was also a new and shiny larder fridge and a dishwasher which had presumably been delivered this morning.

'Everything's ready,' Simon said, heading for the fridge. 'And the table's laid outside. All you have to do is open that door for me and go and sit down.'

'Can't I help carry?'

'No, go and be a lady of leisure.'

There was a brushed-steel latticework table and matching chairs with grey-and-black striped cushions, which was laid for two with blue linen napkins, glasses, plates and cutlery. The shade of the house was still over the table, but the garden was full of sunshine and birdsong. It was a little over-grown from neglect, but there were roses and honeysuckles twining in the hedges, and bees murmuring in the clover that had romped through the shaggy lawn. A rural idyll, she thought facetiously; but it was sur-prisingly quiet for London, with only the occasional car going by, and people's child-ren were all doing their extra classes – ballet, piano, tai-chi, whatever – and so not yelling in the gardens.

She sat with her back to the house so as to be able to look out at the garden, and felt utterly relaxed. And, like something in a film, Mr Big appeared, stalking out of the long grass under the hedge and coming up to stare at her, as if asking what she was doing here in *his* territory. She spoke to him and patted her knee, and he jumped up into her lap to jam his head under her hand, purring loudly, tail up like a flagpole to advertise his love.

Behind her, Simon said, 'What a great accessory. Everyone who's anyone is wearing a cat this year. And the colour's perfect. You must have chosen it deliberately to go with your shirt.'

She turned her head to look at him. 'He's my neighbour's cat. He came out of the undergrowth.'

'The urban jungle,' he said. He was holding two tall, narrow glasses. She hadn't heard anything pop – he must be an expert at opening bottles. His eyes were as blue as the sky and his smile made her heart ache. 'Champagne?'

# Thirteen

Polly (née Walsh) was born in a respectable suburb in northwest London, in a three-bedroom, 1930s, mock-Tudor, Metroland semi. Her mother had been an orchestral violinist. Her father was a mathematics teacher in a Harrow school (though not, as he often jokingly added at this point, Harrow School), but music was his passion and his hobby: in his spare time he sang in the amateur but highly polished Royal Philharmonic Chorus. They had met outside the Royal Festival Hall: he had been to the concert, and she had been playing in it, and they bumped into each other on their separate ways to the station to go home. Their eyes had met, they had liked the look of each other, got chatting, and one thing had led satisfactorily to another.

Polly was the youngest of the four daughters born to them. Clara, Sidonie and Maria Anna (always called Anna) were all beautiful, lively, intelligent girls who amply repaid their parents' love and the aspirational names bestowed upon them at birth. As music had brought the Walshes together, they had given their children musical names in the hope that it would enrich their lives too. Polly's name was actually Apollonia but she very rarely told anyone that.

Those Metroland semis were not large. Six people had to learn ways to live together in the tight surroundings. The main bedroom was twelve by fifteen, the smallest ten by ten. There was one small bathroom and the lavatory was a separate room (thank God!) down a step on the landing. Downstairs there was a sitting room and dining room, and a small kitchen with a hatch through to the dining room and a door to the scullery. The scullery had a door into the garage. The Walshes had no car, so it made useful, not to say essential, extra storage space. Polly remembered it being full of boxes of apples and sacks of potatoes, cases of tinned Italian tomatoes and bags of sugar, cleaning materials in industrial sizes – Mrs Walsh believed in buying bulk. Later, there was a huge old freezer, bought second-hand and rusty at the corners, into which would go whole sheep and half pigs (cut up, of course) bought at farm shops on their trips into the country.

The wooden doors of the garage did not lock, and as age and sunshine warped them, they eventually had to be held shut by means of a large rock set against them on the outside – not for security purposes but to stop them banging in the wind. By day, it was just as usual for the rock to be used to hold the doors open, and the family came and went by route of the garage and the scullery door, which was never locked either. It was more convenient than having to issue front door keys to everyone (and have them frequently lost).

It became customary as the girls grew up for friends to come in this way, too. Neighbours, family and parental friends tended to use the informal entrance as well, for the Walshes were a friendly, relaxed family on whom it was always possible to 'drop in' unannounced, so there was a constant stream of comings and goings all through Polly's childhood.

The house – full, noisy and always with something going on – seemed to Polly interesting and welcoming, exactly what a home should be. It was hard to find a corner to do one's homework, though, especially having to share a bedroom with two sisters. She shared the large bedroom with Sidonie and Anna; her parents had the middle one; and Clara had the small room and a monastic iron bedstead to herself. The dining-room table was the favoured spot to work, but if not being used for eating (the kitchen was too small for a table) it was frequently required for dressmaking, handicrafts, writing exercises of various sorts from thank-you letters to marking bowings, or was annexed by groups of giggling girls playing Scrabble or Cluedo, and family marathons of Monopoly which necessitated leaving the board set up for days.

The upright piano was also housed in the dining room, and there were two music stands in the corner, so the room was frequently taken over for practice. Polly had to learn to concentrate even under aural assault from Bach preludes and endless, endless scales and arpeggios; but when all else failed and she craved solitude, she sometimes took her homework down to the shed at the bottom of the garden and wrote sitting in the wheelbarrow. There in the cool gloom that smelt of peat and sacks and cobwebs, with the metal edge of the wheelbarrow cutting into the underside of her thighs, she would escape into her schoolwork, or into a book. She adored reading. To open the pages of a novel was to leap like a swimmer into the crystal currents of another world, one full of space and possibilities. She would frolic there joyfully like a salmon, until someone, sent to fetch her for tea, would jerk her out, flapping and gasping, on to the dry bank of reality. Then she would almost stagger, disorientated, up the garden to the house – and find, as often as not, the wall of cheerful noise of eighteen people crammed elbow to rib around the table.

Money was always short in the Walsh household, but the girls were all bright and got into grammar school and won scholarships when necessary. Clara took the hint of her name and took up the piano. She went to the Royal College and then for private tuition under Szarowski. She did her first concert at the age of seventeen, receiving the usual lyrical reviews accorded to young musicians (but, in her case, fully deserving them) and now had a successful career as a soloist. Sidonie resisted the call of the harp and took up violin like her mother, and after the Guildhall joined the London Symphony Orchestra. Anna, probably the brightest of the lot, quick-witted, funny, sharp and multi-talented, played cello, piano and flute and sang like an angel. She won Young Musician for cello and everyone expected her to go on to a solo career, but at eighteen she suddenly decided that music was an over-crowded profession and chose instead to study architecture at UCL, her father's alma mater.

Which left Polly. Polly wasn't stupid by any means. She was bright enough for grammar school, and was in the top stream there, but she had, fatally – and astonishingly in such a family – no talent for music at all. She couldn't even sing in tune. At Christmas Mr Walsh used to put Messiah on the record player, and they would all sing along with it, taking different parts – Mr Walsh bass and baritone, Mrs Walsh mezzo and contralto, Clara tenor, Anna first soprano and Sid hopping from first to second as the fancy, or the demands of the music, took her. Sometimes they would take up their instruments and play along as well. Friends and relatives staying for Christmas or just invited in for a drink would form an amazed and admiring audience, or would sing along themselves to the best of their ability, and a very merry time was had by all. Except for Polly. It was years before her parents realized she was a hopeless cause and stopped encouraging her to join in; even longer before her sisters stopped teasing her about it. Then she was allowed to be the one who carried round the plates of sausage rolls and mince pies and refilled people's glasses in grateful silence. Then she would have been happy, were it not for the pitying looks, and the overheard (or imagined) whispers of, *'such a talented family, poor Polly, so strange, so sad!'*

The Walshes did their best to encourage their ugly duckling, but since even Mr Walsh had sung in public concerts and had played the French horn at school, it was hard for them to understand her in the sympathetic sense of the word. The best they could do was to accept her as she was and tell her that everyone was good at something. Polly spent her life with her metaphorical nose pressed against the window, like the Little Match Girl, watching the beautiful people move about in the brightly-lit interior of the world of music from which she was for ever excluded. It was no use telling her that music was *not* the whole world – it was the only world she knew. During sixth form, she chose to study Art, as being at least in the same *hemisphere* as music, and French and History, both of which she was good at. And when the time came to go to university, she applied for and won a place at Manchester, where she did a joint degree in History of Art with Textiles and Design. She knew her sisters thought them very dumb subjects, not even proper academic subjects. Polly suspected her parents agreed, though they would never have said so. Not for anything would she have applied to UCL. To be constantly letting down her father in his own college was not to be contemplated.

From the time the Walsh girls started to grow up, a stream of love-lorn boys joined the trekkers through the garage. Clara, Sid and Anna were all goddesses – tall, full-formed, beautiful, with masses of glossy dark curls and a creamy, sallow skin that never knew the blight of pimple. Add to that their talent and their supreme self-confidence, and it was little wonder that they ruled the kingdom of boys with the touch of gossamer and a rod of iron. Money, as we have said, was short, but they all got themselves Saturday jobs to pay for tights and make-up, and Mrs Walsh's sewing-machine spent longer and longer on the dining-room table, as clothes were let out, taken in, altered and refurbished, and new things were run up from Butterick patterns and cloth bought on sale from John Lewis. As they were all much of a size, there was a great deal of lending and sharing, and complicated bargains were struck on Friday and Saturday nights that would have taxed the brain of any mere man.

'Can I borrow your red scarf?'

'Yes, if you lend me those tights with the stars on them, and let me use your Chick Flick Cherry nail polish.'

'Then it's the scarf and the Alice band as well, and I get to use the bathroom first, and a go of your L'Oreal shampoo.'

'Sid's getting the bathroom first. I swapped it for her Candy Baby lipstick.'

'All right, then I still get the shampoo, *second* bathroom, *and* a spritz of your Lacoste.'

Polly, alone of the girls, resembled her mother rather than her father. She was of medium height, skinny, flat-chested, with rather bony knees and knuckles that were always red. She had a longish face, grey-blue eyes, and that very fine, colourless skin that showed every fleeting blush, and in her teenage years had been prone to large, sudden spots. Washed-out was the adjective that had most often been applied to her. Her hair was blonde, but of that pale, thin, flat, fly-away sort that will not take a curl or hold a style, has no bounce or body, and does nothing but lie limp against the skull getting greasy. If she didn't wash it every day it practically dripped oil down her face. If she did wash it every day there was no doing anything with it, and it was so full of electricity it stuck to low ceilings as she passed under them.

She was not self-confident, particularly where boys were concerned. And she could not fit into her sisters' clothes, nor lend them hers, so she was excluded from the happy Friday-night souk, when half-clad, nubile girls dashed from bedroom to bedroom with armfuls of barter, shrieked to one another until the light fitments rang; sang in the scented steam of the bathroom like full-bosomed nightingales; and finally stepped downstairs delicately as deer, gleaming like racehorses, to meet some smirking boy that all the other girls at school had longed to go out with and known they hadn't a chance of.

Polly had boyfriends. They just weren't very good ones.

Well, that was unfair. They were nice enough boys – probably – but they were the ones no one else would date. The rejects. The nerds. The ones with glasses, uneven teeth, spots. The stammerers. The pathologically shy ones. The boring ones. The ones with moral objections to wearing deodorant. She went out with them mostly because she wasn't quick-witted enough to get out of it when they asked her. And sometimes because she couldn't bear to hurt them by saying no. She felt ridiculously sorry for some of them. It was strange how often *they* turned out to be the ones she had to wrestle

189

with. Maybe because they didn't have many (or any) dates and their hormones were all over the place, the awkwardest, spottiest and nerdiest were always the ones who would have their damp hands inside her knickers at the cinema before she'd even got her coat off and her popcorn opened, and wouldn't desist for anything less than physical violence.

Polly met Seth only because he was Anna's boyfriend. He and Anna had met at college where they were both doing the same architecture course, but they didn't really notice each other until they both joined the Drama Society. Seth with his bouncy outgoingness and huge ego was chosen to play Stanley in the Dramsoc production of *Streetcar*, to Anna's Stella. The cast all went out for drinks after rehearsals, and long before the production reached the stage, Anna and Seth were dating.

It didn't last long. Anna's boyfriends never did. She was so clever and talented, she intimidated them even as she attracted them with her beauty and wit. From her position of superiority she was demanding and capricious, and if that was not enough to put them off, she inevitably got bored with them and ended it herself. So it was with Seth. The relationship was flagging even before the end of the run of the play, and soon after it closed she told him she didn't want to go out with him any more.

By that time, however, Seth had managed

to ingratiate himself with the family and, given the garage-and-scullery casualness of the household, it was easy for him just to keep coming round as he had before. Though everyone knew he was not Anna's boyfriend any more, she was not unfriendly towards him, so neither were they. She treated him, in fact, exactly as she treated any other visitor, while to the parents he was simply one of the girls' friends, a well-spoken lad with nice manners, a familiar enough face for his presence never to be questioned.

When he found there was nothing doing, nor would ever be again, with Anna, he tried to date Clara and then Sid, but they had no interest in him. It was probable that Clara, already dedicated to her career, didn't even notice what he was up to. Sidonie stared in surprise when she realized he was asking her out, then laughed and said, 'Of course not!' as if it had been a joke. She was as dedicated to music as Clara but more forceful about it. When Seth had first appeared as Anna's boyfriend, Sid had questioned him about his musical background and, finding he didn't have one, dropped him, conversationally, like a stone. Around the crowded dining table, the talk was often musical, and Seth, having nothing to contribute, had to sit in silence until a more congenial topic arose. He liked to dazzle, and it came hard to him to keep quiet while the ball flew back and forth above his head.

Polly, coming home from Manchester in vacations, saw Seth being left out and, always sympathetic to outsiders, tried to raise other topics to help him. She wondered, long afterwards, if the Walsh dining-table experience was what had turned him so violently against classical music, which he hated unreasonably. Seth did not seem to notice her, and she saw no reason why he should. She was the plain one, the dull one, the untalented one; and he, though not what one would call handsome, was striking and sexy, exciting and dynamic, and (according to him, but also according to Anna, who had no reason to exaggerate) brilliant in his chosen field.

Polly took her degree and came home for good, with a new haircut and the expectation of a good pass, and Seth suddenly spotted her against the exotic background and asked her out. Polly couldn't believe her luck. To be asked out by someone who had choices! Someone who'd had other girlfriends (her own sister included), who was attractive and amusing and self-confident, who was most of all a catch! She accepted with a gratitude that she could not help showing, and when he was nice to her, fell desperately in love. Once he was sure of her, he was not always nice to her, but she was enough in love always to forgive and find reasons for anything that was not quite what she would have hoped for. She pitied his only-childness, believing that a large family was the greatest blessing on earth. She met his mother and thereafter excused him a great deal. And when at last he asked her to marry him, she was overwhelmed with the sense of her own undeserving luck, and said yes quickly before he could change his mind.

On the evening of her engagement party at the Walsh house, Anna came to her when she was dressing alone in their shared bedroom, closed the door behind her (an action which in itself underlined the seriousness of the occasion) and said, 'I want to talk to you, Pol. Sit down a minute.'

Polly, surprised but obedient, sat on the bed, and Anna stood in front of her, frowning slightly. 'It's about Seth.'

Polly stared up at her sister, wondering what was coming. Anna had finished with Seth of her own free will and long before Polly had gone out with him. 'You don't mind, do you?' she asked timidly.

'Mind? Good God, I've no interest in him. It's just that – are you really sure you want to marry him?'

'Yes,' Polly said, though she looked worried. Anna was the brain of the family, and if she had doubts... 'I love him. Of course I'm sure. Why?'

'Frankly, I don't think he's good enough for you,' said Anna forthrightly.

'*Not good enough?* He's too good! What do you mean? He's wonderful!'

Anna sighed. 'You always undersell yourself. I suppose it's our fault, partly, because you're not musical, and you've always been a bit left out. But you're a bright girl in your way, and not at all bad looking, and you ought to do better than—' She hesitated.

'Yes?' Polly asked in a brittle voice. 'Better than your leavings? Was that what you were going to say? Maybe you have impossibly high standards, has that occurred to you?'

Anna looked surprised, because it never had. She knew what she was worth and she knew she would find it one day, and compromise was not in her vocabulary. She sat down on the bed beside Polly and took hold of her cold hand. Polly's hands and feet were always cold. When she was little, the girls had had to take turns at rubbing them when they all came home from school in winter with Polly weeping in pain.

'Look, I know you're a bit bowled over by Seth,' Anna said, 'and I understand. He's attractive in his way, and he puts up a good front. But underneath, he's not so hot. He's no good, Pol, and I'm worried that you're going to marry him not understanding that.'

'What do you mean, no good?' Polly asked in astonishment. He seemed to her quite godlike.

'I went out with him, remember. I know him very well. He's weak. He has feelings of inadequacy, probably something to do with his mother – ghastly woman – and he has to

194

prove himself all the time. That's why he has to be the centre of attention and do all the talking – you must have noticed that?'

'He talks because he's got a lot to say.'

Anna shook her head. 'I can see he's really got to you. But I really, really, don't want you to marry him, because you're my sister and I love you. Don't you see, he only wants you *because* he's inadequate.'

'Oh, thank you,' said Polly, hurt, and tried to withdraw her hands.

'No, you misunderstand, I don't mean it like that. This is not something against you, it's against him. He can't stand challenge or competition, and he doesn't see you as challenging because he thinks he's better than you.' She held up a hand to stop Polly interrupting. 'What he wants from a woman is abject devotion – and obviously, he's getting it from you. But is that enough to build a marriage on? I think you deserve more. I think *you* should be the one who gets the abject devotion.'

Polly said, 'I know that's what *you* want from a relationship, but it's not what I want. I don't want to be worshipped. I love Seth and he loves me, and I'm going to marry him.'

Anna sighed and stood up. 'All right, I tried my best. I hope you'll be happy, Pol, I really do, and I hope I'm wrong about him. But I do think no one should go into marriage thinking they're lucky to get whoever-it-is. It should be an equal partnership.'

'Is *is* equal,' Polly asserted bravely. Underneath she knew that Anna was right, and that she *did* think she was lucky to get him. However, if Seth wanted abject devotion and she was willing to give it, where was the harm?

Anna never mentioned the subject again, and danced at Polly's wedding as cheerfully as anyone else, and Polly was happy in her marriage. Seth did need her devotion, because it turned out that he did, strangely, lack a certain degree of self confidence, though no one but her would ever have known it because he covered it by being extra assertive. Even she only deduced it: he never admitted it to her, and she would have died rather than suggest it to him. But it gave her an explanation when, early on in their marriage, he was unfaithful to her, and enabled her to forgive him, forget it, and move on. His peccadilloes, as she thought of them, had been simply his way of bolstering his fragile confidence. They didn't mean anything and were not targeted against her. He loved her, and nothing touched that, and once they had settled down into their relationship, the peccadilloes had stopped and he had been straight ever since.

If ever she thought about Anna's warning, it was only to remember with a smile how wrong she had been. Seth and Polly's marriage was one of the great success stories:

how else could they have got through their childlessness so well? And if he was sometimes a bit insensitive or selfish, it was only what one had to expect from a genius. He didn't mean to hurt her, and he always made it up to her. And considering what he was and what she was, she *was* damn lucky to have him.

# Fourteen

Everything about lunch was wonderful. Simon had bought cold things from Fare Trade, and by luck (or perhaps because his tastes were similar to hers?) he had eschewed their wilder flourishes and chosen simple, delicious things: wafer thin rare roast beef, two slices of potato torta with ricotta, parmesan and basil, and baby broad bean and celeriac salad. The flavours were all simple and clear and complemented without overwhelming each other. It was a delight to eat something that tasted of itself, and she told him so. He smiled that lazy, up-one-side smile and said she was a woman after his own heart, and it was important not to lose sight of essentials in one's quest for sophistication. Afterwards he produced some cheeses with Fare Trade's crisp little anchovy and olive biscuits. They had finished the champagne (which went amazingly well with the roast beef and the broad beans) and when he brought out a bottle of Alsace to go with the cheese, she demurred.

'Red wine is too acidic with cheese,' he said. 'Do try this – it really does go well.'

'I wasn't questioning your taste,' she said, struggling not to laugh. 'I was thinking that more than half a bottle of wine at lunch is not a good idea, if you want to get any work done.'

'What's the hurry?' he said. 'I'm not going anywhere. We can do the picture thing any time. Look at the cat. He's got the right idea.'

Big had found a patch of dappled shade close to Polly's chair and was stretched out on his side, his front paws and the tip of his tail twitching gently in contented dream.

So Polly sat back and relaxed (though she stipulated only one small glass of wine with the cheese) and they carried on talking. They had been talking non-stop since they sat down, and it had been wonderful. He was so easy to talk to and was interested in everything she had to say. He asked, and she told him, about her childhood. He seemed fascinated by her family ('Clara Walsh is your *sister*? *The* Clara Walsh?') and egged her on to tell more and more stories about the crowded fun, the make-do's, the ups and downs. He told her he had come from a large family too. 'I think you miss it all your life when you've grown up in that kind of household.'

It was wonderful to talk to someone who understood about shared baths, handed-down clothes and epic family games of Monopoly. Seth, being an only child, had no shared references with her, and was impatient if ever she wanted to talk about her childhood. It made her feel very warm towards Simon, as if they had known each other for years.

They talked about music, about which he seemed to know a lot – or at least, he agreed with what she said as if he knew what she was talking about. It was lovely to talk music again – she couldn't with Seth, of course, and no one else in her circle seemed particularly interested, except for Julian, with whom opportunities were limited by Seth and Ginnie both trashing the subject if they tried to raise it. Even Nigel and Trevor, while *knowing* about music and having listened to it all at some point in their cultured lives, were no use to her. They had a very camp passion for Gilbert and Sullivan and went to every Sadler's Wells and Grim's Dyke concert there was, but their attitude to the rest of the musical canon was that they had 'done it' and never needed to do it again.

The talk wandered on deliciously over a range of topics, and Polly felt she could have sat there for ever, but eventually an attack of conscience got to her when Simon tried again to refill her glass. This was all really too easy.

She roused herself to say, 'Delightful as this is, we ought to go and look at the photographs and the rooms you want them to go in. I can't go in to work on Monday and tell

Nigel I didn't manage even to open the folder again.'

He smiled. 'Pity, when we were having such a nice time. But far be it from me to get you into trouble with your boss.'

They stood up, disturbing Mr Big, who gave them a resentful look over his shoulder, leapt extravagantly to his feet and disappeared bonelessly into the hedge.

The house seemed dark and arid after the garden and the sunshine, and Polly was half sorry she had broken the spell; but, she reminded herself firmly, this was a business relationship, nothing more, and she oughtn't to forget it. They walked about the drawing room and dining room, discussing the colour scheme he was contemplating, with Polly holding up photographs of paintings here and there while he stepped back to get the look. They talked about different painters and she tried to get an idea of what he wanted. It was hard to determine whether the rooms were meant to be showcases for the paintings, or the paintings were merely to embellish the rooms he was planning.

Finally she said, 'Are there any other rooms you want pictures for?' and he said the master bedroom and the hall, and led the way out into the corridor. The light filtered dimly through the glass panels in the front door, and she thought that it would be the perfect place to display old watercolours, where they would not get too much light.

Modern paintings, though, would need their own lighting system to show to advantage here.

She started to say this to him: 'You know, it would be a help if I knew what sort of décor and lighting you plan for this area.' He had stopped abruptly and turned round at the sound of her voice, and she was looking at the walls and walked straight into him. He had to catch hold of her arms to steady her.

At the touch of his hands, it was as though a bolt of electricity had shot through her. She looked up at him, stunned. He seemed surprised, too. He said, 'Polly?' And then he kissed her.

His lips were soft and firm, his breath smelled sweetly of grapes. His hands slid round her back, holding her firmly. For an instant she felt his muscular legs and chest against her and she was kissing him back, her head tilting back like a baby bird wanting to be fed, everything inside her melting.

And then sanity returned and she pulled away, shocked at herself. She placed her hands defensively against his chest (mistake! She could feel the warmth of his skin through his shirt) and said weakly, 'Don't.'

His hands dropped to his sides obediently. 'I'm sorry,' he said.

'I'm a married woman.'

'I know.'

'Happily married.' A thread of anger began to glow in her mind, though it was anger against herself rather than at him. 'What were you thinking?' she said.

'It wasn't a case of thinking – you know that,' he said. 'I didn't mean to do it, but – my God! – I couldn't help it.'

And she couldn't either. It was all part of the warmth and ease that had grown between them, his obvious liking for her, his interest in her. With Seth, she was always the giver of admiration and the supplicant for approval. Simon made her feel she was important and special.

And then there was the sheer, simple physical attraction. That was the hardest thing to forgive herself for. *She had kissed him back.*

'This can never happen again,' she said.

'I know. I absolutely respect that. But if circumstances had been different...'

The doorbell rang. Polly reacted to the sound like a deer to the sound of gunshot. They both looked round at the front door and saw the human shadow outside against the glass. She felt the blood rush to her face and damned her ridiculous skin.

'They can't see us through the glass,' he said.

Did he mean that the person outside could not have seen the kiss, or that they could sneak away and pretend there was no one in? She was never to find out, for the bell was rung again, firmly and with determination, and she said, 'Better answer it.'

'Probably one of those neighbours with the

pies,' he said, but he left her anyway, opened the door, and there stood Ginnie. She looked stunning, in her short, tight, chocolate suede Gucci skirt and the white Donna Karan V-neck silk jersey outlining her boobs. Her magnificent hair, freshly washed, blazed in the sunshine, tumbling down her back and held off her face by an outsized pair of Rayban Wayfarers. Polly knew, because she knew Ginnie, how much thought had gone into the choice of clothes, and how much care had gone into the make-up, which was subtly done to make her look beautiful-without-out-trying. What she didn't know was *why* she had gone to so much trouble. Especially since Ginnie's eyes, flying to Polly's face, told her that she had known she was here.

'Hi there!' Ginnie said cheerily. She stuck out a hand at Simon, which he was therefore obliged to take. 'I'm one of your new neighbours. I thought I'd just pop round and introduce myself. Ginnie Addington. I live next door to Polly.'

Simon shook her hand and smiled down on her in a perfectly friendly manner, and Polly blessed his presence of mind. 'I'm Simon Harte. Well, I guess you must know that as *you're* calling on *me*. Won't you come in?'

'Dying to,' Ginnie said. She was being irrepressibly frank – her cheeky sparrow persona, Polly thought. 'From what Polly's told me about you so far, I couldn't imagine you living in Mrs Tennison's dreary old dump. I had to see for myself. Oh, and I've brought you a housewarming present.' She reached into the depths of her Celine tote and brought out a bottle of wine, which she thrust at Simon with a grin.

'Thank you,' he said, taking it perforce, and then looked at the label, and his eyebrows went up. So did Polly's. Julian was going to *kill* her when he found out. You didn't give away a 1970 Mouton-Rothschild (the one with the Chagall label) to a complete stranger as a hello present. Did Ginnie not realize what it was? She *must* do, after ten years of being Mrs Addington. Polly saw him look at Ginnie to gauge whether she knew what she had given him and fail to come to a conclusion. 'This is better than a pie! Why don't you stay awhile and we'll broach it?' he said.

'No, I ought to be going,' Polly said at once, trying to think of some way to get the bottle back, if she could only stop him opening it.

'That's a nice idea,' Ginnie said at the same moment.

'Let's go out into the garden then. It's a shame to waste the sunshine, and it's not so wonderful inside the house yet.' Simon began to lead the way towards the stairs, holding the bottle upright before him. Polly reflected that as he was fabulously rich, he probably didn't think so much about being

205

handed a five-hundred-pound bottle of fine old claret willy-nilly on his front doorstep. The thought didn't entirely take the sting out of it for her, on Julian's behalf.

Ginnie fell in beside Simon, hustling Polly back into third place. 'You've got a lot to do here,' she said chirpily, looking into the rooms as they passed. 'I *like* those chairs – they must be yours.'

'Yes, I just bought one or two things as a stop-gap.'

'If it was me, I'd have all these walls out, all the horrible cornice and everything, and make one big modern space.'

'My own thoughts exactly,' he said, pausing beside her in the doorway to smile. 'Great minds think alike.'

Polly felt faintly hurt. She had thought he and she had similar taste, and that he had appreciated that as something special between them. *A woman after his own heart.* Now he was agreeing with Ginnie. *Great minds think alike.* What was he up to? More importantly, what was *Ginnie* up to? Polly had been determined to go, but now she felt she ought to stay put to save Ginnie from herself, because in her present mood of restlessness and boredom she was quite likely to make a fool of herself and start something she couldn't finish. Not, of course, that Simon would *do* anything, he was too much of a gentleman, but Polly didn't want to see her friend humiliate herself or be hurt by rejection.

Simon moved away, and as Ginnie followed him she flung a bright, hard look back at
Polly. Why didn't she take the hint and *go*?
Here Ginnie was, flinging herself nobly into
the breach to save Polly's hide (and, boy, had
she been scarlet in the face when Simon
opened the door – what *had* they been up
to?) and instead of making her escape she
was tagging along as if she hadn't any sense
of self preservation at all. Because, let's face
it, Simon Harte was indeed *gorgeous* (Polly
hadn't exaggerated a bit) and any girl could
be forgiven for finding herself smitten.

Ginnie chattered about home improve-
ments all the way down the stairs and
through the horrible kitchen out into the
garden. Polly was glad they had cleared the
table of the remains of lunch before going
upstairs – it would have looked too deca-
dent. Simon invited them to sit down, and
went back inside to get glasses and open the
bottle.

Ginnie at once turned to Polly. 'What are
you doing?' she hissed.

'I was going to ask you that,' Polly hissed
back. 'You can't give away Julian's good wine
like that!'

'Are you kidding me? This guy's a million-
aire. He probably uses *that* on his cornflakes.
You think I was going to bring him a bottle
of Ernesto Gallo?'

'You could at least have made it the '81,'

Polly said despairingly.

'Duh!' Ginnie said, her eyes flashing. 'It's *your* behaviour we're talking about, making assignations while Seth's away. I came here to rescue you from yourself.'

'I'm here on *business*,' Polly began to protest, when Simon – probably fortunately – came back out with the opened bottle.

He poured three glasses, sat, lifted his glass to his nose and sniffed appreciatively. Polly watched in horror as Ginnie slugged half her glass back as if it were alcopops.

'So,' she said to Simon, 'Polly says she came to see you on business?'

'Yes,' said Simon, unfazed. 'She brought me some photographs of paintings I'm interested in. We've been seeing where they might fit in.'

'Nothing would fit in with that awful wallpaper,' Ginnie said. 'Nice plain white walls would be another matter. Are you really going to rip everything out?'

'Pretty much,' Simon said. 'I like everything sleek, modern and minimalist.' He smiled at Polly as he said it, and she realized he thought that was her taste, too. Well, how could he know any different? And she *did* love modern décor, especially Seth's ideas. It was just that she liked history, too, and sometimes she thought they were too quick to sweep it all away these days. 'Trouble is, I'm not really bursting with original ideas, and what I want is to have something

208

completely innovative. I don't want it to look like anyone else's house.'

'I *so* agree with you,' Ginnie said, chucking back the other half. Polly comforted herself that at least Julian wasn't here to see.

Simon topped her up again. 'What I need, I suppose,' he said, 'is a really good interior designer. But one who has a completely fresh approach to each new job. So many of them repeat their effects and you end up with a clone of everyone else's pad.'

Ginnie almost choked, and put down her glass so hard Polly was afraid the stem would snap. 'You should ask Seth,' she said. 'He's the most brilliant, innovative designer in the country – maybe in the world.'

'Seth?'

'Seth Muller.'

Simon stared at Ginnie. 'How amazing you should think of him! I *love* his work. He would be my first choice. But it's not really on. I'm keen to get started on this, and he must be booked up for years ahead.'

Ginnie looked at Polly and shook her head in pity. 'Didn't she tell you? My God, she's so unworldly it's a joke! Polly's name is Polly Muller, didn't you know that?'

Simon's eyes widened. 'You don't mean – you're *Seth* Muller's wife? Seth Muller the designer lives a couple of doors down from me?'

'How cool is that?' Ginnie said, enjoying his amazement. 'And if anyone can get you an appointment with the master, it has to be Polly.'

'Oh, no,' Simon said quickly, 'I couldn't ask that. It wouldn't be fair.'

'Oh, crap,' said Ginnie, now halfway down her second glass. 'What's unfair? I should think Seth would jump at it. It'd be a great advertisement for him.'

'He doesn't need my endorsement,' Simon said, and Polly was touched by his modesty. 'Everyone knows his reputation.'

'All the same, it'd be a big commission for him, and he loves these slash-and-burn jobs – doesn't he, Pol?' said Ginnie. 'There's no harm in your asking him for Simon, anyway, when he gets back, is there?'

'Well,' Polly said. She suspected Ginnie was right, that he would jump at doing Simon's house, maybe trying out the ideas he'd had for their own and never implemented. And on an unlimited budget, to all intents and purposes. But to ask him for a favour would be interfering in his business, which he didn't like. And if he took the job, it would mean she would be brought, inevitably, into closer contact with Simon than was perhaps wise.

'I wouldn't want you to do anything you weren't comfortable with,' Simon said, and she blessed him.

'Why should she mind?' Ginnie demanded.

'I can see that she doesn't feel right about

it, so we'll leave it at that. But I can't get over being a neighbour of Seth Muller's. I have to be one of his greatest fans. He did a loft conversion in Manhattan for my friend David Lauren, and it's fantastic!'

'He's a fantastic guy,' Ginnie said.

'He's a very lucky one,' said Simon, smiling into Polly's eyes.

She felt herself blush again. She looked at Ginnie urgently, meaning, *say something to change the subject.*

Ginnie obliged. 'So, you're in publishing, I understand?'

'Yes,' Simon said, 'and I know, because Polly told me, that you're married to Julian Addington of Addington and Lyon. Another pleasant coincidence. I'm really glad I bought this place.'

'All the best people live in Albemarle Terrace,' Ginnie said. 'But you don't mean you'd heard of Julian *before* Polly told you about us?'

'Julian Addington? Of course. He's very well respected in the publishing world.'

'Well, in book publishing, maybe. But you're in global multimedia. My God, Addington and Lyon's like a corner shop to your outfit.'

'But you forget,' Simon said, 'that book publishing is the historic root and the source of all the rest. Just like Hollywood stars wanting to go back and do live theatre, and never mind the bucks, it's what we all long to

211

shine at, in our secret hearts. It has the authenticity, the romance. Once you've done books, you're a *real* publisher.'

Ginnie blinked a little at this, and then decided he was being polite. 'Well, you'll certainly hit it off with Julian if you talk like that.'

'I'm looking forward to meeting him.'

'You'll have to wait a bit,' Ginnie said. 'He's just gone in the other direction. He's in New York, trying to deal with a temperamental author. With the help of someone called Angela Demarco. Do you know her?'

'Of course,' he said at once. 'Everyone knows Angela.'

'Oh, do they?' Ginnie said, her eyes narrowing.

Polly glanced at her, wondering at her tone, but Simon, not knowing Ginnie, did not seem to notice it.

'She's wonderful,' he said. 'Brilliant. Best commissioning editor in the business.'

'How divine,' Ginnie said. Her stomach clenched at his words. Well, to be honest, everything inside her clenched, and her teeth followed the general trend.

'And she's a fabulous human being,' Simon went on. 'Everyone warms to her as soon as they meet her. If anyone can bring a tricky author to heel, she can.'

'And everyone else as well, I suppose,' Ginnie muttered. She unclenched her teeth.

'Well, isn't Julian lucky to be working with her?'

'I guess he won't be back in time for this welcome party tomorrow, then?' Simon said. 'Pity. When he's back, we must see about having dinner, maybe. Out, I should add,' he said, 'because this place won't be fit for entertaining for a while.'

'Oh, I don't know,' Ginnie said. 'It's the best time to have a wild party, when you've got nothing to get wrecked.'

'I haven't been to *that* sort of party in an age.'

'Nor will you, round here,' Ginnie began. 'However, there *are* things I could tell you!'

Polly saw she was about to say something even more indiscreet and intervened. 'This has been so delightful, Simon, but I really have to be going. I've got a lot to catch up on this afternoon. And I'm sure you have, too. Ginnie, are you coming? We'd better leave him in peace to get on.'

For a wonder, Ginnie took the cue and stood up. 'Yes, I've got places to meet, people to be. It's been great meeting you, Simon.' She stuck her hand out again. 'And isn't it nice that we'll be meeting again very soon?'

'Yes, at the party tomorrow,' Simon said, leading the way back through the kitchen. 'What's the form with the Bickersons? Is it fairly casual?'

'Oh, yes, you don't need to dress up,' Ginnie said.

At the front door he shook Polly's hand and thanked her for bringing the photographs. 'I'll be in touch about the paintings when I've had time to ponder.'

Polly smiled, but refrained from thanking him for lunch, as she wanted to, because she didn't want to fuel Ginnie any further. She could ring him sometime and do it, or thank him discreetly tomorrow.

They were outside on the step when Ginnie turned back to Simon and rummaged in her tote bag again. 'Listen, I know what it's like to be the new guy in a place full of strangers,' she said. 'If there's anything you want, give me a ring. Or if there's any information you need or anything like that. I've lived here for yonks, I can probably help.'

'Thank you,' he said gravely.

She pressed into his hand a piece of paper on which Polly could see at least two lines of writing. Her home phone and mobile number, it must be. Ginnie didn't have a business card. She must have written the numbers on the paper before she came here, with the intention of giving it to him. Polly wasn't sure why she found that ominous.

# Fifteen

Ginnie had known from the moment she shook his hand that he was going to phone her. Over the wine in the garden they had been having so many eye-meets it was getting ridiculous. Then when he'd started eulogizing Angela Bloody Demarco, she'd have been happy to fling herself on the grenade and save Polly from him right there and then. If Julian was going to have his affair, she would damn well make sure to have hers! But of course Polly wouldn't have left without her, so she had to leave as well. And perhaps it was better not to be *too* forthcoming. Let him stew a bit. Men liked to be the hunter, not the hunted.

But even she didn't expect him to ring so quickly. She was hardly back in her house when the phone went. She picked it up and said 'Hello,' and he came in immediately with, 'Well, you did say if I wanted *anything*.' Just like that. No greeting or identification. Straight in. She liked that.

She'd have known his voice anywhere. My God, it was sexy. She wanted to rub it all over her.

'And what sort of anything did you want?' she asked, trying to sound cool.

'Dinner tonight?' he said. 'It's a lonely town, as you so correctly analysed. I don't know anyone in London – in England, in fact – except business contacts, and I sure don't want to have dinner with any of them. Will you take pity on me, come and hold my hand while I eat? Otherwise it'll be a sandwich, choked down by my inconsolable tears.'

She laughed. 'Does the tiger cry over the deer? If anyone was ever at home in the urban jungle, it's you.'

'But you're so wrong! I lost all my friends with the divorce, and I've been too busy building up the company ever since to make any more. I've enjoyed every minute of *that*, don't mistake me, but finding myself here, in an empty house with nothing to do, I suddenly realize how lonely it's been. However, if you don't want to take pity on me...'

'Oh, I didn't say that,' she said hastily. 'If it's a genuine case of charity, how can I refuse? Dinner where?'

'My place,' he said, so promptly that it was obvious he had thought it out. Her heart just had time to sink at the thought of that house, the discomfort, and the danger of being so close to home, when he added, 'Not the one you just came to. I can't stand it here another minute. I'm going back to my apartment in Chelsea Harbour. The company

216

leased it for me furnished, so I can be comfortable there. And I thought if you'd like to come and keep me company, I could cook for you. I'm quite handy in the kitchen, you know. Famed for it.'

Ginnie felt breathless at his sheer cheek. It was a blatant seduction ploy. Or did she feel breathless because she knew, no matter what arguments she might put up in her own mind in the next few minutes (or even hours) that she was going to go? Even if she hadn't wanted to teach Julian a lesson, how could she refuse a man who made her feel like this. Every bit of her was tingling with excitement.

She had to keep it light. 'I'm a very picky eater,' she warned. 'I'm used to the best.'

'I could tell that by the wine you brought me. I promise you shall have the best. It's only fair, if you're going to give up your evening to comfort me. You *are*, aren't you?'

'I am what?'

'You are going to comfort me?'

'Dinner,' she said, 'and that's it.'

'My dear Eugenia, what can you mean? What else could be on my mind?'

'You can have what you like on your mind, as long as it stays there,' she said, wondering how he knew her name was Eugenia. Most people thought it was short for Virginia. 'Thoughts are free. And let's stick with Ginnie.'

'I shall certainly stick with Ginnie as long

as I'm allowed,' he said. 'Now, shall we say eight o'clock? Have you got a pen? I'll give you the address.'

Of course, it wasn't that easy. Quite apart from the question of what to wear (her mind instantly went into review mode over the clothes that were largely still spread out on her bed from her previous trawl) there was the question of what to do with the children. If only bloody *Marta* wasn't in sodding *Poland* she could have got her to come over. Polly's Leela sometimes obliged, but if she asked for her, Polly would be bound to ask where she was going all of a sudden. After some thought she dialled the house where Flora was even now playing with her friend Ruby (retro names had been all the rage ten years ago), and got the crystal tones of Vera Pritchett-Handy's telephone voice.

'Vera, it's Ginnie.'

'Oh, hi!' The voice relaxed. 'Flora's fine, if you're phoning to say you'll be late picking her up. She and Ruby are out in the garden having a My Little Pony gymkhana.'

'Oh, good. The thing is, Vera, I was wondering if you could do me a huge, huge favour and keep Flora a bit longer. I've just had a phone call that my mum's not well, and I need to go over there, but I don't want to take the kids.'

'Oh, God, poor you. Of course I'll keep her. Is it anything serious?' Vera asked with the hope-of-disaster of the bored woman in her voice.

'They think it might be a mild heart attack,' Ginnie said. She'd worked that out carefully. It had to be something serious, but also something that could turn out to be a false alarm, not requiring her to stay away for a long time. She didn't want to saddle herself with a long-term sick mother in the background and constant questions from concerned friends and neighbours requiring elaborate updates.

'Oh my God. Is she all right?'

*Of course she's not all right, you silly bitch, that's why I have to go and see her!* 'Well, they're cautiously optimistic, but I really want to go and see for myself.'

'Of course you do. Well, don't worry about Flora. She can stay here as long as you like. Why don't I keep her overnight, then you won't have to worry about hurrying back.'

A light bulb went on in Ginnie's head. *Overnight?* 'Thanks, Vera, you're a life-saver. I hadn't got as far as thinking about what time I'd get back, but this way I can stay overnight at her place and see her again in the morning.'

'OK, fine. Do you want me to tell Flora anything?'

'No, don't do that. It might turn out not to be anything serious after all. Just let her think it's a sleepover.'

'Fine. Give me a ring when you hear something.'

When she put the phone down, Ginnie had an attack of conscience, a sharp pain as disproportionate as wind sometimes can be. It was one thing to do the dirty on her cheating husband, but lying to the kids (even without speaking the words, and by proxy) was another. However, she would be a simpleton to turn back now, so she braced herself and rang the Leestons. After that she felt the evening had damn well better be worth it, which meant she was determined that it would be.

Simon's place was everything she expected. It was definitely an apartment, not a flat: a penthouse on two floors. With living room, kitchen and study below and two bedrooms, two bathrooms and dressing room above, it would surely market in the multiple millions. The sitting room was a huge, light, open space, with a whole wall of window, and massive sliders that opened on to a full-width terrace looking over the river. The view was spectacular. As people do, who have that sort of arrangement, he took her straight out on to the terrace (which was wood-floored like a deck) and left her to gawp at it while he fetched her a drink. Then he joined her at the rail (it was a bit like being on a cruise ship) and they leaned on it and stared out. The sun was going down bloodily up river, and the dimpled water was like beaten gold and red enamel.

Ginnie had had another crisis of conscience on the way over, but she had driven that back, too, with the thought of what Julian was doing, coldly and calculatedly – and she bet he wasn't suffering any Jiminy-Cricket twinges about it, either. *As long as it never came out* – that's what he would think. Well, two could play at that game. Of course, if *he* never found out about *hers*, it would take away some the pleasure of hurting him by way of revenge. She would have to force him to admit about Angela, then she could slap him right back with Simon.

But all those thoughts melted away at the sight of Simon's apartment, and even more, at the sight of Simon. He was playing it very cool, as if dinner and her company was all that was on his mind, but that only made it more exciting. He looked gorgeous, in an open-necked dark blue shirt that made the colour of his eyes simply shriek, with softly faded jeans, a heavy leather belt that was outright begging out to be taken off, and – surprisingly – bare feet. Ginnie was not normally too fond of bare feet, particularly men's bare feet, which could be so weird and knobbly, like spare bits in an abattoir, as to put you off your nosh permanently. But Simon's were as beautiful as the rest of him, toasty brown above and touchingly pale beneath, kissably clean and with neat, pale pink nails. She was willing to bet he had pedicure, and yet the idea didn't put her off. Normally she liked her men to be manly, and if Julian had done it she would have been checking his wardrobe for dresses before you could say knife. But Simon was so very male he could afford to do something as borderline-nancy as that.

Also, the bare feet emphasized the nautical feel of the evening. She didn't take much encouragement to take her sandals off too. He had laid a wooden table out on the deck by the rail, where they could see the water, and as the darkness came up and the lights began to twinkle, she was so enchanted by the atmosphere she allowed herself to imagine they were the lights of an island and they were moored off-shore. A shipboard romance was just what she fancied right now. Simon produced a very creditable meal of sesame-fried asparagus, followed by griddled sea-bass with a cucumber wakame salad, and the fishy theme fitted perfectly. By the time he produced a decadently-sagging brie and some black Hamburg grapes, she was leaning on her elbows on the table, utterly relaxed.

They had talked and talked, ranging over a world of topics. He told her about his sad divorce and how his wife had taken the children clear across the States to California, so it was really tough for him to see them. 'It's not the money, you understand – I'd hire a private jet just to get to see them. But it's the time it takes. By the time you've done the check-in and got to and from airports, it's a ten-hour journey each way. And my job...' He shook his head helplessly.

'You must miss them,' she said huskily, thinking through a golden mist of Le Montrachet of her own little darlings.

'God, yes!' he said simply.

He asked her about her childhood, and seemed fascinated by the diplomatic background, listened to her in tender silence as she spoke of her adored Bill. He told her he knew just how she felt, because he had come from a small family too, just the two of them, him and his younger sister Betty, whom he had adored.

'Where is she now?'

'She married a South African wine-grower who had a ranch in the Franschhoek valley. She was killed in a car crash. Some drunken guys in a pick-up drove her off the road.'

She placed her hand over his. 'I'm so sorry,' she said.

He met her eyes, and she felt everything inside her turn to liquid. He used both his hands to lift hers, turn it over, raise it to his lips, and placed a gentle kiss in the centre of her palm. Her bare feet, she realized, were caressing his under the table, and she had no memory of how that had started. Her breath was coming shorter and shorter, and she could see his nostrils widening. She visualized his tight, faded jeans and the leather belt and thought she was going to faint.

'Ginnie,' he said softly.

'Oh God,' she said.

He smiled his up-one-side smile, his eyes crinkled, and suddenly she felt as light as a feather, and as happy as the lark it might have come from. Also as horny as the back row of an orchestra. 'Would you like to?' he asked

He was still holding her hand. She stood up, and he used it to lead her round the table and back into the apartment.

If she hadn't been so horny, she might have had doubts about the taking-her-clothes-off-in-front-of-a-strange-man part. When a woman had had three babies, no matter how much buffing, training and yoga she does, she is never going to look the way she did when she was nineteen. As it was, she could not wait to get naked; and anyway, Simon didn't feel like a stranger. She felt she had known him for years. They had so much in common, were so much alike. And, God, he was sexy! In the bedroom as he started to unbuckle his belt she couldn't keep her eyes from the bulge of his crotch, except that she also could not stop looking into his delphin-ium-blue eyes. This conflict (and the fact that as soon as he had dropped his jeans he started on her – those hands!) kept her from thinking about anything but the here and now.

There was just one moment of oddness as she lay down on his bed and he was poised over her, because she had not done it with anyone but Julian since they married (and only two others before, whom she had comprehensively forgotten) and one bit of her brain realized that she did not know what he would feel like or how he would do it. But she was too hot for the thought to be more than a fleeting flash through the brain and out the other side. He sank into her, and it was magnificent. She groaned with simultaneous anticipation and fulfilment.

'God, you're amazing,' he said through a mouthful of her hair and ear.

They moved together as if they had been doing it all their lives. She clutched him and felt herself going, that aching, delicious instant just before climax that is better than climax itself. Going, going – gone.

'Aah!' he said, and he was over the edge too.

Afterwards, he turned on his side, facing her, and they talked some more, while he twined bits of her hair round his fingers in a way she found very endearing. Then they made love again, slowly and luxuriously. And then, curse it, she fell asleep. If she had been ten years younger, she would have stayed awake all night and done it another five times. Damn you, Old Father Time! She didn't even get the pleasure out of sleeping with him, because she fell asleep so suddenly; and in the morning he was already up when he woke her. He was wearing a dazzling white towelling robe and handed her a mug of coffee.

'I'm sorry to wake you so early, but I've got a heap of work to do, so I'm going to have to turn you out. Shower's through there, and there are clean towels and a toothbrush laid out for you.' He planted a kiss on her brow and disappeared.

Oh, well, she thought, he probably *does* have a lot of work to do. But there had been no mention of breakfast, and she was *starving*. She drank the coffee (which was good) and went through to the opulent bathroom. As well as an enormous double-ended whirlpool bath (they'd have to try *that* next time!) it had a six-foot-wide shower cubicle (oblong-icle?) with nozzles at both ends which gave a variety of different kinds of spray, so you could be pelted from several directions at once in a number of different ways. Pity he was so busy. She thought wistfully how nice it would have been to shower with him and then go back to bed. She cleaned her teeth and then dressed. How slummy it always felt putting on the same clothes as the night before. But it would have looked just too slutty to have brought a change with her. The dilemmas of modern dating! Then she went downstairs in search of him.

He was in the 'study', sitting at a big,

leather-topped desk, fully dressed (shoes too) and looking like a different person, very much the businessman, sleek and unapproachable, as he talked on the phone and made notes on a pad in tiny, hard writing at the same time. He looked up as she appeared in the doorway, but his eyes did not connect with her. He was gone.

After a moment he stopped talking, put his hand over the mouthpiece and said, 'There's stuff to eat in the kitchen. Sorry I can't make it for you.' Then he removed his hand and said, 'Yes. Yes. He knows all that! He had the schedule two days ago. I'm not going to go into it all again, for God's sake. Yes. No. Tell him three and a half is the limit.'

She caught his eye again and mouthed, 'I'll go, then,' and, not sure if he had understood, she made a bye-bye gesture with her hand, feeling rather forlorn. He made a wait-a-sec gesture, found a clean page of the note pad, scribbled on it, tore it off and handed it to her. It was a collection of phone numbers. Her heart rose again, and she removed herself with renewed hope.

She didn't fancy raiding his kitchen for breakfast with him next door in the study being the mogul, so she let herself out, reminding herself that he *was* an important businessman and that, as he must know very well, they would see each other again this afternoon at the party. A taxi was idling past as she reached the road and she snaffled it and rode home in luxury.

She was amazed to discover that it was still only half past seven when she got back (these Americans and the hours they kept!). The empty house felt unwelcoming and a bit reproachful; but Mr Big greeted her with his usual effusiveness, and she put down some food for him and then, on a whim, grilled some bacon and made herself a big bacon sandwich and some more coffee, remembering just in time not to go out in the garden to eat it, in case the neighbours saw her when she was supposed to be at her mother's house, and it came out.

Which reminded her, she had to ring up the Leestons and the Pritchett-Handys with a story. *Oh what a tangled web we weave!* She would say it had been a false alarm, not a heart attack at all, that her mother was fine this morning and going to be discharged later so she was coming home at once. That way she could go to the party and not have to skulk indoors all morning. And she could be cheerful and enjoy it without looking heartless.

# Sixteen

The Bickersons had certainly spared no effort in the time available to them. It looked like being a very good party. Everyone had come, apart from the Carpenters, from number 2, who were on their boat, and Tom Butler and Alex Benn, from number 11, who were in the South of France and were going to *kick* themselves for having missed meeting the new guy, especially at a Bickerson party, which they adored.

There were twenty-one children present which, allowing for the absent Carpenters, the Butler-Benns and the childless Wentworths and Mullers, was a pretty impressive average. But these days, extreme fertility was the thing among the new rich. Two or three children was *vieux jeux*: to be really fashionable you had to be in the fives, sixes and sevens. This was particularly true for top bankers and stockbrokers. Having a large family was seen as proving you had emotional depth as well as financial acumen; and it gave a general impression of trustworthiness and maturity which was supposed to make people feel happier about letting you handle their money. So the fifth child was now the top accessory, replacing the third home, the second yacht and the infinity pool, for those with real money. It *took* real money, of course, given the prospect of school fees and the cost of live-in nannies, but when both parents had seven figure incomes, all was possible. The Bussmans had a nanny *each* for Freddie and Frittie – Freda and Fritz, actually, and they weren't even twins.

Most of the Albemarlians were too young yet to have reached the super-family point, but they were working towards it, though only the host Bickersons had got to six, and that was only if you included his sons from his first marriage (who lived most of the year with him as their mother was in and out of The Priory) along with Jethro, Millie, Hector and Theo. But Serge and Irene Paulevitch, from number 3, had four (Boris, Chloe, Rain and Emmanuel), while Alex and Emma Gregory, from number 10, had three (Daniel, Philo, and Augusta) and Emma was pregnant again.

The Bickersons had made ample provision for the Little People at their party. For the five of them who were still babies, a nursery had been organized at the top of the house with the Bickersons' two live-in Filipinas and the Kemp-Parkers' nanny to take care of them. For the rest of the children, a marquee was set up at the bottom of the garden. On Albemarle Terrace, only the Bickersons were naff enough to have a barbecue, but it was perfect for the children, who were encouraged to choose their own food out of the chill box and watch it being cooked (by two catering chefs hired for the occasion), which had the advantage of being slow work and so keeping them eating, and therefore occupied, for a long time. Also on hand were three nannies and two entertainers with a variety of materials and games, and, if the party went on long enough, there was to be a continuous showing of as many Harry Potter movies as it took, on a big screen set up in the marquee, with big cushions for the children to sit on and ice cream in the intervals.

With the young ones corralled as far as possible from the grown-ups (there was even an extractor fan to make sure the barbecue smoke did not drift the wrong way), everyone else was free to frolic as they wished in the rest of the garden and the house. There was champagne and a delicious fruit punch, and pretty well anything else you wanted if you asked for it – Eric Bickerson and George Bussman walked about defiantly drinking beer from the bottle. A sumptuous buffet was laid out under an awning on the 'patio', as Sadie Bickerson called it, and waiters and waitresses circled with trays of the most delicious canapés: slivers of warm roast beef and fresh horseradish in bite-sized Yorkshires, lobster and asparagus parcels, garlic tiger prawns on parmesan shortbread, hot crispy duck and shredded cucumber rolled in tiny pancakes, and delectable miniature steak-and-kidney puddings that you just popped in your mouth.

All the women were toffed up to the nines, and all the men (who wore formal suits to work all week) were equally toffed *down* to the nines. The sun shone benignly from a cloudless sky, but there was plenty of shade from the big trees, and inside the house it was deliciously cool – the Bickersons even had climate-controlled wardrobes and chilled shoe cupboards. Polly liked visiting them, not only because she felt they were basically nice people, and because she enjoyed sometimes being with people who revelled in their wealth and the spending thereof, instead of either angsting about the morality of having lots of money, or complaining about taxes, the cost of everything, school fees, and generally not having enough of it. Sadie Bickerson had started off years back making birthday and wedding cakes for friends in her kitchen, and went on to develop her own catering company which was now huge and successful. Everyone got in caterers for their parties these days, and of course Sadie had used her own, but the thing was that you knew she had done it all herself in the past and could do it all again if she had to.

But Polly also liked going to their house because Seth had done it for them, and she loved some of the things he had done. He had both dug down, to give the semi-basement better head height, and built up into the roof, levelling it out and creating a whole extra floor for the master suite with a loggia roof-garden. Inside the house there was his trademark lack of dividing walls, and some of his wilder ideas: the walls of Eric's study were entirely lined with kudu skin, and the drawing room had polished aluminium panelling. She wished he could have been here for this party. He'd have liked all the attention he'd have been bound to get, and the 'networking' as he always called it. Women gossiped, but men networked.

She wondered whether she *should* ask him about doing Simon's house, or whether he would resent the interference. Probably the latter. In any case, she was loath to mention Simon to him at all, remembering the kiss. She felt guilty and uncomfortable about that, shocked at herself; though they had been carried away by the occasion, that was all – the wine, the conversation, the warmth of shared ideas. It would never happen again. She was determined about that. It was a momentary lapse and there was no reason ever to tell Seth about it, when it would only upset him and cause trouble needlessly. But if she pleaded Simon's case for him, wouldn't Seth wonder why? More importantly, wouldn't she wonder the same thing about herself? It was awkward.

She saw Ginnie arrive, looking glam in her Issey Miyake pleated skirt, black suede knee boots and a black velvet biker jacket with nothing underneath. She hustled her children down to the bottom of the garden, and then started to enjoy herself very much, circulating among the husbands and eating and drinking with relish. Polly kept trying to go over and speak to her, but working through the crowd was slow work and whenever she got near, Ginnie seemed to disappear, and then pop up on the other side of the garden. Almost as if she was avoiding her.

Simon was late. Polly wondered at one point if he was going to appear at all, and felt a sharp pang of disappointment on the Bickersons' account, when they had gone to so much trouble. Tammy Wentworth was holding court about him, with the little bit of information she had gleaned, and a new piece she was making the most of. 'I'm sure he did not sleep at the house last night. I saw him go off yesterday afternoon and there has been no one there all morning, and I saw him arrive about half an hour ago, in a taxi. But he has a flat, you know, in Chelsea. I expect that would be more comfortable for him at the moment.'

'Well, what are we giving him a moving-in party for, if he isn't moving in?' Willi Bussman said irritably.

'Suits me. I like Sadie's parties,' said Sam Wentworth, holding out his glass to a passing waiter to be refilled. 'More for you, Polly?'

'Thanks,' Polly said absently. She was watching Ginnie, flirting blatantly with Alex Gregory, to the obvious annoyance of visibly pregnant Emma, though she was looking gorgeous in a buttercup-yellow linen dress from the Tamiko maternity range that Tammy had recently added to her Mesodo children's clothes. Polly was afraid Ginnie had had too much to drink already. It wasn't like her to be *so* obvious.

She knew the instant Simon arrived, because all heads turned as if pulled by one string. She felt a huge gladness that he had turned up, and attributed it to relief for the Bickersons. She watched from a distance, content just to look at him, gorgeous as ever, and was amused that in a few moments he had a bottle of beer in his hand like his host. Was that tact, or what he really wanted? She wouldn't have been surprised if it was tact. He seemed to know instinctively how to make himself agreeable to each different person.

Everyone wanted to talk to him, of course, and soon he was surrounded by a crowd all babbling at him at once. Over their heads, he suddenly caught Polly's eye and winked, just once and swiftly, in a sort of complicity, as if he and she shared some secret understanding or amusement about the situation. She smiled back and, feeling warm and comfortable, took herself off to chat to the Arrostos. She didn't need to add to the crowd around him. He would get round to her in his own time.

Ginnie had not gone up to him, controlling herself nobly. Of course, they must not appear too familiar with each other in public. They were only supposed to have met the once, yesterday, briefly in his house with Polly present. But she could not help watching him over the shoulders of the Gregorys, thinking that he would be bound to spot her immediately, and would give her some sign of recognition. And sure enough, he caught her eye and gave her a swift wink, which contented her for the time being.

'My, everyone is certainly flocking round him,' Emma Gregory said, a little sourly. She was still smarting from Alex's responding to Ginnie so readily.

'He's a tremendously successful business-man,' Alex said. 'George Bussman said he's looking to arrange some major finance for a new Transglobal operation over here. It's going to be massive if it comes off. The publishing company thing is just an excuse for his presence, apparently, so he can get a foot in the door and set up his lines of com-munication.'

'If he's such a successful businessman,' Ginnie said, 'why is there any doubt that it will come off?'

'Monopolies Commission,' Alex said. 'There'd be a lot of implications if Transglobal secured all the takeovers that are being rumoured.'

'He's quite a charmer, though,' Emma said, as if that were in some way a cursor to her husband's speech. 'Reminds me of someone ... I can't think who. Tall, dark and handsome, and that crooked smile...'

'Well, being personable won't do him any harm,' Alex said. 'These days you've got to be all things to all people to get on.'

A waiter drifted past with a champagne bottle and Ginnie thrust out her glass, though she knew from the way her eyes did not seem to fit their sockets properly that she'd had enough already. A slight crossness was growing in her, as she watched him being a charmer to everyone while not coming near her. The Gregorys had moved away and she tried to flirt with Phil Kemp-Parker, who was probably the most dreary person on earth and didn't notice. She was relieved when Polly came and joined them.

'Hello,' she said. 'You look gorgeous – doesn't she, Phil?'

'I'd have thought that outfit was a bit hot for a day like this,' Phil said.

'It's all right, I left off my mink underwear,' Ginnie snapped. She was watching Simon, who was now on his haunches talking to Ariadne and Allegra Kemp-Parker, adorable blonde angels in pink Mesodo frocks with old-fashioned smocking and puffed sleeves. How Phil K-P produced such cute children was a perennial wonder. Divine intervention, had to be. The girls were giggling helplessly, obviously as bowled over by Simon as everyone else. *Why was he wasting himself on them instead of her?* 'My God, look at him with the children. What does he think this is, a royal walkabout?'

'He's very good with them, isn't he?' Polly said, thinking it doubly a shame that he hadn't any of his own.

'Why shouldn't he be?' Ginnie said.

Phil caught up. 'Oh, you're talking about Simon Harte?'

His wife Jill who'd been talking to Irene Paulevitch, heard the name and turned back. 'Of course she is. Everyone is. That's why we're here, to stare at the poor man and dissect him. It must be a terrifying occasion for the poor creature.'

Polly smiled. 'I'm sure he'll survive.'

'By the way,' Jill said to Ginnie, 'how's your mother? Vera Pritchett-Handy rang me today and mentioned you said she was ill.'

Polly looked sharply at Ginnie, who, fortunately, was not prone to blushing as Polly was. 'Your mother's ill? You didn't say. What is it?'

'Oh, it turned out to be a false alarm,' Ginnie said, glad now she had chosen this story. But what rotten bloody luck that this fool Jill had to bring it up in front of Polly! 'They thought it was a mild heart attack, but it was just low blood-pressure. They kept her in overnight to make sure but she's fine now. They've adjusted her medication and that's all it needed, apparently.'

Jill wasn't really interested and would have been happy with that, but Polly's face was creased with concern. 'When did all this happen? You didn't tell me.'

'Yesterday. Yesterday afternoon. I got a phone call at home and had to dash off.'

'I was home yesterday afternoon,' Polly said. 'If you'd have rung me, I'd have taken care of the children for you.'

'It was easier just to leave them where they were. They were all playing with friends and the parents were happy to keep them so it saved messing about. I stayed overnight at Mum's house, but they said everything was fine so I came home this morning.'

'Poor Ginnie, you must have been worried sick,' Polly said.

'Oh, it turned out to be nothing. Can we please change the subject?' Ginnie said. Desperately she turned to Phil again. 'Aren't you just back from Paris? Was it wonderful?'

'Too hot,' he said. 'Paris is always too hot in the summer. That's why the French all go away.'

Ginnie shook her head. How could anyone find nothing more to say about Paris than that?

'Leaves more room for the Americans, of

239

course,' Phil went on. 'It's full of Americans at this time of year.'

'Is that why you went?' Polly asked politely.

'Conference about that new bridge in Portugal,' Jill explained for him. Phil was a top civil engineer. 'EU money, obviously, like all these big projects. We pay it in and they can't wait to spend it. Completely unnecessary. Motorways with no traffic. Airports in the middle of nowhere.'

'Keeps me in shoe-leather, however,' said Phil. 'Mustn't grumble.' He seemed to realize that he had not engaged Ginnie's attention and searched for something more interesting to say about Paris. Polly was amused to see something quite visibly occur to him. He might as well have snapped his fingers and said, 'Eureka!'

'You'll never guess who I saw in the Boulevard Haussmann,' he said. Boringly, he waited for Ginnie to answer what was a rhetorical question – actually, not even a question, but a device.

'Who?' Polly prompted, since Ginnie obviously wasn't going to say anything and otherwise they'd be stuck at this conversational point for ever.

'Your maid, or housekeeper, or whatever she is,' he said. 'The nice Polish girl.' The Kemp-Parkers had borrowed her for baby-sitting purposes once or twice.

'Marta?'

'That's right. Marta. Pretty girl. Smart,

too.'

'She's in Poland, visiting her family,' Ginnie said. 'It must have been someone else you saw.'

'She was just getting into a taxi but I saw her quite clearly, no mistake about it. I called out to her, but you know what the traffic's like on Haussmann. She obviously didn't hear me over all the racket.'

Ginnie only shrugged, assuming Phil was wrong and not caring anyway.

Polly felt sorry for him when he was trying so hard to entertain, with all the disadvantages of nature against him, so she said, 'She might have gone on to Paris after seeing her family. Tacked a holiday on to the end of her trip.'

'She didn't mention it to me,' said Ginnie. 'Anyway, it wouldn't be worth it for such a short time. You made a mistake. It wasn't her.'

'No, no, it was her all right' said Phil. 'She was with a man, anyway. Secret assignation.' He forced a roguish smile, still trying to be amusing, and Ginnie curled her lip in disdain. He lumbered on. 'I didn't see him clearly, because he was already in the taxi, but he looked like one of these typical French blokes, you know, that the women all go for. Goodness knows why. Short, dark and hairy. Swarthy, that's the word. A French lover – isn't that what all you girls long for?'

241

No one was obliged to answer this as Eric Bickerson arrived at that moment with Simon and introduced him to everyone. Ginnie smouldered as Simon said merely, 'Oh, I met Polly and Ginnie yesterday,' and then ignored her and turned his full attention on Polly. 'We were just going to look at Eric's garage. Will you come and give me the benefit of your expertise?'

Polly blushed. 'I don't have any, except in paintings – and you surely can't want modern art in your garage?' But she allowed herself to be drawn away and the three of them walked off.

Ginnie almost had to close her mouth manually. OK, discretion was one thing, but did he have to treat her like a complete stranger? Furiously she drained her glass and thrust it at Phil Kemp-Parker. 'I need some more of this stuff? God, isn't this a foul party?'

Jill K-P was talking to Irene Paulevitch again and didn't hear, fortunately, because she'd have been sure to tell Sadie Bickerson what Ginnie said. Phil, looking perforce, because of his height and proximity, down Ginnie's cleavage, found himself speculating (unlike himself) about whether she had anything on underneath that jacket, and suffered a surge of blood to the head.

'Let's go and find a bottle together,' he suggested gallantly.

Such was Ginnie's desperation she was

almost glad to walk off with him, and even let him take her elbow, a gesture that normally made her want to scream because it was what Julian always did when they crossed a road together, as if she were an old lady, for God's sake.

But Simon should not think she couldn't ignore him just as well as he could ignore her, and talk to other men as he was talking to other women.

It wasn't the garage itself that Eric was taking Simon to look at, but the complex Seth had created underneath it in an excavated basement, of which Eric was touchingly proud.

'Weights room, sauna, and plunge bath. Not room enough for a swimming pool, sadly. Seth was willing to dig out under the whole garden area, but the planning bods wouldn't play ball. Planning regulations are the devil, as no doubt you'll find out,' he said to Simon, 'though Seth's pretty good at handling the bureaucracy. Sadie's been agitating for a mud room, and Seth reckons he can dig out quite a bit more all round without the planners having a fit, which would mean she could have that and he could make the weights room bigger too, so as to fit in a couple of machines for Sadie – a cross-trainer and maybe a rowing machine or something. It's the benefit of having the corner house, of course. The other houses in the terrace can't have garages, and building out the back means taking everything through the house. Bit of a nightmare. Mind you, it's never much fun having the builders in. Even we had to go and live in our Hertfordshire house while the kitchen was being done. Poor Sadie said she'd go mad otherwise. But that won't bother you, I suppose. Didn't Tammy Wentworth say you had a flat in Town?'

'Yes, but it's a company apartment,' Simon said. 'I can't live there indefinitely, so I need to get the work started on the house as soon as possible.'

'Well, you couldn't do better than get Seth Muller in,' Eric said. He turned to Polly. 'Couldn't you persuade him to take our new neighbour on, and move him up the schedule?'

Everything seemed to be conspiring to push Polly towards this question. Just for a horrible moment she even wondered if that was the reason Simon had taken her with Eric to look at the garage – the reason he was cultivating her friendship at all. But he took a leap up in her estimation and affections (and made her feel ashamed of her suspicion) by saying quickly, 'I wouldn't want to put Polly under any pressure on that point, Eric. She's already been more than kind, giving up her free time to help me choose some paintings.' He looked down at her with an expression that was almost tender. 'I definitely want the Paul Edelsteins, by the way. I think they'll be perfect in the hall. If I buy them, do you think your boss would be willing to store them for me until the house is ready?'

'Yes, I'm sure he will,' Polly said.

'And perhaps you'd be willing to do some research for me, now you've an idea of my taste? I'm not going to have much time for looking for paintings in the next few months, with the company to set up. I know it's a lot to ask—'

'Not at all,' Polly said, a little breathlessly. It really was not good for her to have him look at her like that. 'But of course if I did anything on the firm's time there would be the question of commission. Otherwise it wouldn't be fair on my boss.'

'Absolutely,' he said. 'No question. That's understood. I don't want poor Nigel to be out of pocket. I didn't go into his gallery to steal his employees and his trade away!'

Eric smiled indulgently at them both. 'That's what I like to see – a business arrangement that suits everybody. You know, if you could get Seth on board, Polly, it would keep it all in the family. It'd be quite a shame to let anyone else have a hand in Albemarle Terrace. It's practically Seth's personal bailiwick, isn't it?'

Simon caught her eye and gave a little shake of the head, which she understood as meaning that Eric might be putting pressure on her, but *he* never would.

She loved his sensitivity. But of course, there was a lot in what Eric said. Seth did regard the Terrace as his own province. How would he feel if another designer were to come trampling over his kingdom-stroke-showroom?

And if Simon was going to buy lots of paintings from her, didn't she owe it to him to help all she could without compromising her conscience? This loyalty business was a tricky thing. But as long as everything between her and Simon was above board...

She smiled back at Simon reassuringly, to show him that she knew he was a pretty straight kind of guy and would never do anything underhand. He might not be trying to steal Nigel's trade, but he had already gone a long way to stealing his employee.

# Seventeen

Monday was a work day for Polly, and she was at her desk at Esterhazy, trying to keep her mind on her usual Monday-morning tasks but frequently catching herself thinking about where she could look for paintings for Simon, when Seth rang her.

'I'm staying on an extra day,' he said. 'There are a lot of people here I want to see, and Saturday was taken up with the awards crowd. And of course I couldn't do much yesterday because it was Sunday and the idiot French don't work on Sunday.'

'Poor darling, were you terribly bored?' She imagined him all alone in an hotel with nothing to do. Seth was not much of a reader and French television was the worst.

'Oh, no, it was fine. There's an American guy here who may want me to do his town house in New York, in the east seventies. Sam Cesarino, have you heard of him?'

'The fashion designer? Of course. Very cutting edge.'

'Well, he's in Paris for a show and renting a flat on the Isle St Louis, and he invited me there for lunch. I met some of his colleagues,

247

people who might be useful to me, so it wasn't entirely wasted. Anyway, I've got fabric people and suppliers to see today and Cesarino's invited me again for dinner tonight, so I'll get an early plane back tomorrow and go straight to the office.'

Polly was disappointed. Another evening on her own. Her thoughts strayed in a forbidden direction and she made herself wonder instead if Ginnie would also be alone and like company for dinner. She could take everything over and cook there to save Ginnie having to get a babysitter. 'So I won't see you until tomorrow night?' she said.

'Everything all right at home?' said Seth, who knew a rhetorical question when he heard one.

'Fine. You missed a good party.'

'Did I? Oh, for the new neighbour. What was it like?'

'The usual. The Bickersons pulled out all the stops.'

'What's the new guy like?'

'Rich. Nice. Apparently, according to what Alex Gregory told Tammy—'

'Tell me all about it tomorrow. I've got to go now. Love you.'

'Love you too,' Polly said, and he rang off.

Nigel arrived at that moment. Polly always opened up on Mondays because he and Trevor weekended in Cornwall and didn't like travelling back on Sunday night – they started at about four o'clock on Monday morning to miss the traffic and Trevor dropped Nigel at the shop. It meant she didn't have time to brood over her grass-widowhood because she had so much to tell him, and ask him, about Simon's requirements. Nigel was excited and flung himself at once into the business, speculating about which of his protégés he ought to promote, and mentioning several collections he knew were going to come on the market though nothing official had been said yet.

'And I know of a perfectly *delicious* de Kooning that's almost certain to be coming up – because Sir Adrian Fossett has *another* wedding to pay for (*five* daughters, can you imagine, before that dreadful female he married gave him a son) and nothing else left to sell – and from what you say about our Mr Harte, de Kooning ought to be *right* up his particular Hauptstrasse. I shall get on to darling Sir Adrian right this minute. Possibly a teensy bit tactless?' He paused a beat in thought. 'But on the other hand the poor man might be at his wits' end and welcome the suggestion. Nothing venture, as they say.'

Nigel knew everyone, and people told him things – despite his cruel eyes – that they would not tell anyone else.

Due to a mixture of too much to eat and drink at the Bickersons, too much smouldering emotion, and then some more to drink at home after the children were in bed, leading to a restless night, Ginnie felt terrible on Monday morning. She snapped at the children, making Ben cry by telling him to shut up for God's sake when he was trying to recite to her the poem he was supposed to have learned for today. She couldn't find Flora's favourite hair slide, tripped over Biggie, spilling milk on the floor, and retaliated by throwing him bodily out into the garden (counter-productive as he would have cleaned up the spillage for her if she'd thought about it!) which made Flora cry – though she hadn't hurt the bloody cat – and this time Flora's nose did bleed. So she had to waste time wiping her up and explaining how cats always landed on their feet and didn't mind flying through the air, in fact they rather enjoyed it as a change to having to walk everywhere. And Jasper talked all through it, over the top of everyone else, about some bloody science fest at school which, though she wasn't properly listening, she just knew was going to mean some ghastly home project that she would get lumbered with (making a working scale model of a nuclear power station out of cornflakes boxes and tin foil or something) until she wanted to scream.

And on top of all that, at the point when Marta was supposed to let herself in and start spreading her healing balm and bringing order to the chaos, no Marta was forthcoming. Ginnie, who had been planning to let Marta take the kids to school while she took an aspirin and had a long bath, had to rush upstairs and get dressed at double-quick speed, slap on some slap, find her keys, lock the various doors and windows and get everyone out and into the car with all their multifarious gear to do the run herself. At the school gates the nannies were better turned out than she was, and the bloody Holland Park mummies looked at her as if she was covered with sores, and stopped talking until she had passed them. A real boost to her self-esteem.

She went straight home once the kids were inside, and *then* Marta rang to say she wouldn't be coming in that day at all. Ginnie hardly listened to her at first because her mind immediately started revolving round all the things Marta normally did that now she, Ginnie, would have to do.

Her excuse, when Ginnie made her repeat it, sounded unexceptional enough. 'I am so sorry, Mrs Addington, but my flight was cancelled because of technical problems. It is a small Polish airline and does not have another aeroplane to substitute. So I could not get another passage until today. At least, I could have left if I had flown a different airline via Amsterdam, but it would have cost extra money and I could not afford it. So I will not be home until late this afternoon and consequently I cannot come to work at your house today. I hope you will forgive this, please. I shall be there tomorrow morning without fail and clean everything very well to make up, I promise.'

You bet your hoss you will, Ginnie thought, while out loud she said, 'That's OK. You couldn't help it, I suppose. I'll see you tomorrow.'

As she put the telephone down she thought that with Julian away, a much lower standard could prevail – something, in fact, closely akin to outright sluttery. Fish fingers and beans in their pyjamas for the kids, and an evening on the sofa with a delivered pizza for herself. Slob heaven. It made you wonder why women wanted husbands in the first place. The house could go to pieces, and Bloody Marta could pick them up tomorrow. It would serve her right for taking a day off.

Her second thought was that Simon might telephone her and then she was only a baby-sitter away from an evening of a very different sort of heaven with him. It was interesting (though she didn't pursue it) that Simon-heaven had been the second thought, not the first. However, a shower and hair wash later she felt so much better that it had become the preferred option by a long margin.

By lunchtime, Simon had not contacted her, and she was on the point of getting out the piece of paper with his numbers on it when the phone rang and she flung herself at it precipitately.

'Oh, it's you,' she said when she heard Julian's voice.

'Is something wrong?' he asked of her obvious disappointment.

'Oh – no, only bloody Marta hasn't come in. Her third-world plane was cancelled – rubber band broke or something.'

'Poor darling. Well, don't knock yourself out. Why don't you just leave everything for her to do tomorrow?'

'Oddly enough, that thought had occurred to me. What's up at your end?'

'I was just calling to keep you up to date. Just when we thought we'd got Mark nicely softened up yesterday, Wolf Saltzman turned up, snatched him away, and they were closeted in Mark's study all evening. Bitsy was very embarrassed—'

'Bitsy?' she interrupted. 'What's that, the dog?'

'Mark's wife,' Julian said patiently. He had mentioned her before.

'Sounds like a cocker spaniel.'

'As I was saying, Bitsy was embarrassed because they didn't even join us for supper. Had a tray sent in. So we went to bed not knowing where we stood.'

'Went to bed. As in you and Angela went to bed?'

'Everyone went to bed, but Angela and I still don't know where we stand.'

'Not the only people,' Ginnie muttered.

'Sorry, I didn't catch that.'

'Never mind. So what's happening now?'

'We're about to go into a meeting with Mark, his accountant, Wolf Saltzman – unfortunately – and Bitsy – fortunately, because she's on our side though she can't push it too much. But she believes in the quality of product over sheer crass sums of money, and no doubt Mark knows her opinion. So this is the deciding moment. Either Mark will sign the Transglobal contract, or he'll sign a pre-contract agreement with us.'

'And that will be that?' Ginnie said. 'You'll be on the next plane home?' It was a trick question, of course.

'The meeting is likely to go on all morning, so even if I wanted to come straight home afterwards I wouldn't be able to get anything before the red-eye this evening. But in fact – ' Here it came, thought Ginnie ' – I was thinking of staying a few days longer. Once this Mark business is settled, there are a number of people I'd like to catch up with, and Angela's already tentatively set up some meetings in Boston and New York. Now I'm over here, it would be a pity to waste the trip.'

'Oh, a terrible pity.'

'Angela's being very helpful.'

'I bet she is.'

'Are you all right?' He sounded puzzled.

'Absolutely fine.'

'You sound as though you've got a cold.' He broke off, listening to someone in the background. 'I have to go. They're ready for us now. I'll ring you tonight and tell you what happened and where I am.'

'You do that.'

'Wish me luck.' He still sounded puzzled.

'You've got all the luck you need,' she said, and hung up.

Blatant, absolutely blatant! And that slip about 'We went to bed not knowing where we stood.' Ha!

She got out Simon's piece of paper and rang his office number.

Polly rang Ginnie several times through the morning but the phone was always engaged, and though her mobile rang it wasn't answered. She must have put it down somewhere and forgotten it, Polly thought. In the early afternoon she rang the land-line again and it was picked up on the first ring by a breathless-sounding Ginnie.

'It's me,' said Polly. 'What were you doing, hanging over it, waiting?'

'I was just passing. What do you want?'

'You sound distracted. What's up?' Polly asked.

'Oh, it's just that bloody Marta didn't turn in today, so I've had everything to do myself. Her plane fell to bits and Polish Peasant Airlines only have one, apparently.'

'Oh, dear. Well, I was ringing to say that

Seth's staying on another day in Paris, so I'm at a loose end tonight. I thought you might like me to come over and cook something for us both. Girls' night in.'

There was a silence, in which Polly could almost hear Ginnie thinking, but had no idea what she was thinking so hard *about*. It was a simple enough proposition, wasn't it?

'Or is Julian coming home?' she added, though since Ginnie had said that his Mark Stephens business wasn't going to be settled until this morning, she had assumed he would not be home until tomorrow at the earliest, given the time difference.

'Oh, no, *he's* not coming home,' Ginnie said. 'He's staying on a few more days. Vital meetings. Important contacts. You know how it goes. Business excuses everything.'

'Well,' Polly said doubtfully, 'I suppose it does, really. I mean, they do have to meet people. When you're the boss of your own company, or self-employed, a lot depends on personal contacts.'

'The personaller the better,' Ginnie said.

'Is something the matter?'

'Not a thing. Why would there be?'

'Well,' Polly went on cautiously, 'how about that meal tonight? I know you don't like cooking all that much. I could make us something nice, we could have a bottle of wine, and curl up on the sofa and watch some MTV. I think *House* is on. Or I could

256

pick up a DVD on the way home.'

There was that strange silence again. Then Ginnie said, 'It sounds tempting, but the thing is, I can't make a decision right this moment.'

'Oh. Is something happening?'

Another pause. 'I might be out.'

Polly waited until it was plain that she was not going to tell here where, and said, 'Sorry. I thought since we're in the same boat...'

'You're not in my boat, and you jolly well wouldn't want to be,' Ginnie said with the hot voice of suppressed anger.

'Ginnie, what is it? Is there something wrong? You can tell me.' Then it came to her. 'It isn't your mother again, is it?'

Ginnie said, in almost palpable relief, 'Well, my mother *is* worrying me. I mean, she was let out of hospital and they said she was all right, but I *am* wondering if I ought to go over and see her.'

'Well, do, then. I'll babysit for you, if you like.'

'Oh, no, I wouldn't put you to that trouble. And I might not go. It's all in the air. I can't decide anything just now.'

'Well, if you—'

'Look, just leave it, will you?' Ginnie interrupted her. 'If I want you to come over, I'll let you know. But I don't feel like a girls' night anyway. I'm not very good company at the moment. I've got to go now. Julian might be trying to ring me.'

She hung up before Polly could remind her about her mobile.

Simon had not called. Ginnie had left two messages at his office for him to ring back, and did not dare leave another. She had rung him at the Chelsea flat, and got an answering machine, on which she had left a very light, casual, 'Oh, ring me if you have a minute,' sort of message. She had tried the mobile number and the first time it had been answered by a woman, 'Simon Harte's phone?' who was obviously a secretary of some sort. Ginnie had been thrown, and mumbled that it didn't matter, she'd try again later, and hung up.

The second time she had rung it, the call had expired without being answered. It must have number recognition, of course, so if the secretary was answering it for him, it might be that she had decided Ginnie didn't warrant picking up. After all, Ginnie had not been answering her own mobile when she could see it was Polly, who had rung several times, or indeed anyone else except Simon.

But what American businessman only had a mobile his secretary answered? She'd seen the movies, read the books. Like movie stars they always had a *personal* mobile they could be reached on all the time, whose number was given only to certain people. She wondered, with a swift pain to her heart that took her by surprise by its sharpness, whether he indeed had such a phone *but had not given her the number.*

But it couldn't be, *couldn't* be, that he was brushing her off. Saturday night had been wonderful, rapturous, life-affirming. She wasn't going to believe it meant nothing to him. It was her glorious affair, and with Julian away for the next few days she had to get on and have it while she could. Besides, he'd given her the numbers, hadn't he? Why would he do that if he didn't want her to phone him? He was very busy, that was all it was. He couldn't find a private minute to himself in office time to call her. Once the office day was over, he'd be straight on to her, wanting to see her. Hadn't he said he was lonely, had no friends since the divorce, knew nobody in London? She must make sure she was ready when he did call, which meant she must get on with arranging for a babysitter to be on standby. There was an agency that specialized in last-minute arrangements. Bloody expensive, of course, but at least it would guarantee anonymity.

And she must fob Polly off somehow. She thought a little wistfully of the girls' night in with Polly's cooking, which in other circumstances would have been great. And it would have been great to get Polly to babysit – much more reliable and costing nothing. But she couldn't have explained the situation, and even if she could have, she guessed that Polly, for all that she was her best friend, would not be sympathetic. Not so much the having-an-affair bit (though she suspected Polly was a bit strait-laced that way), but the hanging-around-waiting-for-a-man-to-call bit. Best friends always did warn you about being too available: she had done it herself to friends many times in the past.

Yes, well it was all very well being a strong, centred woman when it wasn't you who was panting for an assignation. It was very different when the boot was on the other foot. And if *you* had no way to contact *him*, what else could you do?

# Eighteen

Polly had not expected to find herself dining with Simon. In fact, with Ginnie more or less brushing her off, she was planning a quiet evening doing some needlework. But Nigel had passed a busy day, and had not only got Sir Adrian to admit that he was thinking about selling the de Kooning, but had even arranged permission to go round to Fossett's Pelham Place house and get a photograph of it. Now he wanted Polly to strike while the iron was hot and get Simon Harte's interest up.

'Hubby's away, dear, so there's nothing to stop you vamping him as much as it takes. Find out if he's free this evening, and if he is, your way is clear. It will mean he doesn't know anyone and he'll be grateful for the company.'

At first he wanted Polly to invite him to her house, but she felt uneasy about that, with Seth away. Not that anything was going to happen, but she had not forgotten the moment when she had *wanted* something to happen, or almost, even if it was only for a split second, and it seemed like a kind of disloyalty to Seth to do anything which *would* have been dangerous and wrong if it *had* been happening. *Thus conscience*, as the Bard said, *doth make loonies of us all.*

Fortunately, Nigel did not require that kind of detailed analysis. When Polly said she'd rather not, he shrugged and said, 'All right, eat out, and I'll stand buff. Somewhere nice, but don't go mad, dear, or bang goes our profit. You know the kind of thing. A decent restaurant, but no fifteen-hundred-pound bottles of wine. And then work your magic on him.'

Polly had one moment of hesitation. 'Do you think it's quite right to take advantage of him when he's new in Town?'

Nigel looked exasperated. 'In the first place, the only opportunity to take advantage of him is when he *is* new in Town. And in the second place, how is it taking advantage? He came to us, darling, don't forget. The de Kooning is just right for him, but he can always say no. And if he gets dinner with a beautiful – or, well,' he added, looking critically at Polly, 'a reasonably attractive woman, anyway – where's the harm?'

Which made her laugh, and eased her conscience. He might be busy, in any case. And he might not want dinner with her. Surely he was worldly-wise enough to know that it was likely to be a sales approach (not that they hadn't really enjoyed each other's company over lunch – twice!) and discount it accordingly.

She rang the mobile number and he answered at once and said, 'Can I ring you back in five minutes?' And did.

'Sorry, I had someone with me. I was going to call you later, but I'm delighted *you* are calling *me* because that looks so much more friendly, and this is a big, lonely town for a stranger.'

'*You* say that, coming from New York?' she said, amused.

'New York is very different from London. Smaller and more compact, and New Yorkers are much friendlier. I'm talking about Manhattan, of course, not Queens or the Bronx or wherever. But then I only meant central London, not – not Walthamstow or Ealing or – what the hell's this? Free-something Barnet? You Brits and your weird place names.'

'Friern Barnet?' Polly said. 'Famous in the olden days for a lunatic asylum. Where did that come from?'

'There's a map of London on the wall of my office and I'm looking at it right now. Hey, I like the sound of Silvertown. Sounds kind of piratey. What happens in Silvertown?'

'Not much. I think there was a munitions factory there during the war. It isn't like it sounds.'

'We won't go there for dinner, then.'

'How did you know I was going to ask you

for dinner?'

'I didn't. I was going to ask you. I'm at a loose end and hoped you were too.'

'Well, as it happens...'

'Perfect. Where shall I meet you? I'd come out and pick you up, but I'm going to be working pretty late so we'd better meet in Town.'

Polly decided to be upfront. 'My boss wants me to give you dinner, because he's found a wonderful painting for you, and he wants me to show you the photograph of it.'

'Fine! If the excuse makes you feel better, so be it. But dinner's on me. That way I can refuse the painting and still see you.'

'You'll love the painting,' she said, laughing.

'Then you have nothing to worry about,' he pointed out.

He took her to Le Caprice this time, which she was quite happy with, because she had often gone there with Seth, and liked the food. And it was always nice in a restaurant to be recognized by the staff and greeted as a friend. They were given a very good table and Simon ordered her a glass of champagne without asking, to go with his Pernod, while they looked at the menu. She chose the asparagus with a soft-boiled duck's egg to start while he had the scallops with wild fennel, then she went for the calf's liver while he chose the confit of lamb with parmesan mash.

'I always have calf's liver when I can because I don't have it at home,' she explained.
'Seth doesn't like it, and it always seems too
much trouble to be cooking two different
things.'

'I know what you mean,' he said. 'Robyn
doesn't like fish, and you can't think how
many problems that causes when we go out,
never mind when I do the cooking.'

'You still cook for her?' she asked, a little
puzzled.

'I mean, when I *used* to do the cooking,' he
corrected. 'Tenses are the worst thing for
tripping a person up. My dad died ten years
ago and I still find myself talking about him
in the present tense.'

The food came and was excellent as
always, and they talked as happily and freely
as before, about families, food, books and
movies, the way old friends talk, and she felt
divinely happy. He had the knack of making
her feel relaxed and completely grounded in
the present, a feeling that nothing outside
the here and now mattered, or would ever
come to matter. Only when they were coming to the end of their main courses did she
feel obliged, for Nigel's sake as much as
anything, to mention the de Kooning.

'It really is a marvellous picture, and judg-
ing from what we've discussed already, I'm
pretty sure it's to your taste,' she said. 'Would
you like to have a look at the photo?' He

265

hesitated, and her heart sank a little. Had she spoiled the evening? Had she come on too crassly? 'I'm sorry. Forget I said that. It's just that I sort of promised Nigel...'

'Don't be sorry. It's all right. I'd love to have a look at the painting, but the thing is, I'm not too sure about buying any more until I have somewhere to put them. I can't expect Nigel to keep storing more and more paintings for me, and I can't put them into the Shepherd's Bush house until I've had it done over.'

'There's no hurry about the de Kooning,' she said. 'It isn't even on the market yet. Nigel knows the owner and knew he was thinking of selling, that's all. I'm sure if you were interested, he'd agree to give you first refusal when it does come up, which isn't likely to be for two or three months anyway.'

'That's very kind, but I've no idea when the house is going to be ready. You see...' He hesitated, and looked down at his hands as though he were reluctant to speak. 'The more I think about it, the more I want that house to be a Seth Muller house. But I know he's fantastically busy. There isn't a chance he could fit me in, and I can't stay in the company apartment for ever. But ever since your friend Ginnie put the idea in my head, I can't get it out again, and rather than compromise, I think I'd rather sell again and buy somewhere else.'

'I didn't realize you felt so strongly,' Polly

said. 'It's a real compliment to Seth.'

'He's the best,' Simon said simply, and suddenly looked up and straight into her eyes. 'And I'm so glad that you married the best. I shouldn't have liked anything less for you.'

Somehow or other his hand was over hers across the table, and she heard herself saying, 'I'm sure he'll want to do your house when he knows about it. And perhaps I can put in a good word for you.'

'No, I've decided I couldn't ask that of you,' he said, squeezing her fingers. 'I would not want to put you in an awkward position.'

'It wouldn't be awkward. Seth's going to be home tomorrow, and I can mention it to him then. I'm sure he'll want to do it anyway, it's just a matter of prioritizing.'

'He wouldn't suffer by it, I promise you that,' Simon said. 'I know what I want and I'm always prepared to pay for it. Like the Rothko – and the de Kooning.'

'Seth loves de Kooning,' Polly admitted. 'He'll love building a house round it.'

Ah, yes, now she was being trapped by a tense. 'He'll love', not 'he'd love'. So she was committed now to helping Simon get Seth. But, after all, it was in Seth's interest too. It would be a great showcase for him. It only meant changing his schedule and putting Simon in ahead of the Coventrys, and the Connaught Square job.

★   ★   ★

Ginnie finally got Simon halfway through the evening, when she had given up expecting him to answer and was simply redialling automatically at intervals while watching television and eating a packet of Wotsits she had confiscated from Jasper's school bag. She was in her velvet lounging pyjamas, with her hair screwed up on the top of her head and held with chopsticks. Biggie was curled on her lap (mad to allow it, with his hair and what it did to velvet) and she had a large glass of Chénas in her hand. She'd had two other large glasses beforehand with the pepperoni pizza she had ordered in, so she was feeling no strife, even though it was bloody Alan Sugar on the TV being a pain in the glutinous maximus (or was that the name of that Russell Crowe gladiator?). She'd have turned him over if only she hadn't dropped the remote earlier and was too lazy to get off the sofa and pick it up. She nearly dropped the phone, too, when Simon suddenly answered, and had to lunge for it, spilling a drop of wine on Big, who sprang from her lap and disappeared in a huff.

'Hi. Sorry I couldn't answer you before,' Simon said. 'It's been the hell of a day, one meeting after another. How are you?'

'Oh, fine, fine,' she said. 'Just wondered if you'd given me the wrong numbers. Except that it was your voice on the answering machine at the flat, so I knew *that* one was right.'

268

'I haven't been home to the flat yet,' he apologized. 'Did you leave me a message?'

'Just to call me,' she said, feeling better. If he'd been *that* busy...'Where are you now?'

'In a restaurant, having a business dinner with three important but boring people.'

She heard the sound of flushing in the background. 'My God, you're calling me from the gents, aren't you?'

'The gents. I love that – so English. Yeah, I'm in the bathroom. The only way I could talk privately. I can't be long, though. My deals are going cold every minute I'm away from the table.'

'Go on, then, go back and be a mogul. Mogul away, *mon brave*! Just say when I can see you.'

'When is that husband of yours coming back?'

'Not for days yet. Can I see you tomorrow?'

'Oh God. Crowded schedule. Wait, wait, let me think. Look, I can see you at lunchtime, but it'll have to be quick.'

'Best not waste time eating then,' she said.

He laughed. 'You're incredible.'

'D'you want to come here?' she said doubtfully.

'No, it's too far out and I won't have long. Besides, you have neighbours. Meet me at the flat. One o'clock.'

'One o'clock it is,' she said. 'I'll wear as little as possible.'

'God, you're gorgeous! I'll see you then. I've got to go.' And he went.

Polly woke on Tuesday with her usual non-working-day promptitude, and lay staring up at the ceiling, wondering why she didn't feel good inside her head. The ceiling was painted with a special Aluko Meyer emulsion, the colour mixed to Seth's order in the precise shade of off-white he had wanted to go with the eucalyptus floor and the pyinkado of the bed. Neither Zoffany nor Farrow and Ball could get it quite right for him. Polly spent a lot of time one way and another looking at that ceiling and she had to admit it was a subtle and satisfying colour, like the very best, most expensive coffee ice cream. Paint colours all had weird names these days. Farrow and Ball would probably have called it something like Dimity or Mouse's Back. Polly had told Seth (to his annoyance, since Aluko were only making it for him and he planned to use it a lot in clients' houses) that he should call his colour Truss or Bandage.

Yes, Seth: that's where the mental discomfort was centred. He was coming home today and she had (somehow or other) promised Simon that she would plead his case; and while logically and intellectually she still could not see that there was anything amiss with that, it still *felt* wrong. She got up and padded through to the bathroom, enjoyed urinating in complete privacy for once, and then ran water into the black glass bath. She usually preferred to shower, but she thought better in the bath. While it was filling she put some music on and switched the speakers through to the bathroom; then she added a few drops of Cawthorpe's organic rose oil to the water and climbed in, to sink back into the healing fragrance and the sound of the home recording of her sister Anna playing the Bach unaccompanied cello suites.

Simon had spoken again about Seth as they were saying goodbye outside the restaurant, asking her if she was sure she didn't mind asking him to do his house. Now, that was probably Simon being ultra-sensitive. It could also be someone manipulative making themselves *seem* ultra-sensitive so as to disarm the manipulee. But why would she suspect manipulation at all? It could not be other than coincidental that he, who admired Seth's work so much, had met her, Seth's wife, as he did. A happy coincidence for all concerned. Could it?

It was sheer chance that he had come into the gallery where she worked. He had known of Esterhazy's reputation and thought it might be a good place to buy for his new home. And there she was. He could just as easily have gone into a different gallery. Panter and Hall's in Shepherd Market. Peter Nahum's in Ryder Street. And then, of course, she would never have met him.

But if he had been actively looking for paintings, wouldn't it have been better to go somewhere bigger, one of the big auction houses like Christie's or Bonham's. Or to have appointed someone to do some research for him (as he had asked her informally to do) or to go to the country house auctions for him. Nigel, of course, would have been delighted to do so, but he hadn't asked Nigel. And then there was the Internet. He (or someone on his behalf) could have looked for paintings on the Internet. It was a quicker way of covering the ground than walking into a Bond Street gallery, and if she knew anything about Simon, she would have guessed he'd want to cover the ground quickly.

And he had said, during that first meeting, that *he always did his research*.

Then it came to her, the thing that had been niggling the back of her mind all along, something small and unimportant, but which had struck a false note in the beginning, though she had instantly forgotten what it was until now.

He had said he'd been divorced for five years, and that his wife had not been able to have children with him. Now she had three – *and they competed in posh horse shows all over the States and won sackloads of prizes*. But if they had only been divorced for five years, the eldest of them could only be four years old – or five at the most, allowing for legal process. A five-year-old, a four-year-old and a three-year-old winning prizes at horse shows? *I don't think so.*

She heaved herself out of the bath, wrapped herself in a dark blue bath sheet and dried herself slowly, thoughtfully. A slip of the tongue, probably. He had meant to say fifteen years instead of five years. But then yesterday he had spoken of Robyn in the present tense. Another slip of the tongue?

She shook her head. It was madness, what she was thinking – that he had come into Esterhazy deliberately to meet her, and had told her a sad story of divorce and childlessness to get her on his side, in order to – in order to what? To get her to persuade Seth to do his house? My God, that was mad thinking! Who could be so Machiavellian? Why not just ask Seth straight out and be done with it?

Because he wanted the house done now, and everyone knew there was a waiting list for Seth, and he didn't even put you on it unless he wanted to.

And Simon had known that because Seth had done the David Lauren loft in Manhattan, and David Lauren and Simon were friends.

She went back into the bedroom and began slowly rubbing cream into various parts of her body and face. What had poor Simon done to deserve this suspicion? He was a nice, sensitive, kind man. How sad he had looked when he had spoken about not being able to have children. And wait, wait, here was the flaw in her thinking! If he had made up the childlessness bit to get her sympathy, how did he know she was unable so far to have children? All their friends knew, naturally, but he hadn't known any of their friends before he met her. And he had met her by accident, anyway, by coming into Esterhazy. No, it was all nonsense and she was nuts to think it.

She dressed and went upstairs into the small servant's bedroom which was her study at the moment. Seth had a study up there too, but rarely used it, preferring always to work in his office in Bruton Street. He was planning to have the top floor redone as a master suite for them, bedroom, bathroom and dressing room, with a glass roof and an observation deck at the back where they could sunbathe nude. It'd be fun getting that past the planners.

She sat down at her desk and switched on her computer, and when it had booted up, she went into Google. Then she hesitated. It was not a very nice thing to do to a friendly, pleasant man, whose company she had enjoyed so much, to go checking on him behind his back. She waited so long, deep in thought, that the screensaver came on and rolled back and forth in that weirdly lifelike, 3-D way. Finally she roused herself, clicked the mouse, and entered her own name in the search box. 670,000 matches, said the screen. There were Pollys and Mullers galore, it seemed. Not specific enough. She put in Seth Muller and Polly.

A lot of Seth Muller stuff that came up was about an American journalist or writer of some kind, but there was plenty on her Seth, of course, and, yes, one or two included mention of her. She clicked up the first one. A 'profile' of Seth, which mentioned that he was married to Polly, née Walsh, sister of Clara Walsh the concert pianist.

The second one said he was married to Polly Muller, the art historian and authority on Abstract Impressionists, who owned the Esterhazy Gallery in London's prestigious Bond Street.

Poor Nigel, she thought. Rubbish in, rubbish out. But it was there, in black and white, that Esterhazy was where she could be found.

Though how would he have found the reference, unless he had already known her name to Google it? She scrolled down to see where the article came from. *New York Times*. It was a review of the David Lauren conversion. Easy peasy. She felt a little sick, and it was mostly with herself.

All right, he could have found out that she worked in Esterhazy. In fact, if he had read that review of David Lauren's apartment, he had certainly known that much about her before coming to London.

But he couldn't have known about her childlessness.

Except – she remembered now that Sukey Arrosto had said Sam Wentworth had rung Simon and given him a rundown of his new neighbours. Was it possible he had said the Mullers were trying for a baby and failing?

Maybe he hadn't read that review. But look, that Saturday lunchtime at the house, Simon had seemed not to know that Polly Muller's husband was Seth Muller until Ginnie had spilled the beans. But it was hard to believe Sam Wentworth wouldn't have bragged about *that* when he was giving the rundown. Seth was their big celebrity.

Simon *must* have known. And if he had pretended about that, what else might he not have pretended about?

Sadly she keyed Simon Harte into the search box, and added Transglobal to narrow it down. And pressed enter.

She scrolled down the resultant hits to find the most detailed profile, and chose the one from *Forbes* magazine; scrolled down until she got past his business career and into the personal life bit. Married Robyn Carnegie – yes, she was a lawyer. Married twenty years ago. Blah blah blah. Here it was. Three daughters, Rebecca, Kate and Sarah. The Hartes divided their time between their New York home and their ranch in northern California, where they bred fine quality equitation horses. Daughters show-jumped and evented. Simon Harte, the proud father. Robyn Harte quotation about busy lives, private jet enabling them to keep in touch, treasured family holidays together. Wasn't she worried about his new job in London? 'The world's a smaller place now,' said Robyn Harte. 'London's practically commutable these days.'

*I bet she said it with a light laugh and a toss of the head*, Polly thought.

But she had liked him so much, they had got on so well together! They had talked and talked and had so much in common he had felt like an old friend. It couldn't *all* be false, not all of it. He must really have liked her, even if he had pretended not to know things he had known, and to have experienced things he had not experienced. He hadn't done all that just to get her to help him get Seth – not all of it. He had liked her, too.

Well, perhaps he *had* liked her, she thought sadly. It had made his job easier, that was all. It was probably the only real coincidence in the whole business.

# Nineteen

It was not the same this time. Simon had been there waiting all right when she arrived. He had let her in, offered her a drink, pressed a glass of wine into her hand and led her straight to the bedroom. And though all the way over she had been hornier than a ram's forehead, and she couldn't really say it wasn't pretty hot stuff, afterwards it all seemed a bit tawdry. Whatever Julian might be getting up to with Angela Demarco, it would not be a hurried lunchtime bonk like this. She knew him well enough to know that whatever he did, he would do it with his own particular style, which would include making Angela feel like a lady. OK, being a lady was not what she was up to with Simon, but she did feel as though he were not valuing her highly enough.

Especially when he started looking at his gold Tag Heuer Monaco, which was rather too soon after they had stopped panting and before she had had anything like enough lying mindlessly in his arms enjoying the moment.

'You're wonderful,' he said, kissing her,

and stroking some hair out of her eyes. 'But I've got to go. I know this is awful of me, but I did warn you I didn't have much time.' Before she could say something tart about 'thanks for fitting me in', he crinkled his eyes, smiled disarmingly and said, 'I should not have done it, I know, but I couldn't resist the chance of seeing you. You're dynamite.' He kissed the end of her nose and sprang out of bed with a sort of Spiderman litheness, and headed for the bathroom. 'Next time,' he said over his shoulder, 'we must arrange things better.'

She lay with her arms behind her head feeling sulky and bad, dashing and daredevil, pleasantly tingling and unpleasantly used, cross and hopeful, doubtful and determined. And hungry. Sex always made her hungry, and it was lunchtime anyway, and she hadn't had any. Surely they would have something to eat together and talk before he rushed away?

But he came in through the main bedroom door fully dressed in a suit and adjusting his tie. The bathroom had another door on its far side which must lead, she supposed, to the dressing room. His eyes were bright and his hair was just a little tousled but otherwise you'd never have known if you didn't know.

'Look,' he said, 'I feel bad about dashing away like this, but I really have got to get back. If you knew what my schedule was like ... We'll do it better next time. Or maybe we can go away together some time. Would you like that?'

'That'd be nice,' she said, but without great enthusiasm. Once Julian was back it would be impossible for her to go away anywhere.

He came over to the bed. 'You stay here, take your time, let yourself out when you're ready. Don't feel you have to hurry just because I do. There's food and stuff in the kitchen, help yourself. Sorry I can't give you lunch.' His eyes crinkled again. 'You were better than food, though.' He stooped and kissed her lingeringly. 'Mmm. If they could market that, they'd make a fortune.'

And then, amazingly, he was going.

'When will I see you again?' she asked before he got to the door. 'What about tomorrow?'

'I'm not sure about tomorrow,' he said. 'I'm pretty well booked up all day. But something might come up. Someone might cancel. Look, I'll ring you. I've got your mobile number.'

And then he really was gone. She heard the front door close, then lay listening to the expensive silence: the double glazing was too good to allow any sound in from outside. So this was what it was like, being a mistress. Her body had had a good work-out, but her mind was completely unsatisfied. She sighed and hauled herself out of bed. She might as well get what she could out of the situation. A shower in the amazing multi-jet cubicle, and then she'd see what there was in the kitchen to eat. Another glass of wine, anyway. She had plenty of time. Marta had turned up this morning, looking amazingly brown, fit and pleased with herself, and was even now (or she'd better be!) scouring the house from top to bottom and doing the ironing Ginnie had left for her. And Ginnie had told her to do the afternoon school run as well, not knowing how long she was going to be with Simon, so she didn't have to hurry back. Pity he hadn't organized things better for himself.

In the afternoon, when Polly had just got back from her Tai Chi class, the phone rang, and it was Julian.

'Oh, hi,' she said, surprised. 'Are you still in the States?'

'Yes, I'm in Boston. Polly, do you happen to know where Ginnie is? I've tried her at home and she isn't answering her mobile.'

'Oh, dear, I expect she's forgotten to take it with her. She did that yesterday and I could not get hold of her.'

'But you don't know where she is?'

'No, I'm sorry. She didn't tell me she was going out.'

'Oh,' said Julian. There was a brief and expensive Transatlantic silence. 'Can I ask you something? I wouldn't normally trouble you, but being stuck over here makes me feel rather helpless.'

'Anything I can do to help,' Polly said. She had always liked Julian, but she didn't want to come between husband and wife, and from the sound of his voice he was going to ask her something awkward.

'Ginnie's seemed rather odd on the telephone the last couple of days. Do you know what she's up to?'

'She hasn't been on a spending spree, if that's what you mean,' Polly said in quick defence of her friend.

'My dear girl, what can you mean?' Julian asked.

Polly felt herself blushing. 'Oh – well – it's just that she does tell me things, and I know you've been cross with her once or twice about exceeding her budget. And just recently I've thought that you looked rather worried, so I thought, perhaps...' She ran out of steam.

'You thought I had an expensive wife and couldn't afford her?' he said, sounding oddly amused.

'I'm sorry. I didn't mean it rudely.'

'I know you didn't. It's nice of you to worry on my behalf, but I'm not short of money,' he said. 'Apart from the firm, which is doing very well, I have private means. And I've never tried to keep Ginnie on a short rein because I couldn't afford it. It's her I'm afraid for, not the budget.'

'I don't quite understand,' Polly confessed.

'I hate waste,' Julian said, 'and particularly

the sort of conspicuous consumption that's lauded in books and magazines these days. The shop-till-you-drop thing. It's pointless and vulgar. Ginnie goes out and buys armfuls of things she doesn't need and doesn't even want. And even the act of buying them doesn't make her happy. I just don't think that's the right way to fill a life, or even a useful or sensible way.'

'Well, no, of course not,' Polly began, but he cut in.

'She accuses me of being mean, does she?' he asked wryly.

'Oh, not exactly. I don't know that she really feels she ought to be able to buy anything she wants on the spur of the moment,' she said (though she suspected sometimes that Ginnie did indeed feel just that). 'The only thing she really complains about is only having Marta three days a week.'

'Well, that's not because I can't afford it,' Julian said. 'I made the rule for her own good. I felt she needed something that she *had* to do, at least part of the time, if only to give her life structure. My God, if she'd get herself a job, do some charity work, even take up an interest of some kind – *something!* – she could have Marta seven days a week with my blessing. I'm just afraid if she didn't have the housework and the children to look after one or two days a week, she'd never get out of bed at all. She isn't interested in *anything,*' he concluded quietly, 'and it frightens me.'

Polly said hesitantly, 'This is about Bill, isn't it?'

'Yes, I think it is,' Julian said, and he sounded tired to death. 'Or at least, that's the way it seems to me. She really changed quite fundamentally when he died, though it perhaps wasn't apparent to people who didn't know her well.'

'I noticed,' Polly said.

Shortly after Ben was born, Ginnie's beloved brother Bill had been appointed to the embassy in Addis Ababa. A couple of years later, he had been working late there one evening when a group of armed Somali militants had broken in and machine-gunned the whole staff that were present – Bill, an under-secretary, three clerical staff, two radio operators, a groundsman and a caretaker. The Addis Massacre, it had been billed in the papers at the time. There had been lavish coverage in the press and on TV. It seemed to have been a random act of violence against the West. No demand or statement had ever been made about it and the group involved had never been brought to justice. Questions had been asked, but no answers had ever been given. There had been no conclusion to the incident, apart from the full stop of the bullet.

For Ginnie, the sun had gone out that day. And though to all intents and purposes she had got over it and was able to function normally – hadn't taken to drink or started popping pills or anything – she *was* different. Polly sometimes felt she was walking on a thin crust with Ginnie that she might easily put her foot through.

After a pause, Julian said, 'She never cried, you know. I never once saw her cry for him.'

Polly nodded, forgetting he couldn't see her.

'I'm not a great believer in this modern fad for talking about everything, wearing one's heart on one's sleeve. The Diana syndrome. Does more harm than good in most cases. Everyone has painful things they have to live through. You come to terms with it and get on with your life. But I'm not sure she ever did. She never grieved, you see. There's something not right about her now, and I don't know what to do about it. I wish I did.'

There was a silence. Polly thought about that day in Fare Trade when Ginnie had complained of being bored. It wasn't quite boredom, really, but a restless desire to escape from herself. Julian wasn't wrong – she did need something to do.

Julian said, as if he'd heard the thought, 'If only she'd take up her photography again. She was really good at it, and it got her out and about.'

'I suggested that to her the other day.'

'Did you?' he said eagerly. 'What did she say?'

'That she didn't have the contacts any

285

more. And,' reluctantly, 'that she didn't have time between school runs because you wouldn't let her have Marta every day.' He groaned. 'I told her she was just making excuses.'

'Of course she is.'

She hadn't taken out her camera since those pictures in the newspapers of the embassy with the bullet holes everywhere and the blood on the ground. Why did papers put that sort of thing in? They never thought about what the relatives might feel. It was sensationalism of the worst sort. For Ginnie, all photographs were now tainted. But it was ridiculous. She *had* to get over it and take up her life again. Julian felt frustration balling up in him, because he didn't know how to reach her. It was one of those occasions when he felt the different worlds they had come from like a chasm between them.

Polly said, hopefully, 'But at least she did raise the subject with me – of being bored, I mean. So maybe she's ready to move on, and just needs some encouragement.'

'Yes. I'll certainly bear that in mind when I get home.'

'Are you staying away much longer?'

'Probably the rest of the week. Why? Is that a problem?'

Polly hesitated, not wanting to get into it. But it was possible that Ginnie was right about him and his affair, wasn't it? And if so, Julian shouldn't be allowed to get away with

286

it when it was hurting her friend so much. 'It may be,' she said. 'I don't know if I ought to mention this, but Ginnie is upset about your staying away longer.'

'Is she? Any specific reason?'

'She thinks – no, she suspects – well, you talk a lot about this Angela person, and you're spending a lot of time with her.'

There was a short silence, and then Julian said, 'She's jealous of Angela Demarco?' Polly didn't answer. He said, the laughter breaking through, 'She doesn't think I'm having an affair with Angela? My God!'

Polly felt cross not only with him, but with herself now for having told him. If he was going to make a joke of it. 'I don't think it's funny,' she said.

'I'm sorry,' he said, sobering, 'but you would if you knew Angela. She's nearly seventy, around five foot nothing, wears those bottle-glass spectacles ... Did you happen to see the film *The Incredibles*? We took the children to it. Think Edna Mode, but quite a bit older.'

Polly was wrong-footed. 'But you keep saying how wonderful she is.' And Simon had said the same, now she came to think of it.

'She is. She's the best commissioning editor in the world. She's a legend in the business. She has a mind like a steel trap and an encyclopaedic knowledge of publishing. Any publishing company would give anything to have her. It's a privilege to work with her.' Polly said nothing, having nothing to say. 'She's also married to Brad Bradley of Warner Brothers, and has been for over fifty years. They're devoted. Ask anyone.'

'I believe you,' Polly said hastily. 'But it isn't me you have to convince.'

'I'll talk to her,' he said.

'Don't tell her I said anything about it,' Polly begged.

'Of course not. I'll just drop it into the conversation naturally that Angela's a little old to be my fantasy date. Though that brings us back to the initial problem of trying to get hold of Ginnie when she's not answering the phone.' He sighed. 'I'll have to try ringing in the middle of the night so as to catch her before she goes out in the morning.'

When Julian had gone, Polly wondered again about Ginnie, who had been a little strange the last couple of days. Where was she? Then she remembered that Ginnie's mother had been ill over the weekend. Why had she forgotten that? She should have mentioned it to Julian. But, wait a minute, Ginnie would of course have told Julian herself. And wouldn't that have provided all the reason he needed for her to be 'rather odd' on the telephone? And wouldn't that be where she had gone? She might have forgotten to take her mobile, but he could have called the hospital or her mother's house and caught her there.

She felt guilty now for mentioning the Angela Demarco thing, because it was more than likely worry about her mother that was making Ginnie snippy. She was probably no more serious about being jealous than about many of the other things she came out with. Ginnie did tend to say a lot more than she ever meant. Polly hoped she had not dropped her in it, or stirred up something unnecessarily. It showed the positive virtues of keeping one's mouth shut, especially when talking to men, who were all unreliable bastards (*oh, Simon, did you use me?*), even the formerly saintly Julian.

Edna Mode, eh?

# Twenty

Seth did not telephone all day Tuesday, which left Polly with plenty of time to ponder on Simon's sincerity or otherwise, and debate with herself whether she ought to mention his job to Seth. It was good business for Seth which he probably would want to do anyway, so where was the harm? Especially as the Coventrys would probably not mind being postponed – it was their third home and they weren't actually living in it. And she suspected he didn't really want to do the Connaught Square job anyway (because some of the things the owners wanted were a bit naff, and the extreme security demands were going to compromise his design), but felt he ought to because it was big money and high profile – both of which Simon's job would be a replacement for. But was mentioning Simon to Seth at all a betrayal, of herself if not her husband?

But they would, after all, be neighbours and it was important to keep on good terms with neighbours, especially in a place like the Terrace where they all knew each other and socialized frequently. And Simon hadn't actually done her any harm, had he? So he was insincere, so what? Most rich people were, in one area or another. He had engineered a meeting with her, purely for the purposes of queue jumping, but although it was Seth he had been trying to get to, she was sure he actually *had* liked her and enjoyed her company. As she had enjoyed his. She had come out of it two lunches and a dinner ahead, not to mention the commission on the pictures. If you wanted to be crude about it, she was in profit.

She decided at last that she would tell Seth about the job, but in cool and unemotional terms. Simon had said he would sell the house rather than let anyone else do it, but she wouldn't mention that, and in any case he was probably exaggerating. She didn't suppose it would cause him any pain to go on living in the company flat, especially if he would be 'practically commuting' back to the States to see high-flyer Robyn and the three horsey children. (Good for Robyn. She made herself feel glad for her.)

When she saw Simon again, or spoke to him, she would be friendly and neighbourly and that was all. There would be no more lunches or private consultations, and if he wanted research done on pictures it would be Esterhazy who did it and Nigel who would bill him.

Cool and friendly, that was the thing.

But she would miss the conversations. She

dismissed from her mind the image that leapt to it unbidden, of the sapphire blue eyes and the up-one-side, self-mocking smile. She shuddered. The man was *dangerous*. Bloody Robyn ought to keep better tabs on him.

She wished Seth would call. She assumed he was back – he had said he would go straight to the office – but she could not call him there, because of the no-calls-at-work-except-in-an-emergency rule, and she hadn't an emergency to her name. She could hardly ring to ask what time he'd be home to dinner.

She started thinking about what they should have, though. Or should they go out? That would be nice (and take the taste of Simon-dinner out of her mental mouth). They could go to E&O in Blenheim Crescent. They hadn't been there for a while. Or The Ledbury. Or Mediterraneo on the KPR. But, no, probably he wouldn't want to eat out, having spent the entire weekend in restaurants. Probably he would want a good, simple, home-cooked meal and an early night. Her period was over now (they never lasted more than four days, five at the very outside) so an early night would be a doubly good thing. She thought about his hard, masculine body, dark and hairy, dominating her, driving into her, and shivered pleasurably. They had some catching up to do. And soon it would be Baby Night again. Well, she wouldn't think of that right now. She'd think about tonight's menu. Something simple and delicious. A slab of foie gras with toasted brioche. And prawn and lobster cannelloni would be quick to do. And then her white chocolate and coffee mousse. She could knock that up right away (she always had eggs and various sorts of chocolate in the house) before she went out to buy the rest.

He finally rang her at half past five when she was making the pancakes for the cannelloni.

'Hi, darling. Good day?' she said.

'Busy,' he replied. 'Things pile up when you're out of the office for five minutes.'

'Well, I've got lots to talk to you about. I thought after eating in restaurants for four days you'd like a proper home-cooked meal for a change. What time do you think you'll be home?'

'Sorry, I'm going to be late,' he said. 'I've got to see a client tonight, so I won't be home to dinner. I expect they'll feed me, so don't worry about getting anything in for me.'

'I already got it,' she said, trying not to sound disappointed, which would only annoy him.

'Won't it keep?' he asked, and she could imagine his brows pulling down as he said it.

'It'll be fine, don't worry about it,' she said. The mousse would keep, but not the fish or the foie gras. She thought of eating it herself and felt daunted. It wasn't the sort of eating for two she was interested in. 'Any idea what time you'll be back?'

'None at all,' he said. 'Don't wait up for me if I'm very late. But don't forget to leave the chain off when you go to bed.'

'OK,' she said. She felt like a deflated balloon. Then she thought of Ginnie. With Julian in America and her mum giving her anxiety, she'd probably be glad of a good meal. She could take it all over there and they could have that girls' evening they didn't have before. Assuming she was in and not at the hospital or whatever. She'd give her a ring now and find out.

Ginnie was in an odd mood, half-elated, half-anxious. But most of all restless. When Polly phoned and offered to bring dinner over, her first instinct was to refuse, as if Polly were trying to tie her down, keep tabs on her. But she wasn't going anywhere tonight, that was for sure. Simon hadn't rung her again and his mobile number went straight to voicemail when she tried it, and belated pride had kicked in to stop her ringing again. It was too complicated anyway, going out in the evening, with babysitting considerations.

Marta had fed the kids when she collected them from school, improvising with what she found in the kitchen – tomato and mushroom risotto (with dried mushrooms from the store cupboard) followed by cinnamon and brown sugar eggy-bread (which was starch plus starch, but fine by the children even if it was nutritionally unbalanced). Then she had seemed eager to get away, which was not like Marta, who was usually good for a chat. But perhaps having been away so long she had householdy things to do for herself, like washing and ironing. Ginnie only had time to tell her about dopey old Phil Kemp-Parker swearing he had seen her in Paris with a French lover. 'Ah, Paris, City of Dreams,' Marta had said wistfully. 'I always wanted to go to Paris.'

'Better in the spring when the chestnuts are out,' Ginnie had told her, 'and French lovers are all front and no back.'

'What does it mean, please?'

'Disappointing,' Ginnie had translated. 'Not like Polish men.'

Then Marta had rushed off, stuffing her cardigan into her string bag because the afternoon was so warm, and striding down the road in her sensible shoes, which despite being flat still did not make her legs look any less sensational, Ginnie thought sadly.

It was only when Polly rang that Ginnie realized she had nothing in the house for her own supper, so she swallowed her first instinctive refusal of Polly's offer and said OK, and then, realizing that eating the planned meal with her rather than Seth couldn't be Polly's first choice, she added, a little gruffly, 'Poor you. I'll get up a bottle of Julian's wine and we'll comfort each other.'

'Not one of the expensive ones,' Polly said.

Ginnie scowled. 'I own half of everything in this house, according to the law. I'll drink what I bloody well like.'

'Fine, fine,' said Polly hastily. 'I'll see you later, then.'

Ginnie got the children to bed, had a quick shower (she had the weird superstitious feeling that the smell of Simon was clinging to her in such a way that Polly would notice it) and, to keep her morale up, put on her cashmere leggings with her Benjamin Cho silk print mini-dress – comfortable but not slobby. She brushed out her hair (it was getting very long – could probably do with a trim) and held it back with two of Flora's sparkly slides so that it hung down her back almost to her waist. She put on some smoky eyeshadow, looked at herself in the mirror, and said, 'My God, Simon Harte, what *are* you missing?' Then she went to Julian's cellar and, not knowing what Polly was bringing to eat, got out a bottle of red and a bottle of white, set the one to chambré and the other to chill.

Then she put a jazz cassette on the old kitchen player, envied Polly her sound system where you could switch the music into any room or combination of rooms you liked, and thought, to hell with it, she deserved a glass of wine right now, no matter what Polly was bringing. So she opened the Puligny Montrachet and poured herself a big glass.

The food was delicious. 'God, Polly, you're a good cook! Old Seth doesn't know he's born!' They talked easily as friends do about neutral things, about food, the new restaurant that was opening on the Green, the lack of a decent fish shop (Polly had had to go to Notting Hill for the lobster), why white chocolate was white, why on earth everyone had raved about the movie *Chocolat*, other movies, television, why men found Natasha Kaplinsky attractive, how Marta could wear flat shoes and still her legs looked like a gazelle's.

'I'm glad she turned up all right,' Polly said.

'Oh, she's very reliable. It was the plane that wasn't. I can't think why she bothers with domestic service, though. With her looks she could replace old Natasha tomorrow.'

'Maybe she enjoys it,' Polly said. 'Some women are born domestic.'

'Not me, that's for sure,' Ginnie said, refilling their glasses. 'Though I'd sooner clean someone else's house than my own. I expect someone will snap her up soon, and then she'll find out about wife-and-motherhood from the other side. It's not all it's cracked up to be. You ought to rethink this baby thing before it's too late.'

'You wouldn't give away any one of yours.'

'I might sell them, though,' Ginnie said.

'By the way,' Polly said, 'talking of motherhood, how's your mum? Have you been to see her again?'

'She's fine,' Ginnie said, feeling uncomfortable. She dug out a spoonful of mousse so as not to have to meet Polly's eyes. It would serve her right, of course, if her mother really did have a heart attack now. *It's just the sort of thing that happens to me*, she thought with a touch of self-pity.

'So it wasn't anything serious after all, then?'

'I said, she's fine. Change of subject, please.'

Polly shrugged. 'Have you spoken to Julian today?'

Ginnie scowled. 'That's not a new subject, that's still family. Why are you so concerned about my nearest and dearest all of a sudden?'

'You're my friend. I'm concerned about you.'

'Well, you don't need to be. I'm fine. And bloody old Julian is obviously fine, swanning about the States with his precious Angela. Probably in an open-topped car, with her raven tresses flowing back in the wind. With any luck, they'll get caught in the wheel and snap her neck, like Isadora Duncan.'

It was meant to be funny, but Polly could

hear the hurt underneath. 'Look, about Angela Demarco. I don't mean to interfere, but you've got completely the wrong idea about her.'

'How would you know?' Ginnie scowled. 'What makes you such an expert all of a sudden? You've never met her.'

Polly was prepared for this question. She didn't want to tell Ginnie she had discussed it with Julian. She said, 'I Googled her.'

Ginnie stared. 'Now why didn't I think of that? Genius! So, what did you find out?'

'She's apparently very highly respected in the publishing world—'

'Oh, highly! Especially by Julian Addington!'

'Her date of birth is in nineteen thirty-nine. She's been married to the same man for fifty years.'

'Fifty years? What are you talking about?'

'Nineteen thirty-nine, Ginnie. Work it out. She's sixty-eight years old. And I got a picture of her from the web. I printed it out for you.'

She reached into her handbag and handed the folded sheet of paper across to her friend. Ginnie opened it out suspiciously, and then began helplessly to smirk. Angela Demarco wasn't quite Edna Mode, but there was a definite resemblance: the big, thick-lensed glasses, the heavy-lidded eyes, the large nose, the old-fashioned page-boy hair-cut (though the thick, coarse hair was grey, not black). She was good for her age, but she didn't look a day under sixty. Ginnie began to giggle. 'Oh my God. Poor Julian! And I imagined her bringing him champagne in bed and licking it off his bare chest. I imagined...' She was overcome with what she had imagined. 'She looks like Rosa Klebb!'

'Oh, come on, she's not that bad,' Polly said, smiling herself. 'But anyway, you can see you were wrong. Julian admires her professionally, that's all. You know now there was nothing going on, don't you?'

'Poor Julian!' she said with a giggle. And then abruptly, in the course of saying, 'Poor Julian,' again, she was crying. She put her face in her hands and sobbed, 'What have I done?'

'I don't know,' Polly said anxiously. 'What have you done?'

'I wasn't at my mother's on Saturday night,' she sobbed. 'Mummy wasn't ill.'

'Oh, God, Ginnie, what have you been up to?'

'I wanted to pay him back. I thought he was having an affair, and being so bloody casual about it. They're like that. His lot.'

'Not Julian,' Polly said. 'I've always said—'

'Oh, I know what you've always said,' Ginnie moaned, lifting a reproachful, tear-stained face to Polly. 'You w-were always on his side. You're supposed to be m-*my* friend.'

'I *am* your friend,' Polly said. 'And I'm always on your side. But for God's sake tell

300

me what you've done. Where *were* you on Saturday night?'

'With S-Simon,' Ginnie wailed, and sobbed again.

Polly felt everything inside her go cold and still. 'Simon Harte?' she said in a voice that seemed to come from a great distance away.

'How many other Simons do we know? Oh, I know you like him and you went to his house and everything, but I knew you wouldn't approve so I didn't tell you, but he rang me up straight after I met him with you that time. He invited me out and gave me the big come-on, and well, you know how g-gorgeous he is. How could I resist, especially with Julian being such a bastard? Thinking he was being, anyway.'

'How far has it gone?' Polly asked from the same vast distance.

'I spent the night with him on Saturday at his flat. That's why I had to say I was at my mother's. And I saw him again today. At the flat. We made love, but he had to dash off. The b-bastard was busy.'

'Oh, Ginnie!'

'Don't "oh, Ginnie" me! I wouldn't have done it if I hadn't thought Julian was bonking this Angela woman. And it was *he* came on to me, not vice versa. And you don't know what he's like. It's not just that he's a stud – which he totally is – but he's kind and caring as well, and we have s-so much in common. And now I know Julian isn't, I can never see him again, and I'll m-miss him.' The tears flowed.

Polly came and sat down beside Ginnie and hugged her in sympathetic silence, and then handed her tissues until she stopped crying. Ginnie wiped her face and blew her nose. Polly pushed the glass of wine into her hand and said, 'Take a slug. I've got something to tell you.' Ginnie obeyed, and looked at her apprehensively. 'I *do* know what Simon's like. I do know how sympathetic he seems, what good company he is. I've spent a bit of time with him, and I thought we had so much in common as well. He told me he and his divorced wife couldn't have children together. You can imagine how that made me warm to him. And he said he came from a big family like me and missed the noise and fun of it.'

Ginnie sat up straighter, frowning indignantly. 'That's not true. He told me he only had one sister, who he adored, and she was killed in Africa, in a car crash.'

'Did he? I'm not surprised. He lied to me, too. It turns out he has three children.'

'I know that. He told me his wife took them when they got divorced so he hardly ever sees them.'

'That's not true either. He isn't divorced.'

*'Bastard!'* said Ginnie.

'That about sums it up. I'm afraid he'll say anything to get people – women, anyway – on his side. To get what he wants.'

302

Ginnie thought of something and her eyes flew open. 'Oh my God, you didn't sleep with him as well, did you?'

'No,' said Polly sadly. 'That wasn't what he wanted from me.' But she remembered the kiss, and thought that it could easily have gone that way, had she not resisted.

'Well, thank God for that. That would have been too gruesome for words, both of us shagging him at the same time. And poor old Seth doesn't deserve that. He's devoted to you.'

'Julian's devoted to you.'

'Is he? I don't know. Oh, I accept he wasn't banging Angela Demarco, but I still think he's pretty fed up with me. He's never really taken me seriously, you know. He laughs at me. He thinks I'm a complete idiot – and even if he wasn't off with Angela, he might easily do it any time, with someone else.'

'I think you're wrong.' Polly thought it was time to come clean about the phone call. 'I spoke to him today—'

'How come?' Ginnie said with a quick frown.

'He rang me to ask if I knew where you were, because he hadn't been able to get you on the phone. You forgot to take your mobile with you again.'

'I didn't forget. I just wasn't answering it.' She gave Polly a look. 'Well, how could I? Going to Simon's apartment, at Simon's apartment, coming home from Simon's apartment. I'm not completely hard-boiled, you know. I couldn't talk to Julian under those circumstances.'

'I'm glad to hear it. Anyway, he phoned me, and we had a chat. He's worried about you. He loves you.'

'How do you reckon that?' Ginnie said derisively.

'Come on, Ginnie. I'm not a fool. I could tell from the way he talked about you. The way he always *talks* about you, come to that, here at home, and the way he looks at you. And he does take you seriously. He said – he said he wished you'd take up your photography again, because you were so good at it.'

'Did he really? He said that?' Ginnie's eyes moistened again.

'Yes, and you are. You're really good, Gin, and it's a shame to let all that talent go to waste.'

'But how can I do anything like that with the house and the kids to look after?'

'I don't think you should let that consideration put you off,' Polly said carefully. 'Talk to Julian about it. I'm sure if you were serious about it he'd let you have Marta every day, or as often as you needed her, anyway.'

She looked gloomy. 'I don't know. He probably thinks a wife ought to *want* to take care of her own home and children.'

Polly laughed. 'Oh, come on! If he'd wanted that sort of surrendered wife, he'd never have married you, would he?'

'Well, no, I suppose not,' Ginnie said, smiling reluctantly. 'OK, I'll think about it. It might be rather fun to get the old camera out again. I'll talk to Julian when he gets home.' Her face fell again. 'If he ever comes home, after this. My God, what have I done? I'll have to tell him about it, and then he really will hate me.'

'No! No, you mustn't!' Polly said urgently. 'Listen to me, Ginnie, whatever happens you mustn't ever tell him about Simon. It was an aberration and it's all over, but if you tell Julian, it will break his heart. Confessing won't do anyone any good except maybe make you feel better at his expense, and that's not what you want, is it?'

'But suppose it comes out? Suppose Simon tells?'

'Simon won't tell. He's got too much to lose. Just make it clear to him that it was fun while it lasted but it's all over.

'I think it *is* all over,' Ginnie said. 'Not that there was really any "all" at all. I bet he'd be very pleased never to hear from me again. He certainly doesn't like answering the phone when I ring.'

Polly hugged her. 'Oh, poor Ginnie! But it's for the best, isn't it? Write it off to experience. It's what I'm going to do. He can't help what he is. It's for us to be more careful and avoid the trap in future.'

305

Ginnie sighed and reached for the bottle. 'You're right. And he's the loser, not us, two sensational birds like us. The proverbial two in the Bush. Have some more wine.'

They sipped in silence for a while. Then Polly said, 'It was all illusion. And illusion isn't in anyone's interest. Not even the conjuror's.'

'But it's fun for a bit,' Ginnie said.

'As long as you don't mistake it for the real thing.'

'You never did say what he wanted you for,' Ginnie said after a while. 'Simon, I mean. Why did he tell all those lies to you, if he didn't want to have sex with you?'

'He wants Seth to do his house up, and he thought I could put in a good word for him.'

'Is that it?' The corners of Ginnie's mouth were twitching, and finally she broke down and howled with laughter. 'Oh, poor Polly! Knocked back for your own husband! Second fiddle to hairy old Seth!'

'Laugh away,' Polly invited. But she smirked a bit, too. 'He'll never know what he missed.'

# Twenty-One

Seth didn't come home at all that night. Polly got back late from Ginnie's and thought he might be already there, but the house was empty and there was no message on the answering machine. Polly went to bed, leaving the chain off as instructed, but she slept lightly and fitfully, expecting to be woken every minute. However, in the morning the other side of the bed was still empty.

He must have stayed with the client, she thought. She was not worried for his safety (you didn't worry about a full-grown, muscular man like Seth the way you would about a teenage daughter), but she did think it was a bit mean of him not to telephone and say he wouldn't be back. However it was not unprecedented. He was not the world's greatest communicator, and had stayed out all night before. Usually he said afterwards that it had been so late by the time he thought about it that he didn't want to wake her up. She knew he did get completely wrapped up in his work and didn't notice the time pass. However, at the moment that the client said, 'Would you like to stay the night?' she'd have preferred he rang and told her, however late it was.

Of course, he still had his Paris suitcase with him, so he wouldn't even need to come home and change. That was probably what swung the decision for him. Even if he didn't feel pressed to come home and sleep with her, he would never have gone to work (or anywhere) in a dirty shirt. There had been occasions, though, when he had simply sent someone to buy him a new one. Turnbull and Asser knew what he would and would not wear.

If she'd known who the client was and where he was staying, she might have rung him before she went to work, but as it was, she had to wait for him to call her. Which he did in the middle of the morning when she'd just got back to her desk after making the coffee.

'Sorry about last night,' he said.

'What happened?' she asked mildly.

'Oh, things developed,' he said.

A quotation came into her mind: *'Events, dear boy. Events.'* Where did that come from?

'I shall be home this evening. I've got a lot to talk to you about. There isn't anything in the diary, is there?'

'No, it's just you and me.'

'Good,' he said. And then, as if remembering it, 'We can have what you bought for supper last night.'

'I ate it with Ginnie yesterday. It wouldn't

have kept.'

'Oh. Well, don't go to any trouble. I shall probably have to lunch someone today, so I shan't want much. I'll see you around six thirty.'

Ginnie slept badly again – too much wine and emotion – but Marta arrived on time and took up the strain, and drove the children to school without even being asked. Ginnie pulled herself together and went up to shower. Under the fall of water she was trying to work out what time it was in America – she always forgot whether you added or subtracted – and wondered whether she dared call Julian. It would have to be on his mobile since she didn't know where he was, and it cost the earth to receive a call from England on a mobile in the USA. But she hadn't spoken to him yesterday and given what Polly had said, he had evidently tried several times to reach her and she felt guilty about it. Would he be more cross at having to pay for her call, or at having to wait until lunchtime to speak to her? Except that it was *her* lunchtime, wasn't it, not his? Wasn't it *his* early morning? Bloody hell, why couldn't everyone be on the same time?

She wanted very badly to talk to him, to make sure that it was still all right, that she hadn't irrevocably destroyed something in these past few days. She was angry about Simon and his lies to Polly. She was not so concerned about his lies to her because that wasn't what it had all been about between them anyway – if she was honest it has just been sex, hadn't it? The nice, friendly stuff had been an add-on. As far as Simon and she were concerned, she was more angry with herself for having been so stupid and so easy. The thought of how often she had phoned him made her cringe, and she had a horrible image of herself in his bed at the flat saying, 'When can I see you again?' Pathetic! It made her want to scream, *'rewind, rewind!'* She must have come across as so *needy*. No wonder he had run a mile. *Bastard!*

And she had this dreadful, compulsive desire to tell Julian *everything,* to 'get it off her chest' and be forgiven. She wasn't even a Catholic. But there was something horribly tempting about that whole confession-absolution thing, and, let's face it, Julian was that much older than her and there had often been a bit of the father–daughter in their relationship. She wondered suddenly, and painfully, if Julian had minded that, minded being cast as her dad, having to take the strain while she swanned about being irresponsible. Well, this was one case where she was going to bloody well have to behave responsibly, no matter what it took. Because Polly was absolutely right. She must never, never tell him. She had made a terrible mistake and done a terrible thing, and keeping it to herself was going to have to be her punishment.

But was Polly right that Julian loved her (still loved her – that was the point)? That was what she needed to know. Had it gone too far or could she get it back? Things had not been good between them for a long time, not since – well, she didn't want to think about that. Of course, Julian *hadn't* had an affair, and he would never know that *she* had, so the situation wasn't as bad as it felt inside her head. But she had been snapping and sniping at him over the phone for days and he had sounded fed up with it all. Who could blame him? When he came home she would make it up to him. And somehow, she must get her life under control again. She thought involuntarily of Simon, remembering that he was going to be a neighbour, present at the various social gatherings in the Terrace. She would have to meet him and be cool about it, behave naturally with him. An irrepressible grin tugged at her lips as she imagined him working his way through all the wives on the Terrace. Tammy Wentworth and Sukey Arrosto were gagging for it already. *Go Yale!* When he got to the far end he might have to sell up and leave through sheer sexual exhaustion.

This thought did her good, and she was out and dressed and more or less human by the time Marta got back. She heard her let herself in and mentally followed the footsteps down the hall as she went to the kitchen. Ginnie had started sorting through her clothes to see what needed taking to the cleaners when a light quick step on the stairs heralded Mr Big, who must have just come in from his morning walk-about. He chirruped to her and she picked him up and pressed her cheek against him. He purred like a motor-mower and flexed his big paws bluntly on her shoulder. His fur was cool and smelled of grass and outdoors. 'Gorgeous boy,' she said. His purr accelerated as if he was agreeing that he certainly was.

Then Marta came up the stairs after him and appeared in the doorway. 'Mrs Addington?'

Ginnie lifted Big off her shoulder and set him down, and he did his front-end stretch, and then shot past Marta and down the stairs as if he thought she was going to kick him. Ginnie looked enquiringly at Marta. She had picked up a bit of a tan in Poland, which quite suited her, because normally she was a bit too pale.

'Something wrong?' Ginnie asked, because for once Marta wasn't smiling. 'If it's Jasper swearing, don't worry, I know about it. It's a phase he's going through. He doesn't really know what those words mean, but he hears the other boys saying them. When Mr Addington comes home he'll sort him out.'

'Oh – no, it is not that. I have heard him say those words too, but my mother always said it is better not to make a fuss. Like with the cat when he scratches the rug. If you pay attention he does it all the more.'

'I don't pay attention, I just kick the little bugger,' Ginnie said. 'The cat, not Jasper.'

But Marta didn't laugh. 'Mrs Addington, I have something to tell you. I am very sorry, but I must give you notice. I cannot work for you any more.'

Ginnie's heart fell like a demolished wall. 'You're leaving? Oh, Marta, no! Please don't go. I can't manage without you.'

'I'm sorry,' Marta said again, but her face was adamant.

'Is it something we've done? Or has someone offered you more money? When Mr Addington comes home—'

'No, please, it is nothing like that. It is that I am getting married.'

'Good God!' Ginnie said. Now there was a coincidence, given she and Polly had only been talking about it last night! 'But that's marvellous – for you, I mean, not for me. Congratulations! It is someone from back home – from Poland?'

Marta hesitated a beat. 'It is something that has been arranged this past weekend,' she said.

'Arranged?' Ginnie said. 'But I hope you love him?'

Now she smiled. 'Oh, not arranged like that. Yes, I love him. Very much. Otherwise I would not do it. But please forgive, Mrs Addington, that I cannot work any more

313

after today.'

Ginnie was taken aback. 'Blimey, that's quick. When are you getting married – tomorrow?'

'No, not for some time,' Marta said gravely. 'But he wishes that I begin to live with him at once.'

'Well, I don't mind that! We're broad-minded, for goodness sake. You can give us a week or so, can't you? Or a few days, at any rate, until I can make other arrangements.'

Marta lowered her head a little and sighed. 'Please forgive,' she said again. 'I will finish today and then not come any more. It is best.'

Ginnie's eyes narrowed. 'Is it *him* insisting on this?' Marta didn't say yes, but she didn't say no. Ginnie gathered from what Marta had said that men from her hometown were sometimes very macho and didn't like their women working outside the home. She imagined him telling Marta to give her notice at once, and Marta – well, that was the odd bit, wasn't it? Marta agreeing? Marta with her good degree, who had come to England to get a second one, bright, intelligent, capable Marta. She shrugged inwardly.

'Well, if that's the way it has to be,' she said. 'I hope you will be very happy, Marta, and if ever you want to come back and work again, don't hesitate. And of course if you want a reference—'

'No, that will not be necessary. But thank

314

you very much, Mrs Addington. And – again, I am sorry.'

She went away. Well, that was a bugger, Ginnie thought. The image of everything Marta did, even on her three days a week, piled up like avalanche snow in her mind. So much for getting the camera out again! Until she could get someone to replace Marta, she would be tied hand and foot to the house and the kids. And where would she ever get anyone as good as Marta? She realized how spoiled she had been. As soon as Marta had disappeared out of earshot she dashed for the telephone to call Polly.

Polly had had an awkward telephone call from Simon. Awkward for her, that was, not for him, since he didn't know she had rumbled him and she wasn't about to tell him. She didn't want anything emotional creeping into their relationship, which had to be completely businesslike from now on. So she didn't call him a lying, manipulating, friend-bonking bastard. She simply said she hadn't had a chance to speak to Seth yet, and then asked him if he had given any more thought to the de Kooning. He said he was still considering it.

Then he said, 'Polly, is there something wrong?'

'Of course not. What could be wrong?'

'Your voice sounds different, that's all.'

'Well, it's the same one I always use.

Perhaps it's a bad line.'

There was a pause, and he said, 'Have you thought any more about doing some picture research for me?'

'I thought everything was on hold until you could get your house done.'

'Well, I'm relying on you for that,' he said, and she could hear the smile as he did it, the slopey one that made her knees go weak. 'I have every faith in your powers of persuasion.'

'Let's just see how it goes, then,' she said. 'When and if we know what the situation is, then we can proceed.'

There was a silence as he tried to pick the bones out of that, and failed. 'Right,' he said at last. And then, 'How about lunch? I can't do tomorrow, but the day after?'

She had to admire his cheek. 'I'll have to get back to you on that,' she said, remembering how he wouldn't answer the phone to poor Ginnie. Let him be the one to sweat it for a bit.

But when she put the phone down, she had a horrible moment of missing him – the Simon she had sat and talked to over three wonderful meals. He hadn't been the real Simon, she knew that now, but she still missed him.

She felt very tired by the time she got back to Shepherd's Bush that evening. She was very hungry, too, not having managed much

316

for lunch. It was a pity Seth only wanted a snack. Oh well, good for the figure, no doubt. She stopped at Fare Trade and bought one of their French stonebaked round loaves and an olive ciabatta, some thinly-sliced Bradenham ham, some kipper pâté, some ripe gorgonzola (Emil's brother, Julian called it, as she remembered with a smile) and two different salads.

The house was cool but a little stuffy when she got back. Leela had been in, of course, and whisked away the minute traces she had left of her existence. When Seth was away, there was very little for the maid to do. Polly had not grown up in a confined space with five other people without learning how to be clean and tidy. She dumped the food in the kitchen, opened the back door to let in the green air and birdsong, and went upstairs to take off her work clothes. It was a quarter past six so there wasn't time for a shower if he was going to be home at half past, but she washed at the basin, put on some more deodorant, and slipped into a pair of pale fawn cargo pants and a sleeveless, loose-necked, rose-coloured silk top. She brushed her hair, thought about shoes, rejected the idea, and padded downstairs, enjoying the cool silkiness of the wooden floors against her feet.

She didn't know where he would want to eat so she laid the food out ready, assembled plates, glasses and cutlery, got out fresh napkins, and put the cold jacket on a bottle of Gros Plant, a wine Seth was particularly fond of. Mr Big walked in cautiously, testing the air for Seth. She gave him a bit of kipper pâté on the end of a finger but he wasn't keen, and having circled her legs three times, like someone doing a spell, he wandered out again to try the other gardens. There were murmuring grown-up voices, and children calling, from several of them up and down the Terrace, and the satisfying clink of suppers beginning to be taken out of doors. She looked at her watch. It was nearly seven. He was late.

She heard his key in the door upstairs at last, and found, to her surprise and pleasure, that her heart was beating faster. It was nice that she still felt that way about him after all these years of marriage. It was good, she thought, for married couples to spend a day or two apart now and then so that they could rediscover the delights of meeting again. She grabbed the wine, pulled out the cork, which she had already extracted and replaced lightly, poured two glasses, and posed herself holding them, facing the door, with an inviting smile.

His footsteps came down the stairs and then he was there, her Mr Rochester, Corsair-dark, swarthy as a Frenchman, fashionable in his exquisitely-cut suit, with the end-of-day shadow around his chin and lips. He never had to try for that designer-stubble look. It just came naturally. She caught the faint tang of his cologne, which had almost worn off by now – she liked it better when it was just a hint on the air rather than the full morning gust.

'The wanderer returns,' she said, crossing the floor to him with a glass held out. He took it automatically, but he looked a little dazed. 'Ithaca is yours, my lord. How do you like your lotus done?'

A faint frown deepened the cleft between his black and vigorous eyebrows. 'What are you *talking* about?'

'Odysseus,' she said. 'Returning to the faithful Penelope.'

He took a swig of the wine without seeming to notice it. 'Now, you see, that's just the sort of thing I mean!'

'Mean what? What do you mean?' she said, thrown. She began to suspect the tender reunion wasn't going quite to plan.

'I come home worn out from work – not to mention a tiring trip away – and you throw a lot of Greek mythology at me.'

Well, credit to him, he'd recognized from the name Odysseus that it was Greek. 'I'm sorry,' she said meekly. 'I'm just glad to see you. It's been a long weekend.'

He wasn't to be placated. He walked past her to the back door, looked out, turned again restlessly, examined the food on the table briefly, picked a piece of artichoke out of the salad and put it in his mouth, and said, 'I've got to talk to you about something.'

'So you said,' she remarked equably. 'I've got lots to tell you, too.'

'Well, mine's important,' he said. 'You'd better sit down.'

His face was inscrutable but there was no welcome in it for her. She began to feel very bad about what was coming. Had he heard about her meals with Simon? But he couldn't object, surely? Simon was a client. She sat down at the table, and he pulled out the chair opposite and sat facing her.

'Look,' he began, 'there's no easy way of saying this. I'm just going to come straight out with it. But I expect you've guessed already. You women always seem to know this sort of stuff. I expect you've talked it all through with everyone already.'

'Talked about what?' Polly said, bewildered.

It seemed to exasperate him. 'I'm leaving you. I want a divorce,' he said. She could only stare. 'Well, don't pretend to be so surprised. I can't believe that oaf Kemp-Parker hasn't spilled the beans already. I know he saw us.'

'I don't know what you're talking about,' she said, but the tears were rushing to her eyes. She didn't want to cry, but some system inside her seemed to be operating on its own. 'You can't leave me. Why? What have I done?'

'It's not about you! Why does everything have to be about you? You're just like your bloody sisters – it's all me, me, me.'

'But—'

'Look, it's perfectly simple. There's someone else. I'm going to marry her. I'm leaving you. I want a divorce. Can't you understand that?'

She couldn't speak. The tears welled over and she gave a convulsive choke as she tried to pull them back. He scowled. 'Here come the waterworks.'

'Why are you being so horrible to me?' she gasped

'I'm not being horrible. I'm trying to be practical and keep this thing on an even keel. There's no need to get all emotional about it. Marriages end. People move on. I've *told* you it's nothing to do with you. *You* haven't done anything, so there's no need for you to get upset. I've met someone else, that's all. She and I are better suited. You and I were never really a couple.'

'I thought we were,' Polly said, trying desperately not to cry, though she couldn't for the life of her have said why she shouldn't.

'No you didn't. You've always held aloof from me. We were just two people living in the same house. It's different with Marta.'

'*What?*'

'Don't tell me you didn't know.'

Even after what Ginnie had told about Marta leaving to get married, even after the mention of Phil Kemp-Parker, she had not expected this. How could she have guessed it? She could do nothing but stare.

He examined her face and sighed theatrically. 'Look, I'm telling you because you were bound to find out sooner or later anyway, but otherwise I wouldn't have, because it isn't any business of yours who I marry after we're divorced, any more than I would want to know who you ended up with. Marta and I have been – seeing each other for a while now. I took her with me to Paris to see whether it would work over a longer time. I know now that she's the right woman for me. We were spotted in Paris by Phil and I knew he'd lose no time in telling everyone, so we decided to make the break now. Otherwise we'd have left it a few weeks longer until our plans were ready.'

'How nice of you,' she managed to say.

'Well, it couldn't make any difference to you *when* we moved.'

'Phil said he'd seen Marta in Paris, but of course we all thought he was mistaken,' she said, as if to herself. 'Poor old Phil. He didn't see you, though. He just said there was a man in the taxi, very short and dark like a Frenchman.'

'I am not short!' Seth shouted.

She shook her head, distracted. Thoughts were tumbling through her head. 'But why Marta?' she asked. 'I mean, I know she's pretty and everything, but it can't be just that.'

'She's a great homemaker. She'll be a proper wife, and a support to me in my business. And I'd like to have children.' A peculiar expression crossed his face, which puzzled Polly for a moment until she realized he was trying to look sentimental. 'If *we* could have had children, things might have been different.'

She didn't even feel the cruelty of the blow for the puzzlement. 'But you haven't had the tests yet. You don't know that it isn't you.'

'It isn't me. I know that for a fact. I didn't tell you before, didn't want to upset you, but there was this girl at college. She had an abortion, of course, but all the same ... Marta can give me children. I'm sorry, Pol, but what with that, and your career – and we don't share the same tastes or anything, you have to admit. We just aren't suited. You'll be better off without me. You can find the right person for you, and we'll both be happier.'

It was an attempt at kindness, but she was hardly listening. She was back in her bedroom at home, on the night of her engagement, with Anna telling her Seth was no good. 'He only wants you because he's inadequate.' He couldn't stand competition or challenge. He wanted abject devotion from a woman. And he thought he was going to get it from Marta, because – this was the good bit – because *she was the Addingtons' cleaner*! Marta who swapped erudite jokes and classical tags with Julian.

'My God,' she said, awestruck, 'you are such a *snob*!'

His face reddened. 'And you are just like your bloody sisters! *So* superior, the lot of you. You all think such a lot of yourselves, no one's good enough for you! Well, Marta's worth two of you.'

Polly was shaking her head, laughing weakly. It was not real laughter, but the tightness in her chest demanded some outlet. 'You poor fool, of course she is! Don't you know? Don't you understand? She's pretty and bright and clever and God knows why she wants to marry you, but it isn't because she sees you as her slave-master. She's got a *degree*, for heaven's sake!'

He waved that away. 'Oh, yes, from some Polish university. That isn't going to make her swollen-headed. She knows how a proper woman should behave.' He stood up abruptly. 'Look, I'm sorry you're taking it this way. I hoped we could be civilized about it. I was going to have supper with you and talk through everything, but since you're taking up this attitude I don't think there's any point in going on now. I'll pack a bag and go back to Marta's place. We'll have to meet some other time when you're ready to talk sensibly.'

She didn't answer him. She was still thinking of Anna's words and fitting them to this new situation. Yes, he had married her because he thought she was inferior to him, and over the years as she had proved to be her own woman, he had drawn back from her. Now he was attracted to Marta because he thought *she* was inferior. Poor Marta, when he found out the truth! But what did Marta want? Seth was successful and rich, and would be richer yet – maybe it was as simple as that. She had family back home in Poland. She had come to England to better herself. Married to Seth, she would be able to send money home. Polly had a brief and satisfying vision of Marta's mother coming over to live with them, of Seth sharing a house with his little old Polish-peasant mother-in-law. Marta's mum might find his interiors rather hard to stomach, of course. The lack of doors on the bathrooms to begin with...

'Are you listening to me?'

'I'm sorry, what did you say?'

He was looking at her more kindly. 'Are you all right? I don't want to leave you in a state. Look, let's not be enemies over this. We've had a good run, and these things happen. It's time to move on. There's no need to be hostile to each other, is there?'

Was he worried about how much alimony she'd claim? No, to do him justice, he really didn't see why they shouldn't just part and move on. He had never invested emotionally in her, the way she had in him. And – this was the hardest thing for her to face – it had been a mistake on her part. She had – stubbornly, wilfully – mistaken him for someone he was not.

'I can't talk any more,' she said. 'Just go.'

He hesitated. 'I'll ring you tomorrow, then,' he said. 'You'll be all right?' It was a plea rather than a question, and she didn't answer it.

He got as far as the door, and then she spoke. 'Wait!' He looked at her. 'The girl in university, who got pregnant, who had an abortion.'

'It was mine all right, if that's what you're going to say.'

She shook her head. 'I just wanted to know – it was Anna, wasn't it?'

He paused so long she thought he was going to deny it, and then he said, 'Yes.'

She nodded to herself, and he went.

It was almost dark when the phone rang. Polly hadn't moved since Seth left, God knew how many hours ago, and found herself rigid, cramped and cold. The back door was still open and the air coming in now was chill. She struggled to her feet and hobbled across the room to the telephone. She thought it would be Seth, but it was Ginnie. Her mind was so hurt and stiff from its bruises, and Ginnie's voice was so unlike her own, that she could not understand at first what she was saying. Then she understood that Ginnie wanted her to come over at once, and feared for some reason that someone had broken in and attacked her.

'Have you called the police?' she heard herself asking.

Ginnie screamed with frustration. 'It was the *police* phoned *me*! Don't you understand? You've got to come. I can't cope. For God's sake Polly, *come now*!'

'I'm coming,' she said.

The Ginnie who let her in was white as a sheet but not bloodied, and there were no signs of violence or intrusion. She held out a hand and Ginnie grabbed it and held on to it like someone hanging off a cliff.

'Tell me what happened. Try to speak slowly,' Polly said.

And so, fairly slowly and more or less clearly, Ginnie told her that the police had rung trying to find out where Julian was. His brother Rupert and Rupert's wife Amanda had been in a car crash on the A34 on their way down to Addington Hall. They had been airlifted to Southampton hospital, but they were seriously injured and not expected to live.

# Twenty-Two

Ginnie couldn't cope at all, couldn't make the simplest decision. Polly had to take over, which was good in its way because it drove her own disaster right out of her mind. She only thought about it once, fleetingly, when Ginnie suddenly said, 'Bloody *Marta*, leaving now, just when I need her!' But it wasn't the time to tell her the rest of the story.

First Polly made tea and forced a mug into Ginnie's hands and made her sit and drink it while she rang Julian. She felt she could explain things more succinctly than Ginnie at the moment. He was in Boston, at a meeting, and booked into a hotel there for the night. He was wonderfully calm and practical, took what details he wanted from her (she could imagine him jotting them down) and said, 'There's a flight from Logan in a couple of hours, which would get me in around seven thirty tomorrow morning. If I can't get on that, I ought to be able to get the one around tennish tonight, which would mean ten tomorrow morning. I'll let you know which one I make. I'll drive straight to the hospital from Heathrow. Get Ginnie to ring my mother right away. She can be there before any of us. How is Ginnie?'

'She'll be fine,' Polly said, trying not to look at the little, staring white face. What use in upsetting Julian more?

Perhaps he knew anyway, because he said, 'Thank God for you, Polly. Can you stay with her?'

'Of course.'

When he had rung off, she said to Ginnie, 'He wants you to ring his mother.'

'Oh God,' she said.

'Do you want me to do it?'

Ginnie pulled herself together visibly. 'No, it ought to be me.'

But it turned out that Mrs Addington already knew. One of the policemen involved was a local man who had known who Rupert was, knew the family, and had rung her straight away. She was just leaving for the hospital.

'I'll have to go there,' Ginnie said when she had rung off. 'God knows I don't want to, but I have to. Julian will expect it and I can't let him down.' She stared at Polly and her eyes seemed enormous.

'Do you want me to come with you?'

The eyes filled with tears. 'Would you?' She seized Polly's hand again in wordless thanks. 'But what about the kids?' she remembered suddenly. That was the point when she said the thing about 'bloody Marta'.

'I'll ring Leela,' Polly said. 'I'm sure she'll

come over when she knows it's an emergency. She'd be at my house tomorrow anyway, so she can be here instead.'

She organized Leela (who was wonderful and said she'd be over in half an hour) and then packed a bag for Ginnie in case she stayed down there, and laid out a change of clothes for her and made her put them on, rang the hospital for instructions on how to get there. Julian rang back to say he was on his way to the airport, he had got on the seven-thirty flight, and she told him about the arrangements so far. He thanked her abruptly and was gone.

She asked Ginnie, 'Are you fit to drive?' and Ginnie said yes, but she was staring and shivering. Polly had intended to go down in two cars so that she could come back independently, but that was obviously not a good idea. They would have to wait for Leela and go together. She used the waiting time to knock up some sandwiches – she hadn't eaten yet and she had no idea how long it would be before they could eat again – and to write the details of the hospital on the telephone pad for Leela in case she needed them.

And then finally they were off, in Polly's car, with Ginnie hunched beside her with the bag of sandwiches in her lap. Polly could not begin to imagine what was going on her mind, but it was obviously bad. She put the heating up full and put some Bach on the

CD player and headed west towards the last bit of red in the evening sky.

Mrs Addington was amazing, a tiny, slender figure, exquisitely dressed, as though for a committee meeting, in a knitted suit, with pearls and full make-up. She seemed absolutely calm. She thanked Polly for her help, and dedicated herself to comforting Ginnie, as though it were Ginnie's son rather than her own lying grievously injured in the operating theatre. But of course, Polly reflected, that was her way of coping. Not for anything would she allow anyone to see her other than controlled and perfectly turned-out, and thinking about someone else kept her mind off her own suffering.

As Ginnie had been so thoroughly clasped to the bosom, as it were, and knowing that Mrs Addington needed to go on doing the comforting, Polly offered to remove herself, but Ginnie at once turned to her with wide, panicky eyes and begged her not to go, and Mrs Addington seconded the request with more than mere politeness, so she stayed. They sat in a horrible 'lounge' which hurt the eyes, on the cheapest of 'lounge' furniture, which made every muscle ache, waiting for news. Polly, now starving, offered the sandwiches generally. Mrs Addington accepted graciously, just as she would have accepted a glass of sherry from a cannibal chief before the meal at which she was the principal dish. Polly fetched horrible coffee from a horrible coffee machine, and they ate and drank in a bizarre simulacrum of real life – which after all was all you could ever expect in a hospital, she reflected.

Eventually a doctor came in, looking hauntingly young and frighteningly tired, and told them that Amanda had not made it. Her injuries had been too severe and they could not save her. She had died half an hour ago. Rupert was alive, but his head and spinal injuries were serious and his condition was still critical. He had been taken up to the intensive care ward and they would be able to go and see him in a little while.

Mrs Addington thanked him graciously, but Polly could see the stark pain in her eyes.

When Julian arrived in the middle of the morning, looking pale, tired and grubby from the journey, the situation was unchanged. Rupert was still unconscious in intensive care, hooked up to a drip and various monitors, but breathing for himself, which was the only positive in a strong field of negatives. Until he regained consciousness, there was no knowing what neurological damage he had suffered. And it was still entirely possible that he would not live.

Julian received the news with an expressionless nod, and said, 'Can I see him?'

'Yes,' said his mother, and looked at Ginnie with exhausted kindness. 'You go with him, my dear,' she said gently.

Ginnie looked at her, startled, out of her daze, but got up obediently. Mrs Addington watched them go, and said to Polly, 'You may not believe it, but I had hair that colour when I was a girl. Rupert's was very red when he was a little boy, but it faded as he grew up. And Julian was never more than light brown.'

Polly wanted desperately to press her hand in sympathy, but knew enough to know that it would offend deeply, coming from a stranger. Probably even Julian wouldn't initiate such a movement uninvited. Poor Ginnie, she thought, so very much at sea in such a family.

Ginnie had been in several times already to the ICU, and seen Rupert, unrecognizable with his head hugely bandaged and two black eyes, tubes in and tubes out, and a softly bleeping monitor counting his seconds out like tokens in a deadly game. He was no relative of hers, and she had never much liked him, and the sight had meant nothing to her beyond the pity she might feel for any stranger. She walked up to the bed with Julian and he said something under his breath, a small mutter of pain. She looked up at him and saw his lips shake as if he were trying not to cry, and it hurt her as much as if it were Jasper or little Ben trying to be brave.

Then suddenly the veil was ripped aside,

and it was all real, not an episode of ER. The reality of it, the terrible injury suffered, the agony of love hardly daring to feel itself for fear that life could not be endured under it, came over her in crushing waves. She wanted to cry out, but couldn't – for Rupert, for his mother, for Julian – most of all for Julian – and for herself, as if 'herself' was a separate person. Not self-pity, but a great agony of sorrow for anyone who was bereaved, for that most human condition, and the fragility of hope, that must always, in the end, be betrayed.

The tears tore out of her, and she couldn't bear it. She turned to Julian and he put his arms round her and held her against him, and she shook and shuddered as the ravaging grief soaked through his shirt to his skin. He wept too, but she never knew it, because he did it silently, as men do, his body rigid and his face, unseen above her, contorted. He held her until she eased a little, and then bent his head and laid a kiss on the crown of her head, gently, as though even the touch might hurt her.

In the afternoon of that day, the doctor reported that Rupert's condition had stabilized, and Polly felt able to go home. She had that strained, arms-length feeling you get when you have missed a night's sleep, and she was desperate for a shower and a change of clothes.

There was the question of what to do with the Addington children. Leela had slept at the house and got them off to school in the morning, and was willing to collect them again in the afternoon, but she had her own home and family to take care of. But neither Julian nor his mother was willing to leave the hospital, and Ginnie was obviously not fit to drive anywhere. It was decided that one of the chauffeurs from Addington should drive to London to pick them up and take them back to Addington Hall. Polly volunteered to supervise their packing when she got back, and stay with them until they were collected.

It had to be said – though Polly never did say it to anyone – that Flora, Jasper and Ben were far more excited about missing Friday school and going down to Addington for an unspecified length of time than they were upset about their uncle Rupert, whom they knew very little and cared for less. At the last minute, when they and all their bags were packed into the car, Flora said, 'Where's Mr Big? Isn't he coming with us?' He was nowhere to be seen and didn't come to call. Cats always had that ability to absent themselves in moments of stress, Polly thought.

'Don't worry, I'll look after him for now,' she said, bundling them into the car. 'Come on, you mustn't keep Mr Rogers waiting.'

Rupert regained consciousness briefly that evening, long enough to exchange a few words with Julian. He and Amanda had been quarrelling, he said, and he had been driving too fast. He didn't remember the accident at all. She had said she wanted a divorce, he remembered that, and they had been screaming at each other. That was all. He asked how she was, and Julian told him she was also in intensive care. It didn't seem the time to tell him she was dead.

'I'm sorry,' Rupert had said to his brother, weak tears on his cheeks which must have hurt to cry, his eyes being so swollen.

'It was an accident,' Julian said, trying to comfort him.

'No, I'm sorry to do this to you,' Rupert said. 'You never wanted it.'

Soon after that he lapsed again into unconsciousness, leaving Julian to wonder what he had meant. He never surfaced again, and died from an embolism a week later without ever knowing he had killed his wife. That, Julian had thought, was a small mercy. Rupert had never been an easy person to live with. His first marriage had ended in divorce, his second had been heading that way, and now he would never have the chance of a third, or the opportunity of redemption.

Rupert was buried in the churchyard just outside the gates of the Addington estate on a beautiful summer day, and the children had cried, Mrs Addington had cried, and Julian had bitten his lips and managed not to cry. But Ginnie had cried more than anyone. That moment by the ICU bed had opened the floodgates. She had cried for days after that, could not seem to stop crying, and it was not for Rupert, of course. It was the end of something that had begun long ago under the big oak tree at Horn Hill, and when it was over, it was over for good.

Julian came into the Esterhazy gallery one morning in October, and Polly got up in surprise and went to him to hug him, though they had never really been on hugging terms. He was not generally demonstrative in that casual, modern manner. But he pressed her shoulders briefly before she released herself, and smiled at her as though he were not offended by the gesture. She had spoken to him on the phone, but she had not seen him since the hospital. He looked older, she thought, and no wonder, new lines etched into his face. Thinner, too. He was wearing what looked like a new suit – dark-blue, expensive, in his usual unemphatic style, but with a gold watch-chain across the fob. He had never worn such a thing before, and she wondered if it had been his father's, in-herited via Rupert. She couldn't ask, of course.

'How are you?' she said.

'Oh, bearing up,' he said. 'Ginnie sends her love.' He looked around the gallery, empty of customers, and said, 'I don't suppose you could sneak out for a bit? Have coffee with me?'

'I think it might be arranged,' she said. She excused herself to go and see Nigel and explain. Then she collected her handbag and they walked across to the Ritz and sat in a corner of the Palm Court, blessedly quiet at this time of day, and ordered coffee.

'So, tell me the news,' Polly said, when the coffee had come. 'How's Ginnie?'

'She's doing well,' Julian said. 'She still has bad days, when she can't cope with anything, but they are fairly rare now. And on the other days, she's a new person – or rather, the old person. She's like the girl I married, bright, funny, cheerful.'

'You must be so relieved.' Polly hesitated, but this was a new Julian, willing to speak about personal things, and she guessed he had no one else to talk to on this subject. 'You went through a bad patch after Bill, I know.'

'More than a patch,' Julian admitted. 'Things were never right. Rupert's death seems to have brought it all to a head. But we're getting back on an even keel now.'

Polly had spoken to Ginnie a few times on the phone, and they had exchanged letters, but she had only seen her once since the crash, when she had come back to Albemarle Terrace to pack some more clothes and belongings. It had been about a month after the funeral, and it had struck Polly to the heart to see her friend so ill-looking, white and pinched, and somehow *smaller*, as if in weeping so much she had actually been shedding her substance. She was wearing a dark cloth two-piece, not at all her usual sort of thing, and her hair was done up behind. Neither style suited her.

'How are you coping?' Polly asked her, as she helped pack suitcases.

Ginnie made a face. 'I thought you of all people would know that coping isn't my thing. And this! My God. "Yes, my lady", "no, my lady". Even the vicar at church on Sunday calls me Lady Addington.' She snorted. 'Me, at church! Can you imagine? But I have to go, no arguments allowed.'

'Poor Ginnie,' Polly said. It took her an effort, every time she thought about it, to grasp that Ginnie – her friend Ginnie, *that* Ginnie – was now a countess. Both Rupert's marriages had been childless. On his death, Julian had become the Earl Addington. Well and good – Julian had always looked the part. But Ginnie? 'I find it hard to take in. It must be very strange.'

'It doesn't feel like me,' Ginnie admitted. 'Neither of us ever really thought Rupert *wouldn't* have children. I mean, though he was older than Julian, of course, he was still young enough. And it wasn't as if he didn't like women. He already had another one lined up – did you know? – to take Amanda's place when they were divorced. So if it hadn't been for the accident...' She shuddered, and met Polly's eyes reluctantly. 'I feel so guilty. My mother used to talk – when I first met Julian – about Rupert having a car crash. I hated it even then. Julian keeps on at me, but I can't bring myself to go and see her yet. I suppose I'll have to ask her down eventually, but she wanted it so much I can't help thinking we somehow ill-wished him.'

'Don't,' Polly said. 'It doesn't work that way.'

'Well, you believe in God and everything, so I suppose you have to think like that. I don't know what I believe in. Irony, I think. Here's me, always hated the country, and hated Addington most of all, and now I'm going to be stuck there for the rest of my life. Doing all the county stuff and pretending to be a country gentlewoman.'

'Is it really so bad?'

She shrugged. 'I have to lump it, don't I? It's such a dump. Rupert never did much to the house or the estate. When things are more settled, Julian says we'll do the place up. I've half a mind to suggest we have a Seth Muller Special – pull out all the walls and fireplaces and burn all the antique furniture.'

'I don't think that would be appropriate.'

'Are you kidding me? He wouldn't even let me touch *this* place ... Never mind the furniture, maybe we could burn Addington down, come back here and forget any of this happened.'

'You can't ever go back,' Polly said.

'No.' She shut one suitcase and started on another. 'Well, at least there's plenty of money now. We can all have everything we want.'

'And what do you want?'

'I don't know. I haven't found out yet.'

'But you've got Julian.'

'Yes, there is that,' Ginnie said.

Later, when Polly helped her carry the cases to the car, Ginnie said, 'I'm taking up my photography again.'

'Are you? That's good. What brought that about?'

'Well, *Country Life* wanted a photograph of "the new countess" and there was simply nothing suitable of me they could use – I mean, I've never had a studio portrait done (can you imagine?) and a snap of me in the garden in hotpants fooling about with a garden hose isn't really the sort of thing they wanted. So they asked if they could send someone. I got talking to her, and she was very nice and friendly and put me in touch with the right people. So I'm going to do some interiors for them. Starting with my mother-in-law's house in Winchester. They hinted they might give me a series. How rich widows live, sort of thing. Actually, finding a series title will probably be the hardest bit.'

'How about Dowagers' Dens?'

'Or Old Bats in their Belfries?' Her smile

faded. 'They're very excited at having "Lady Addington" do photos for them. I can't decide whether it's just the title itself, or they think because of it I'll have unusual access to top people. They didn't remember I used to do stuff for them before as me, until I reminded them,' she finished sadly.

The last bag was in, when Ginnie said, 'I forgot to ask – where's Mr Big?'

'Oh, he's around somewhere,' said Polly, feeling a little pang. Of course Ginnie would want him back, but she would miss him. He had filled a gap for her these past few weeks. 'We'd better look for him.'

'No, don't bother. He might be anywhere and it would take for ever.' She slammed down the boot lid and turned to Polly. 'Look, I don't suppose you'd think of keeping him, would you? I know it's an imposition, but—'

'I'd love to keep him. I always wanted a cat but Seth wouldn't let me have one. But surely the children will be asking for him?'

'Are you kidding? There are three cats there already, and they've got farms full of animals all round them and they're going to have dogs and I don't know what else. Poor old Biggie wouldn't get a look in – besides which he'd probably get eaten by a fox the first time he stuck his nose out of doors. Addington's not like Albemarle Terrace.'

'I imagine not,' said Polly. So she kept Mr Big.

★ ★ ★

Polly leaned over and refilled Julian's cup, and asked, 'So what brings you to Town?'

'Business with the family solicitor. And I want to pop into the firm to see to a few things. I've missed Addington and Lyon, and if it's not vain to say so, I think it's missed me.'

'Nothing beats the single vision, or the personal hand on the reins.'

'That's true. And I have to instruct an estate agent to sell Albemarle Terrace and to start looking for something else for us.'

'So you're never going back there?'

Julian shook his head. 'We will want to keep a place in Town. But I'm not sure that's the best house for us. Too many memories. And it's not the most convenient, either. Something further in would be better.'

'It's a shame. You loved that house.'

'It served its purpose. But after Bill, everything got tainted. It would be better to make a new start.'

'So you'll be living mostly down at Addington?'

'For now,' said Julian. 'I have to take care of the estate. Eventually I hope it will more or less run itself, and then I shall be able to come up to Town more often, but at the moment there's so much to do.' It was a huge weight on his shoulders. Sometimes he thought that was what Rupert had meant when he said, *you never wanted it*. The title.

The estate. He hadn't ever wanted it, but fate decreed otherwise and he was not going to shirk his responsibility. He knew, at least, that he would make a better steward than his brother. 'Ginnie begged me to sell at the beginning, but, well, it's the family seat. I couldn't just let it go.'

'No, I see that,' said Polly.

'The children love it, of course – all that space to run around. The freedom. And Flora has her pony at last.'

Polly smiled. 'She must be thrilled. But does Ginnie still hate it?'

'Oh, she's not so totally against it as she used to be. She likes the space as well, and she did grow up in the country.'

'She always said Denham wasn't classed as country by the landed set.'

He avoided that one. 'My mother is being a great help to her with the county side of it, the social duties and so on. It's good to see them getting on so well. Mother keeps saying she ought to go back to Winchester, but Ginnie won't hear of it. And – ' his smile broadened – 'she's taking riding lessons.'

'Ginnie? But she hates horses!'

'Not so much any more. Flora's so dotty about riding, she keeps begging Ginnie to get a horse so they can go out together. She was nervous at first, but of course she *had* ridden as a child, so it wasn't a matter of having to learn from scratch. She's even talking about hunting this season.'

'Wonders will never cease,' Polly said, shaking her head in bemusement.

'But what about you?' Julian asked. 'Here I've been talking about my own affairs, and never asking about yours. You've had your own trouble. I was so sorry to hear about it.'

'You needn't be. Seth said when he told me he wanted a divorce that we weren't suited, and he was right, really. It was a shock, and hard at first, but we are better off without each other. Marta is a much tougher person than me. She runs him like a business. He'll go from success to success with her behind him.'

'It was unforgivable of him to turn you out of your house.'

'Oh, it wasn't quite like that. It was always his house rather than mine, you know. That's the problem of living with an interior designer, you never get to choose the way things look. He and Marta wanted to live there, and I didn't particularly, especially as I guessed you and Ginnie weren't coming back. Seth bought me out very generously, so now I have a lovely flat in Kensington, which suits me very well. And I can have it painted any colour I like. *And* have a door on the bathroom.'

Julian laughed. 'You're a real trouper.'

'No, really, you don't need to worry about me. I'm fine. I have my own place, and my career is taking off. Did Ginnie tell you that Nigel and Trevor have made me a partner?'

'Yes, she did. I'm very pleased for you.'

It was Simon, really, that she had to thank. When news of the divorce became common along the Terrace – which took about two days – Simon had gone straight to Marta. Polly had to admire his single-mindedness. Marta had seen the benefits at once. She made Seth take the job, postponing the Coventrys and cancelling Connaught Square (which he had thoroughly gone off by then). During the planning and the work, he and Simon had hit it off and become close friends. As soon as the security systems were in, Simon started living at number one, which was not as much of a hardship as it might seem, since he had the run of Seth and Marta's place a couple of doors down. Polly did wonder a little what the relationship was between Simon and Marta, the worldly little minx, but it was not her business any more.

Anyway, Simon had had his paintings delivered, and had gone to Esterhazy, asking Nigel to have Polly research and track down more for him.

It could have been uncomfortable, because it was not just finding paintings for Simon. The corner house was Seth's baby as much as his. There was no way of escaping frequent contact with Seth (in the course of which he said more than once, triumphantly, how he had always *told* her they could be friends). Now he was talking about getting her to source paintings for other houses for him in the future. And it was all because of Simon. Seth had not even seen her as a person when she was married to him. It was Simon who had made him respect her abilities in her own field. She felt she would never properly understand Simon, or know how much he meant of anything he said.

Still, the result was that she had made so much good quality business for Esterhazy that Nigel and Trevor had felt it was only just to take her into partnership.

'It's nice knowing that I have a stake in the business, and that anything I do is benefiting me as well as Nigel. He's been amazingly generous to me. He says I'm the daughter he and Trevor never had!'

'So you really are all right?' Julian said. 'You are happy? Ginnie wanted me to find out the truth on that point.'

'I *really* am,' said Polly. 'Except that I miss my friend.'

'You must come down and stay, see Addington for yourself. Come for a long weekend.'

'I'd like that. I will.'

'Soon,' Julian insisted.

They parted soon afterwards, Julian to Green Street station and Polly back to Esterhazy. There was one bit of news she hadn't told Julian. It would have to wait until she saw Ginnie, because it was more something for a female friend's ears. And it was early days yet, anyway. But she was seeing someone.

His name was Mark and she had met him at a country-house auction where they had been seated next to each other. After a bit they had caught themselves looking at each other's catalogues to see what was marked – very different items, which was probably fortunate as it meant they weren't bidding against each other. Eventually they had got talking in between lots, and when the break for lunch had arrived they had walked out together and it had seemed natural for him to say, 'Do you fancy grabbing a sandwich or something? The pub across the road's supposed to be OK.'

In the time left to them after fighting the crowds at the bar (everyone else had had the same idea) she had discovered that he was not a dealer – which was good, because she tended not to like them – but had been buying on his own behalf. By profession he was a conservator, specializing in furniture, fabrics and wallpaper, but consulting more widely on everything from stonework to stained glass. 'Jack of all trades,' he had admitted cheerfully, 'but when I'm out of my depth I know the right people to call in.' Inevitably he did a lot of work for the National Trust – which was probably why he had looked so at home in the surroundings – though he also worked for museums and for private customers. He asked what she did. She thought his job fascinating; he was impressed with hers; and when she admired the nineteenth-century landscape he had bought and they both admitted to preferring less modern works than the ones she sold, a definite warmth had started up between them.

They sat together through the second half, and a certain frivolity had come over them, though given the time they'd only managed one glass of wine each at the pub. But he had turned out to have a rather wicked sense of humour, and there was so much giggling between them that it was fortunate they were seated in the back row, and that she didn't have any more serious buying to do.

Outside, when it was over, he had said suddenly, 'We didn't get round to music. Do you like it?'

'It depends,' she said cautiously, 'what you mean by music.'

'Classical, to use a loose term,' he said – endearing himself to her on two counts. 'A friend gave me two tickets to a concert at the Festival Hall tomorrow night and I have no one to go with. I wondered if you'd like to help me use them?'

It was a carefully neutral question, implying nothing and conferring no obligations, but after all, they were both old enough to have past histories, and she liked him for the caution. Many things rushed through her mind, warnings and doubts and questions and memories, but in the end what came out of her mouth was only, 'Yes, I'd like that.'

They'd been out six times since then. She was trying to be sensible and take it slowly, not get too carried away too soon, but things were heating up most satisfactorily between them and it was taking her all her control not to pounce on him. The nice thing was she was pretty sure it was taking all his, too. He was dark, good-looking in an unflashy way – so unflashy it would be easy to overlook him, and she guessed most women did – but he had an air of coiled power that intrigued her. She suspected he had a deeply sexual nature and that when the moment came they would both go up like tinder. She was looking forward to this rather tremulously and had been glad to put the moment off, because when something was important it was not to be rushed into. She thought he felt the same. But it wouldn't be long. They shared so many tastes and opinions, had laughed together so much about so many things, that they were already good friends, and there was only this one step more to take.

After that – well, who knew? It was a bit teenagery to leap at once to thoughts of marriage and babies, but she couldn't help it. Sometimes she looked at him when his attention was elsewhere (when he was driving, for instance – she loved the quiet power of his hands on the wheel) and he would feel her thoughts and turn and look at her with an expression that made her shiver deliciously. She thought she would like to have children with him. She hadn't managed it with Seth, but perhaps that had not been meant to be. *Maybe some people just don't go with other people*, as Simon had said. More true than he knew! You had to find your niche in life, your right place, your right person. Mark was solid, capable, real – a grown-up. It occurred to her that he *was* what Simon had only *seemed*.

Thinking about it all, she crossed Bond Street towards the gallery, threading through the traffic, seeing her reflection come towards her in the window, a slim, smart young woman in a fawn Nicole Farhi suit, capable-looking, her own woman. A beneficent God, she thought, had endowed human beings with the gift of being able to dream and to hope. It was a tool they needed for survival. But it meant there was always going to be the danger of mistaking illusion for reality. What you needed to tell them apart, it seemed to her, was practice.